Also by Jamake Highwater

Journey to the Sky:
Rediscovering the Maya
novel

Anpao:
An American Indian Odyssey
novel

I Wear the Morning Star
novel

Song from the Earth:
American Indian Painting

Ritual of the Wind:
North American Indian Ceremonies and Dances

Fodor's Indian America:
A Cultural & Travel Guide

Dance:
Rituals of Experience

Many Smokes, Many Moons:
An American Indian Chronology

Masterpieces of American Indian Painting
8 folios

The Sun, He Dies

THE SUN,

HE DIES

A Novel About the End of the Aztec World

JAMAKE HIGHWATER

Lippincott & Crowell, Publishers   *New York*

FIRST EDITION

Designed by Abigail Moseley

U. S. Library of Congress Cataloging in Publication Data

Highwater, Jamake.
    The Sun, he dies.

    Bibliography: p.
    1. Aztecs—Fiction. I. Title.
PZ4.H6385Su [PS3558.I368] 813'.5'4 79-25859
ISBN 0-690-01695-6

---

80 81 82 83 84 10 9 8 7 6 5 4 3 2 1

In Memory of Anaïs Nin

*"We write," she once told me, "in order to create
a world that is truer than the one before us."*

He who fights the future has a dangerous enemy. The future is not, it borrows its strength from the man himself, and when it has tricked him out of this, then it appears outside of him as the enemy he must meet.

—Søren Kierkegaard

I

In the Days of the Dawning

Tenochtitlan's legendary founding is depicted in this Mexican drawing. The two ideographs at the bottom represent the subjugation of various neighboring cities of Anahuac, the Valley of Mexico. *Codex Mendoza.*

One

Call me Nanautzin. For I am the one who threw himself into the fire so the Sun would rise. And I am the last of my race which has fallen into a reckless night. Call me *tlamatini,* for I am one of the wise men, a broken mirror in which the world makes its fragile shadows. I alone have escaped to tell what has come down upon my people.

Night falls upon my words, for I am old and filled with black thoughts and dark memories. I have covered my face with soot. Nothing but broken flowers and songs of sorrow are left to me. In the road are broken spears. The houses are torn apart, and their walls are red with blood. My people have chewed twigs and sour grass. We have filled our mouths with dust. We have eaten rats and worms. Though we must perish, we still live. Earthquakes stomp the ground and terrible omens appear everywhere. We must perish, but we live. The day dies slowly.

All around us are the strangers. They growl. They spread their thick saliva everywhere and multiply like beetles. They roar. They hurl lightning. They hunt us down and destroy us. I can hear them scratching among the boulders, barking as they sniff the ground for my scent. Soon they will find my cave and throw themselves upon me, sinking their teeth into my body.

Great Huitzilopochtli stumbles as he strides across the sky, and his dream of bright yellow plumes is shattered. The Sun strangles on the darkness, weeping great silvery tears as he falls to his knees.

But my songs will not end. I, the singer, raise myself on my songs. And I will sing until this longest day is ended and all that I have known can be known no more. I will sing of the new fire and the new years. Of the days when our city ruled the world. When great Montezuma was Lord and his prayers kept the heavens turning. All this I shall tell. Of the Four Suns and the ones called Toltecs who carried with them the black and the red ink, the songbooks and the music of the flutes. Of the Lord named Quetzalcoatl, and the long journey to this good land, and the founding of the mighty city of Tenochtitlan. I shall tell these many things before the last day of my people is ended and all our fires have gone out. All this I shall tell.

Two

It is midnight. And in the vast darkness of the world the gods silently take their places around the divine fire. They watch the sky and they wait. They wait very long. Then a small red bird comes into the night. The horizon slowly opens its flaming wings and spreads its yellow plumes. The Fifth Sun comes flying into the blackness, and its morning song is heard among all the people of the Earth below.

As the long night departs, its dream remains, and the dream is called Tenochtitlan . . . great city of flowers and warriors. City of polished jade sparkling in the Sun. Glorious stronghold of the Valley of Mexico from whose gates stretch forests of oak and sycamore and tall cedars. And beyond the forests are wide valleys of maize and maguey mingled with nine times nine thousand flowers, making riotous colors in all the gardens. At the center of the vast valley are many lakes, their shores wearing a precious necklace studded with handsome towns and villages. And in the midst of this valley of jewels is the great city of

Tenochtitlan, with her white towers and pyramids and awesome temples that are the eyes of the gods.

I come to her from a very great distance. I walk two days and I paddle two nights. Then I hear a faint hum of life in the distance. The clay landscape reverberates with the sound. Then the land ends in a great water and I lower my grass boat and cast off into the brown stream. The wide waterway that leads into the city becomes narrow as little islands of floating vegetation appear one at a time—drifting gardens made of mud dredged from the shallow lake and suspended on the water's surface on wickerwork rafts. These random garden barges gradually entangle, becoming large stationary plots of rich land. Lush plants have sent their roots down deep into the lake's bottom, creating so many artificial earthworks that the lake has been transformed into hundreds of narrow canals through which white-clad farmers swiftly pole their dugouts as they cultivate their watery gardens. These canals are the causeways of Tenochtitlan. Along the banks and among the flowers and trees are the thatched huts of farmers. Then, as the boats loaded with city-bound produce become numerous, the adobe walls of richer homes appear among the foliage—at first made simply of naked clay and then plastered more elegantly and colored muted shades of red. Narrow roads appear beside the canals where merchants with armed guards and trotting carriers bring their goods to the markets. Soon people of rank are seen along the banks of the canal. Clan leaders wear the rich mantles of their office. They alone are permitted to carry an aristocratic bouquet of flowers, which they sniff lavishly. They meander among the black-garbed priests whose faces are painted black, whose ears are scarred by self-inflicted penance, and whose long black hair is matted with blood.

There is much excitement in the city. Everywhere there is a holiday atmosphere. It is a special day in the history of our land. And all the people are filled with happiness. In various little houses fiestas are being celebrated. The jubilant sounds of wooden drums and flutes and conchshell trumpets come from every direction. It is a day of many flowers and many precious feathers. The old men smile and the young girls are dancing. It is the day when the great city Tenochtitlan and all her vast domain called Mexico will have a new Lord, a new Great Speaker.

This visit to Tenochtitlan happened many years ago when I was still a poor boy of only sixteen summers, living with my mother in the marshy lands near the city of Tlaxcala. I was the boy who had traveled to Tenochtitlan, and I had seen Montezuma. But the people of Tlaxcala hated the Lord of the greatest city of Mexico. They scoffed at him and belittled him though they had never seen him. But I had seen Montezuma and I did not loathe him. I had seen him in Tenochtitlan, the city of enemies of my Tlaxcalan ancestors. But Montezuma was not my enemy. He was the most glorious being I had ever seen in my life, while my own people were wretched and savage. I, Nanautzin, had seen the immense Plaza of Tenochtitlan, but among my own people I was despised for my ugliness. Stealing whatever I could, chopping wood, and doing whatever I had to do to survive, I grew up through many bad days and many sad and hungry nights.

That is when I got the name "the Ugly One"—

Nanautzin—because I had stumbled into the cooking fire when I was a small child and, like that forlorn god who sacrificed himself in the divine hearth, I was deformed by scars and terrible wounds which were slow to heal. My mother hid me in her arms. She wept when boys and girls called out unthinkable names and abused my deformities. She held her hands over my ears and surrounded me with her warm body. But my father could not tolerate the shame. The men turned their eyes away when he walked among them, for he was father to a monstrosity. And so my father turned his back on me and disowned me. He urinated on the ground where I had been born and said I was no longer his child. But my mother could not let me go into the wild land alone. She hid me in the darkest corner of our hut, and when we were alone she knelt before me with tears on her cheeks and wrapped my swollen ankles, trying to relieve the pain with herbs and prayers. My childhood was filled with her tears and her prayers.

Then the day came when my father did not return to our home. He had thrown my mother and me away. He brought no food; he brought no water. And we were alone.

All these things I have known, and knowing them has taught me something of disdain and something of loving.

Each day of my life I wanted him to come back, taking me upon his shoulders, smelling from the fields and from the sweat that rolled down his body. Each day of my life the young men laughed at Nanautzin, and every day the young women turned their heads so they would not have to see the terrible speckled scars that covered my shoulders and face. Every day I was hungry and every day I wept. And in the darkness where I lay blessedly invisible, I listened to the night birds on the far distant royal hill of Chapultepec where the Great Speaker of Tenochtitlan, Ahuitzotl, called out from among the gigantic cypresses for more tribute from my wretched people of Tlaxcala. Each night my dreams were filled with transformations that changed me into a man of wisdom and a reader of the wondrous stories written in the Stars of the evening sky. Each night I walked slowly toward the Great Speaker, but just as I came close enough to peer into his face, the daylight broke into my dream and the glorious palace walls dissolved into the interior of my hut. In the morning my reflection in the water was the same reflection, and my empty stomach was the same empty stomach. And so it was that they gave me the name of the ugly god, Nanautzin, and they gave me an ax and they called me woodcutter and then they forgot about me.

I tied my dugout to the shore and slowly made my way past a handsome house of many cool and spacious rooms. The polished red floor was strewn with mats and straw cushions where a young fellow idly smoked a cigarette in a cane holder and picked at the scarcely healed lobe of his ear, which was tattered by penitential bloodletting. I nodded to the young man and his fat little sister who squatted in the doorway, but they acted as if they didn't see me. I lingered for a moment before climbing to the roadway leading into the city, sniffing the marvelous aroma that came from the kitchen at the back of the house, where rhythmic clapping hands prepared tortillas and threw them with a daring gesture onto the hot stone griddle.

I was not welcome here, but in my dreams I often ate the finest tortillas and the noblest of men greeted me as a

Celebrants carrying festive foods. The symbols coming
from the mouths represent speech. *Codex Florentino.*

friend. And though I was little more than a slave and hadn't the least hope of ever setting foot within the temples or the high places of the lords, I had come this long way to see Tenochtitlan and to see the installation of the new Great Speaker. For if I were to be a wretched fellow for the rest of my life, I was determined that I would have one thing that I alone among all the people of the marshes could tell. I would go to the mighty city of Tenochtitlan and I would stand among the throngs of celebrants during the coronation of the Great Speaker, Montezuma II, who is the Lord called Xocoyotzin, "The Younger."

I made my way through a little grove of blossom-filled saplings where a group of old men lolled drunkenly, sipping cups of pulque. The old ones smiled ecstatically to the music of flutes and nodded to festive drumming. They alone were permitted to drink the intoxicating pulque—the reward in their old age for having passed with honor through rigid years of self-denial. Now they could sit and dream. Now they could dismiss restraint and dignity. The pulque released the sacred clown within each of them and they laughed at misfortune and destiny and death.

Farther along the road there were large groups of priests and men of high office. Everywhere I could see the glorious vestments of the nobles: mantles, jingling necklaces, and glittering translucent jewels.

A distant music resounded louder and still louder, and throngs of people from many different causeways spilled suddenly into a magnificent open square, where great temples rose high above the huge white pyramids that supported them. Incense billowed into thick clouds, and the rich amber sunlight of the afternoon rebounded against the rippling, unearthly outlines of the immense temples. I could not believe what I saw before me, though I had always heard marvelous stories of the mighty city. It was my old dream come out into the sunshine.

Drums thundered and the shouts of people rose into a vast, mysterious drone. Everywhere was the smell of blood. And in the skull rack thousands upon thousands of human heads were threaded on poles and piled high in perfect symmetry, a testament of those who loved the gods and had given their precious blood to the Sun, without which it would quickly die of exhaustion and hunger.

The music and the shouts of the people rose into a tumult of jubilant sounds. My pulse soared with excitement and I was so overwhelmed by the spectacle of the Great Plaza that tears came into my ignorant eyes. I had never seen so great a world as this!

Then suddenly there was silence. Far across the Plaza I could see the royal procession coming into view. Stripped of their elegant mantles and jewels, the Lord Montezuma and his councilmen walked in humble quietude. They paused at the wide base of the Great Pyramid to Huitzilopochtli. And there before the deity they were dressed in the simplest garments. The dark-green cotton cloak was placed on Montezuma's shoulders. It was painted with the faces and the bones of the Dead. Over one shoulder they suspended a gourd filled with sweet herbs, and in the great Lord's right hand they carefully placed an incense burner filled with bright coals. Over his face they then placed the mask painted with a skull so the people could not see their god.

Now priests take his arms and guide him, as he climbs the one hundred and fourteen steps to the house of

Huitzilopochtli—a wooden temple at the summit of the pyramid where the huge image of the god is sheltered. There Montezuma bows very low, touching the stone floor and sprinkling dust on his head in submission to the ancient tribal protector and god of the sunlight.

Then he pours the fragrant herbs upon the coals, and clouds of adoration billow from the incense burner. I stand among the huge crowd of people and I am filled with such reverence that I begin dreaming. I press forward through the awed people. I cannot take my eyes off Montezuma II as he pierces his ears with a needle made from the tiger's bone and his blood falls upon his shoulders. And all around me the people softly murmur. I can hear somewhere deep within my body a whimper. I press forward through the silent throng, never once taking my eyes off the figure of the great Lord of Tenochtitlan high atop the pyramid. The black priests drift among the clouds of incense, swarming slowly around Montezuma with their power and magic. Putting the insignia of the Great Speaker upon him. Placing the obsidian diadem upon his head.

I am very close to the pyramid now. I strain to see him—to see each finger of his graceful hands. I stare up at him so intently that I fly into the air and hover over his head like a butterfly. In my heart I can see Montezuma. As the mask is taken from his face I groan. His face, it is a night sky filled with turbulent dark clouds. Now and again a great, luminous Moon appears unexpectedly in his expressionless eyes. Then it is gone and it is dark again.

Suddenly the music of rejoicing bursts in the immense Plaza. From the pyramid platform come the great booming voices of the wooden drums and the cry of the conch-shell trumpets and pipes. Down the steep steps comes his council, and then countless priests, and finally the people who humbly trace his divine steps. The Lord Montezuma! He is surrounded by a multitude of great men and powerful wizards. He moves across the Great Plaza and I press forward unfalteringly, dazed and haunted by the splendor of his image. Now Montezuma draws near. He passes just in front of me. All around me the people drop to their knees, but I cannot move as I gaze at him. All around me the people dare not lift their eyes to look upon his face. But I stare at him until the guards shout and push me to the ground.

When I look up, Montezuma is gone.

Three

After that marvelous day in Tenochtitlan I was prepared to live out my life in the gray world of the marshes, resigned to the fact that seeing the Great Speaker Montezuma was to be the only grand event of my existence. But I was satisfied. And so I left the great city and returned to my home, where I buried my heart in drudgery, never hoping to know another exceptional moment.

And yet I was somehow changed by what had happened to me in Tenochtitlan. When I looked at my reflection I was still the same ugly lad, and my hands were still coarse and pitted by calluses. My mantle was made of the coarsest maguey fiber and my feet were bare. But nonetheless I felt deeply changed. I began to feel something that no one else had ever felt before. I began to think about Nanautzin. I started thinking about what and how I felt about things . . . all kinds of little things I had never noticed before. And I grew to loathe my woodcutter's hands and my woodcutter's life.

For the next five summers I chopped wood. At dawn I began and at dusk I returned to the hut, where my mother fed me silently; until one morning she could not get up anymore. And she died.

For five summers I chopped wood. Dreaming of giant pines while searching for timber in the swollen ground of the marshes where nothing grows tall and everything grows old too soon.

Then in the twenty-first summer of my life, it was time for me to become a man. All the young males of my clan went to see the old women who make marriages. But I was Nanautzin, the Ugly One, and I was the poor woodcutter, so nobody wanted to be my woman. I, Nanautzin, had gone alone to Tenochtitlan and I had seen the Great Speaker. All this I had done, and yet I was a man without a wife and without a family. For me it was a bad time. But for the great Lord of Mexico it was a good time.

After a year of sacred seclusion, Montezuma was established in a new palace in honor of the festival called the Second Bringing of Stones from Malinalco, commemorating the ancestors who had brought the stones used, four hundred years earlier, to build the first temple of Huitzilopochtli—the War God, the incarnation of the Sun and the protector of his people. The god had promised us dominion over all Mexico. But there were still enemies to be subdued. The prophecy of greatness was not yet complete, and Lord Montezuma proclaimed that his armies would crush those who stood between him and his people's destiny. That winter, in the year of 11 One Reed (1503), great snows fell in the Mixtec highlands. The severe frost threatened the hills of maize, but the storm also brought much water, and the drought that had endangered the crops came to an end. In this way, all things were good and plentiful. And all of this was achieved by Montezuma, who understood the weather signs in the sky.

And then in the year 12 One Reed (1504), caravans of merchants returned from long journeys to the land in the south where an ancient people lived . . . a people who wrote in glyphs and made magnificent temples. There was much rejoicing in Tenochtitlan, for the bearers brought many hampers of the precious cacao bean. This too was achieved by the Great Speaker, for he had seen the Pleiades in the heavens—the sky market that glimmers beside the great river of light called the Milky Way. And so Montezuma encouraged the daring of the merchants, for if they traveled the roads of all Mexico they would be like those wide-ranging Stars of the heavenly marketplace. They would therefore bring great power to Tenochtitlan. And all this Montezuma saw in the sky, and all this he achieved on the Earth. In the past the cacao bean had been so precious, it took only four hundred beans to transact the most important business of the traders and chiefs. But now, under the rule of Montezuma, cacao beans were sold at the marketplace for the first time since the glorious days of the Toltecs. This is how great was the achievement of Montezuma!

These were the stories that traders and farmers brought to us from Tenochtitlan, reports of good omens and marvelous victories that were told and retold until eventually the people of the remotest marshlands beyond Tlaxcala had heard the astonishing tales of Montezuma's greatness. Even woodcutters like me sat gloomily rubbing their large hands together while the news from the enemy city of Tenochtitlan was told.

My people were very proud of their independence from the great Lord of the Mexicans who ruled all the Great

The forlorn Lord Montezuma meditates in ancient
Tula, land of Quetzalcoatl. *Codex Florentino*.

Valley of the lakes and many of the tribes beyond the valley, but our freedom was false, for we were continually abused by the warriors of Tenochtitlan and forced to give tribute. Many of our young men were taken to the Great Plaza and offered to the gods. But still the people of my humble village were awed by the wonder of Montezuma's greatness. And so they recounted all the stories of his deeds again and again. I used to close my eyes and, as I listened, I would try to recall the image of the great Lord, but all I could remember was the angry shouts of the guards who had thrown me to the ground for trying to look into the face of Montezuma. Though I worshiped his power and his godliness, and though I had been forever touched by his grandeur, I also hated him for his seclusion that kept him remote from us. I might have loathed him as all my people loathed him, I might have shouted out against his pompousness; I might have groaned about the tribute he took from Tlaxcala, but having come so close to him I was forever changed, and I knew that whatever made me what I had become was somehow dependent upon the existence of Lord Montezuma II.

It was summer, and the young men came from the fields and rested in the shade, where their women fed and fanned them until they fell asleep to the buzzing lullaby of ten thousand black flies. Dogs panted under the thatched roofs and only the tireless red ants continued their frantic work in the glare of the Sun. I could not sleep. I sat staring blankly at the long strings of red peppers hanging motionless in the humid air. Sweat collected on my face and chest. I was despondent and disgruntled, but I did not know what it was I wanted. I got up from my mat without knowing where I was going and, after fetching my ax, I stumbled blindly into the blaze of sunlight and started out through a cloud of dust as the villagers laughed and called me a fool for leaving the comfort of the shadows.

I walked for many hours, unconscious of anything but the heat and the sweat running off my limbs. When I stopped I found myself at the edge of a wide, wooded slope. It was the most beautiful grove I had ever seen . . . truly a woodcutter's dream! I had spent my youth in miserable thickets collecting sticks and twigs. There had been no sturdy logs for my woodcutter's ax, no wide-limbed giants perched handsomely on their broad trunks. But these trees were lords among trees. They were surely part of the guarded reserve of some man of very high rank. A man of power and wealth. Someone, perhaps, who had even entered the Council Chamber of Montezuma!

I knew, of course, that I should not enter this forest. I knew that I could forfeit my life if I were to trespass on the land of some great man. But I could not turn away. I could not simply turn and go away. For a very long time I remained there on the edge of the lush forest, peering into the mysterious green shadows. Listening to the opulent, endless trill of those remarkable birds which nest only in the tallest of tall trees.

I do not know why I did it. I do not understand the voice in me that spoke so strongly. I could not resist the beauty of this forbidden place and, feeling amazed by my own actions, I picked up my ax and stepped into the leafy shadows, where I was drawn forward by the magic song of the birds.

Soon I found myself standing in a small clearing surrounded by such stately trees that in the amber twilight they seemed to be the lofty walls of some forgotten green temple. Now it was utterly still in the forest. The birds had returned to their nests for the night, and already the evening air came tumbling down from the mountaintops. With the Sun's setting it became much colder, and I was about to turn for home when I noticed in the middle of the clearing a pile of dead wood that would surely make an excellent fire. Without thinking of the consequences, I decided that I would cut up the wood and enjoy a comfortable night's sleep next to a nice fire.

When I swung my ax the whole forest rang out with the echoes of my work. I dropped to my knees in fear and peered into the fading daylight. Nothing moved. There were no sounds except the windy whispers of the treetops. I slowly stood up and, closing my eyes and trying not to hear the din sent up by my ax blows, I started to chop the wood into kindling and logs.

At just that moment a voice shouted out from behind me, and I whirled around and lifted my ax to the intruder. I was terrified to see vaguely in the dimness a man glaring at me. I quickly dropped my ax to the ground and, before he could call for his guards, I greeted him as humbly as I could, putting on a sad face in the hope that he would be compassionate enough simply to shout at me and send me away.

"What are you doing here?" the man asked quietly. "And why have you been cutting firewood on this land?"

The great man's voice was so compelling and his manner so composed, I could not raise my eyes to his face. I was dumbfounded. And yet I did not fear him, for I was enchanted by an aura of solemnity that surrounded him.

After a moment I began speaking to him in a whisper,

telling him things I knew I was never supposed to tell a nobleman. "I am poor," I said. "I am alone. And I need wood to warm myself."

Then I glanced up into the man's shadowed face. I moistened my lips carefully and I began to speak to him as I sometimes spoke to myself. "I am tired of being a woodcutter," I said. "I am tired of having nothing. And I am tired of the tribute exacted from the villages and the work service we are forced to give."

The nobleman looked at me with amazement; and then he smiled very slowly and I was not certain if he was planning some terrible punishment or if he was genuinely amused. "Is that so," he said flatly. Then he smiled again, took a few steps toward me, and continued to speak in his serene voice. "Is this what your people think about their lives?"

I answered at once. "It is his fault!" I blurted out in anger. "The Great Speaker of Tenochtitlan does not love the Tlaxcalans. He loves only war."

"Is that so?"

"Yes!" I barked as I turned away from him. "Yes, it is so. All of it is so. Since Montezuma has ascended to the Palace he has become a lover of power. It is true! What I say is true. And besides," I muttered gloomily as I became aware that I would surely be punished for the things I had said, "in the old days, before Montezuma was the Great Speaker, my people, the Tlaxcalans, were allowed to cut all the dead wood they wanted for their own use. Only Montezuma prohibits us from warming our bodies."

The nobleman nodded several times in silence. He looked around as if he were about to summon his guards, but instead he seated himself in the midst of a golden heap of dead leaves and pine needles and looked at me very calmly with a trace of friendship in his eyes. It was the first time in my life that I had seen so great a man sit upon the ground.

"I will not punish you," he said to me quietly. "This much I know for certain . . . I am not going to punish you because you are far too exceptional a man. You may be a problem," he mused, "and yes, of course, you are probably dangerous, for all exceptional men are dangerous. But I will not punish you."

I continued to gaze at him, but he paid no attention to me as he arose in the darkness that was quickly surrounding us. Then he walked slowly toward me. "This honesty of yours," he said, "let us hope that it is a *most* exceptional trait in Mexico, Woodcutter. For I would not be happy to discover too many outspoken men like you in my land." Then for no apparent reason the nobleman smiled, drew his mantle around his waist, and, as he turned and walked away, said firmly, "Tomorrow at midday you will come to me at the Palace of Tenochtitlan."

I nodded in amazement.

"What is your name, Woodcutter?" he asked in a commanding voice without looking back at me.

"Nanautzin," I said.

Trembling, I watched him until he was gone. Then I fell into the leaves on the cold ground and closed my eyes. Soon it would be the new day, and I would be judged in Tenochtitlan. Surely this would be the end of the Ugly One called Nanautzin.

Four

I had expected never to see Tenochtitlan again. yet here I was rushing toward that great city. Despite my premonitions of punishment for the theft of firewood and trespassing on a royal reserve, I was nonetheless overwhelmed with excitement as I found myself among the same canals and floating gardens, among the farmers and the priests, the officers and men of rank whom I had not seen since my boyhood.

It was a big market day, and the crowds were larger and noisier than they had been when I saw the marketplace as a young man. Humble and great men hurried in every direction, the rich carrying flowers and the poor carrying burdens. In a small ball court, with its sloping masonry sides and narrow playing field, a few men were practicing the game we call *pot-a-tok,* and so I momentarily forgot the punishment that might await me in the Palace of Montezuma and stood amazed by the skill of the difficult game. The expressions of the young players were unusually grim as they raced after the hard rubber ball and, using their heads, their thighs, and their feet, tried to keep it from striking the floor of the court. It was a sport of great daring and deep significance. And I watched the ball fly through the air. Again and again the players on the two teams tried to score. They thrust and leaped and sang as they played, trying to put the ball through the rings set at intervals in the walls of the court. But neither side could score.

It was a game that only the best and strongest young men were permitted to play, and even in my simple village, where we did not have even the rudest ball court, the boys nonetheless imitated the movements of the game and chased wildly after a sand-filled gourd that they invented as their ball. All the boys of my village had rushed and butted and bounded in the dirt playing their imaginary game of pot-a-tok, but I was Nanautzin, the Ugly One, and they had not let me play with them. So I stood entranced by the game. Now, here in great Tenochtitlan, I was seeing a real game of pot-a-tok.

Yet I did not dare linger, for I had already annoyed a nobleman and did not dare enrage him further by keeping him waiting.

I hurried away and pushed through the Great Plaza. I could see nothing but human bodies and human baggage as I pressed forward. Then suddenly I stepped out of the tangle of the crowd into a vast open space at the entrance of the Palace. Here, before the door of Montezuma, there were no crowds. Only men of power and rank walked here. One by one they came to the Council Chamber of the Great Speaker to plead for favors or to beg for his forgiveness. This was a place where even fearsome men were afraid, for no one was greater than the Great Speaker Montezuma. And I was Nanautzin, the woodcutter who had nothing. And as I

touched the gates of Montezuma's Palace I trembled and my
heart died.

But somehow I gained entrance without a word, for no
one seemed to want to bother with me. A guard glanced at
my feet and, seeing that they were bare, he did not give me
any further notice. And it was only with difficulty that I
managed to get the attention of a young man who listened
to my story patiently and then asked my name.

"My name is Nanautzin," I told him. "And what is
your name?"

The young man turned away without answering me.
With his back to me, he muttered, "We will call you when
it is time. Wait here quietly."

Because I did not want to get lost in the crowd of
waiting people and perhaps miss my summons, I stayed
close to the door through which the fellow had disappeared
and gazed silently at the exceptional people who had come
to the Palace of Montezuma. Of them all—priests, judges,
merchants, and even the humblest farmers—I was surely
the humblest and most frightened.

Soon I was told to enter the large chamber beyond the
doorway where many guards stood silently staring at me. I
was told to wait at the foot of a massive staircase that
ascended through the wide, empty space of the large room.
I stood there tearfully, for in this grand place, among these
men of rank and power, I realized how very foolish I was. I,
a mere woodcutter, had always known how truly low I was,
but here, awaiting the nobleman who would judge me in
this greatest of all great places, I felt smaller and lower than
I had ever felt before. I must have been insane to enter that
forest and to insult a nobleman! I could not imagine what
had possessed me to behave so arrogantly.

In the midst of these appalling thoughts, I suddenly looked up and was terrified to see a slender man descending the stairs. He was wearing the blue cloak of Montezuma! Quickly I covered my eyes and fell to my knees, sobbing with fear as I threw dust on my head and trembled. Surely I had not been so incredibly unfortunate as to have trespassed in the forest of the Great Speaker himself! I was overcome with dread. I crouched on the floor, waiting to hear what he would do with me.

"Ask him if he is the one who calls himself by the name of a god," a soft, eloquent voice instructed one of the orators through whom Montezuma spoke. "Ask him if he is the one called Nanautzin."

I was about to protest that I was named for a god not out of pride but out of misfortune, since like the god Nanautzin I had been disfigured by fire. But suddenly, as I lay there on the floor trembling for my life, I could not help feeling that I knew the voice of Montezuma. I was absolutely certain of it. I had heard that voice somewhere before. I dared one quick glance at the magnificent figure on the steps and, with a sick heart, realized with horror that this absolute ruler and god before me was the same "nobleman" who had caught me stealing firewood!

I was certain that Montezuma would tear my heart from me at once or summon the power of his divine ancestors and kill me with a glance.

"Do you see what trouble there is in the truth?" Montezuma said through his orator. "Trouble for you and trouble for me. I went out into the countryside and there in the wilderness I learned far more than I ever need to know about the people of Mexico!" Then the Great Speaker was silent, and this made me more frightened than his words.

37

"Woodcutter," he barked at last, "stop groveling! Get up on your feet and come with me!"

Trembling and repeatedly bowing as low as possible, I crept along after the great Lord, following him through the clusters of murmuring people who dropped to their knees and crouched on the floor with their hands covering their eyes as we swept past them. I could not speak or think. I barely could breathe. But as I followed along frantically in the footsteps of Montezuma I knew one thing: whether I was killed or allowed to live, nothing could change the things that existed in my head. I knew that such thoughts were mad. And I knew that I would surely die for thinking them, but I was glad that I had finally become *someone,* even if I had achieved it at the cost of my own life.

Montezuma hurried through kitchens and storehouses and immense dining rooms where hundreds of guests were being served by countless servants. As our great Lord swept past them they tumbled to their knees and covered their eyes. We passed the treasuries where clerks were making elaborate picture lists of the objects of jade, the mantles of feathers, and the baskets of food that had been sent as tribute to the great Montezuma. We passed the lavish apartments where the Great Speaker's two wives and many concubines occupied magnificent chambers. Everywhere people scrambled to get out of our way. Everywhere people knelt and murmured respectfully.

Then we entered a small white room and Montezuma waved his arms and then stood silently. At once the priests bowed and quickly rushed away, followed immediately by the attendants and guards. The door was pulled closed and suddenly I found myself alone with the mightiest ruler in the world.

The war chiefs come before Montezuma II. *Codex Florentino.*

"I wish to speak to you," he said, taking no notice of my astonishment at being addressed directly by the supreme ruler of men. "And I want you to answer me as honestly as you did last evening when I found you in the forest. Is that clear?"

I blinked with confusion, but I nodded my head in agreement. Then Montezuma spoke to me in a very soft voice, asking the same questions he had asked the prior night. I answered as politely as I could, for I had a love of words and I hoped to be eloquent in my speech even if I was crude and primitive in all other ways. And so I gave my answers as I had given them originally, except this time I tried to be as humble as I was honest.

Montezuma listened patiently and then he reached out and touched me just once on the shoulder and told me to remain in peace and without fear. The Great Speaker opened the door and at once the rules of ceremony were resumed. The official interpreter stepped forward and spoke the words of Montezuma. "You will be changed," I was told. But I did not understand what these words meant. I tried to ask the interpreter the meaning of his statement, but he ignored me. Meanwhile attendants were being called and the room was in an upheaval, with people hurrying in and out to bring clothing and jewels. All of these precious things Montezuma had them place at my feet. And as I gazed around in astonishment, new commands were issued, and gradually I began to understand that I was to become a new person.

I was thrust to the floor, and while my eyes streamed with tears and I made every effort to conceal my pain, an attendant sent a blade through my lower lip and through the septum of my nose. Then into these raw wounds marvelous jewels were quickly inserted: the lip plug worn only by men of power and a beautiful nose plug that was the mark of the men of art. Then, as my head still spun with pain, I was pulled to my feet and a handsome new blanket was wrapped around me, while great bundles of feathers were hung from my shoulders, and the priests came forward to paint my face.

"This man called Nanautzin is changed!" the Great Speaker Montezuma said through his orator. "He is no longer the woodcutter. He is no longer the man of Tlaxcala. He is the one who is highest among those who speak my words for me, and he will accompany me throughout Mexico and speak my words in honesty and with eloquence as he has spoken so honestly and eloquently for himself. Nanautzin, you are transformed!"

Five

Great Montezuma sat on his wicker throne in the Palace of Tenochtitlan, and I sat beside him. When he spoke, I spoke in his behalf, for I was his voice. When he walked, I walked beside him, and when he was particularly satisfied with himself he would momentarily glance into my eyes and then a very small smile would creep slowly into one corner of his mouth.

My Lord was magnificent. And by comparison I was nothing. Whereas the noblemen bowed with eloquence, whereas the servants and even the slaves bowed abjectly, I could only grovel in my awkwardness, for I knew nothing. Though I wore the mantle of the Chief Orator of Montezuma, I had the memory of a woodcutter, and I knew nothing of my people's history among the gods. I did not know the Days or the messages of the night skies, written against the darkness in the motion of the Stars. I was like a child again, learning everything for the first time. I was sent to the Telpuchcalli where the young men were trained in war. And I was also sent to the Calmecac where the sacred ways of Quetzalcoatl and his priests were taught.

"Nanautzin, do not be in such a hurry," the Great Speaker would advise through one of his lesser orators while he sat quietly at his dinner. "Inside you are already what you need to be. It is only the outside that needs a new whitewash."

Montezuma spoke to me in this friendly manner, but he never addressed me directly while we were in the presence of his entourage. When we were alone in the Council Chamber or in the lovely rooftop gardens of his apartments, then he called me by the name he liked best for me. "What do you think of this war of ours, Woodcutter?" he would ask me. And when I answered him honestly, he would say, "Well, Woodcutter, don't talk about such ideas with the elders or the scholars, or they may realize what fools they are!" And then he would laugh. Montezuma's laughter was a sound so rare and so private, I was embarrassed to hear it.

Sometimes the great Lord would sit down among the flowers with the book of fate called the *Teoamoxtli,* in which he could read the wide dreams of the future. He would speak of the glorious things he could see while gazing into this puzzling book, as I sat at his feet and listened to the splendid stories of the gods and of the people.

From the rooftop of the Palace, voices from the Great Plaza far below rolled through the clear, warm air. Flowers grew rampantly in the abundant sunshine of the serene gardens of Montezuma. Vanilla orchids sent delirious fragrances into our nostrils, and the hibiscus and jacaranda interlaced, piling strident blossoms in the air, while among the musky herbal shrubs honeybees made their way on

43

thick, yellow feet. At a respectful distance, in the broad, plastered patio adjoining the garden, acrobats were practicing their perilous feats and humpback dwarfs rehearsed antics and outrages in the hope of winning a subtle smile from their ruler. But if the Great Speaker was in a gloomy mood and did not want the company of fools, he would call to me impatiently: "Woodcutter!" And we would go to the buildings that housed the royal zoo, where huge serpents dangled sleepily from trees, and the blazing yellow eyes of ocelots and jaguars watched us with shameless ferocity from within the cages.

There were splendid diversions to entertain the Great Speaker, but of all his many preoccupations the one that most obsessed him was the knowledge and mysterious power of the ancients called Toltecs. There were days when I could see in the eyes of Montezuma a terrible darkness that slowly covered his face like the fearful shadow that sometimes falls upon the Sun. The antics of a thousand merry dwarfs could not relieve that sadness. On such days the great Lord sat silently on his wicker throne and stared into the vast Council Chamber, his black, oiled hair hanging heavily about his shoulders, his splendid mantle draped over his tall, athletic body. He looked like a god exquisitely carved in brown stone and turquoise, but in his eyes there was the sorrow of a man.

I was only a woodcutter and yet I had been chosen by the great Lord to speak his words. I was a man of Tlaxcala whose people were called barbarians and whose hearts were taken by the thousands in our flowery wars to feed the Sun. Yet I was the one whom Montezuma trusted. And I loved him for his trust. I was an ignorant man of the country, and yet I could see in his dark eyes a little island of time surrounded by infinite sorrow. For this sadness I also loved him.

One gloomy day Montezuma called for his guard and his litter and we made the two days' journey to a forsaken place called Tula—a vast ruin sprawled out in the golden grass. "Here is my wilderness," my Lord said in a whisper as we neared Tula. "Over there—on that heap of rubble which was once the sacred House of the Frog, that is where I had a vision of unhappy Topiltzin, the last Great Speaker of the Toltecs. I saw him go sadly into exile. That is what I saw in my vision. Then it was gone and I was left in the dust and silence of Tula. This is a place of great tragedy and power, Woodcutter. It is a place of strong visions."

It was also a place of utter desolation and decay. Among the broken roots were burnt timbers and the charred stones that once had been grand temples. Faint traces of pigment clung to shattered stone portraits, vague footprints in time that vanished into the shadows when the Sun dropped below the broken city wall with its crumbling procession of carved ocelots. The wind remained when the sunlight withdrew.

In the midst of this vast ruin was a small temple that Montezuma, when still a boy, had petitioned his uncle to erect within the shambles of ancient Tula. No one but Montezuma cared about the ruined city. No one ever came this way. Only the priests remained, making offerings in honor of Montezuma's visit to Lord Quetzalcoatl and to Huitzilopochtli the Warrior.

These ceremonies did not raise my Lord from his gloomy mood. He sighed and turned away from the priests. "We are torn and we are broken into many pieces," he murmured, "just as Huitzilopochtli once dismembered the Moon. We serve two gods. We revere one while we await

the return of the other. We are broken by our devotion."
And then Montezuma became silent and beckoned to the
litter carriers.

Soon we were ready for the journey back to Tenochtitlan. We started out at a jogtrot, the guards chanting songs
while their captain played on a conch-shell trumpet, sending a fragile music across the wide windy plateau as our
grave Lord bobbed above our heads like a precious bird upon
the water.

We had taken only a few steps when Montezuma
looked down at me and said, "No, Woodcutter, not you.
You will remain here with the priests."

I started to complain, but he waved me away with a
stern gesture that made me step back in fear. I stood looking
after him until he was gone and it was dark, and the priests
came out into the moonless night and stood beside me.
Finally I turned back to the temple. Montezuma had given
the priests their instructions, and there was nothing I could
do but obey their commands. "It is our task to teach you,"
the head priest told me as he wished me good night.

The discipline of the temple was very strict, and the
boys sent there by their parents were as miserable about
their situation as I was. The priests gave me a mat and told
me to sleep among these callow youngsters, though I was a
grown man and the Chief Orator of the Great Speaker of
Tenochtitlan. But this made no impression upon the
priests, who turned away and left me alone with the
children.

The boys stared at the spotted scars that covered my
body. They whispered, and the youngest among them
whimpered in the darkness. I rolled over and went to sleep.

Night, however, was the time when the temple came

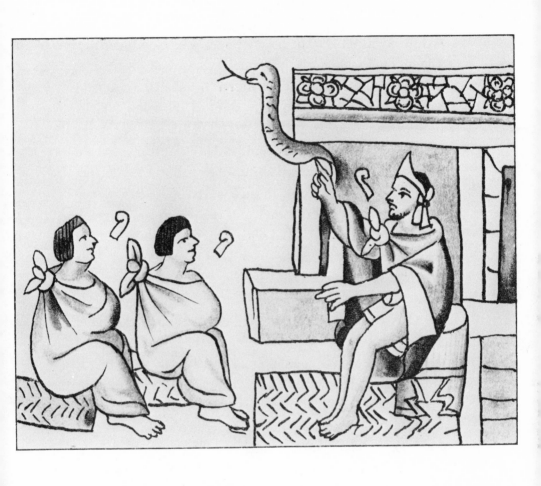

Montezuma knew more about the history of his
people than any other man. *Codex Florentino.*

to life. At midnight the boys were awakened and sent in a solemn procession to the uppermost platform of the temple, where their voices awakened me with sorrowful chants. I arose from my mat and quietly climbed the stairs. Yellow light flew up from the fires burning in the stone vases on the highest platform of the pyramid, and in these flames I could see the boys thrusting needles into their earlobes and letting blood flow in large drops to their naked shoulders. When the bleeding ritual was completed, the priests stood among the weary boys and pointed with emaciated hands into the heavens, teaching them the odysseys of the Stars. And while the older boys searched the heavens, the youngest were sent out naked into the utter darkness on their Night Journey. It was the first test of manhood, and they were more fearful of failing than of the perilous deep night that surrounded them. Each group of trembling boys was led by a black-clad priest who understood the laws of time and the words that charmed away the dangerous beings of the dark. The Night Journey was a search for the elements needed to make the God Food, *teotlacualli,* a thick pitch which the priests drank and with which they painted their bodies. It was the duty of the youngest boys of the temple to search for centipedes, scorpions, lizards, spiders, vipers, and other deadly beings which they caught with twigs or, if the youngsters hoped to be warriors, with their fingers. They took all these things and burned them in the brazier that stood in the temple, after which the ashes were placed in mortars together with an herb called *tobacco.* After crushing these precious things, a ground seed called *ololiuhqui,* morning glory, was added to the mixture together with hairy black worms and soot.

When the *teotlacualli* was prepared, the priests care-fully poured the liquid into a ceremonial gourd. Then, without a word, the gourd was placed in my hands.

I stared dumbfounded at the black-painted faces of the priests. But they did not respond. Though their eyes were open there seemed to be no life within them . . . just small mirrors in which I could see a perfect image of myself. I stepped away and shook my head with dread. I tried to thrust the gourd back into the hands of the priests, but they turned away from me. I started to run down the temple steps, but hands restrained me and from every direction came black figures, forming a circle around me.

Then I realized I would have to drink the hideous potion.

A luminous lake rose slowly until it became a green horizon cut into delicate slices by a blinding rain. In this place where nothing moves, Ometeotl walks on two im-mense feet, each wishing to go its own way and tearing Ometeotl in two, so that the one part engenders and the other conceives, and from this came everything that fills the green sky—rain, wind, and the place called the Region of the Dead. Mother of these many things and of the Four Directions spread out slowly on the navel of the Earth, and within the turquoise circle the being who lives in the bluebird water, who dwells also in the clouds and inhabits the shadows, took hold of me by the hair and threw me down upon the ground, sending up a shower of sparks and flames where I landed . . . making fire and time in one instant. Then came the Four Suns. But they were destroyed by deluge and hurricane, volcanoes and the hammers of

Earth and Air, Fire and Water together. The First Sun was the Sun of Atonatiuh, the Water; and during this time the world was filled with giants who could not sow the ground and ate only pine kernels. And they were destroyed by water. The Second Sun was the Sun of Ehecatonatiuh, the Air, and during this time the world was occupied by deformed people who neglected the temples and ate only bread made with the fruit of the mesquite. They were destroyed by a gigantic hurricane that swept them away. And the Third Sun was the Sun of Tletonatiuh, the Fire. The people of the Earth knew how to sow but did not possess the divine maize, and they could eat only a grain born in the water. And volcanoes shook and threw their crimson veils over everything, leaving nothing but the scorched barren mountains; so the world ended again. The Fourth Sun was the Sun of Tlaltonatiuh, the Earth, and its people lived in a green place where crops flourished and the animals multiplied. But the gods who watch us saw that not all people gave prayers of thanks to them. They came together in council to decide how they could save those people who were good while destroying those who had not obeyed the ancient laws. They chose Chicomecoatl, goddess of the Earth, to carry out the fourth destruction of the Earth. She turned the crops brown and trampled the forests under avalanches. She tore herself open and gorged herself on fields and orchards, which fell into her ragged canyons. She shook and she trembled and she brought down the houses of the evil ones. But in the night she sent food and water to the good people of the Earth.

"O gods in the sky, you must help us or we shall perish!" the evil ones cried. "It would be better to be eaten alive by tigers than to die of hunger and thirst!''

"Haaaaaa!'' cried the gods, and they released the lean,
hungry tigers upon the Earth, which devoured all the evil
ones. And so the world came to an end once again. Now
there was nothing but the light of the gods and the drone of
broken stones falling through time . . . reverberating
everywhere but being heard by no one . . . making a long
vast storm of emptiness.

Then it was midnight, and the gods gathered at
Teotihuacan and took their places around the divine hearth.
At this holy place the fire blazed for four days. And then the
gods spoke. "We shall create the Fifth Sun, but to do so one
of us must throw himself into the fire.''

No one spoke. The fire burned brightly, but no one
spoke. Then someone . . . some shadowy person arose
. . . an ugly god, a terrible god with pimples, warts, and
scabs. He arose timidly and trembled as the other gods
gazed down upon him. He turned slowly, moving toward
the light, so I could begin to see his face.

It was my face! It was the face of Nanautzin!

When the arrogant god Tecuciztecatl, the Lord of the
Snails, saw that such a deformed little god had volunteered
to become the Fifth Sun, he jumped to his feet.

Silence!

I stared fearfully around.

The immense fire leaping and roaring and sending the
Stars into their flight. The universe beating frantically at its
mother's womb and everywhere the sound of drumming.
The sound grows louder and the flames reach higher. Then
the gods speak: "Now, Tecuciztecatl, it is the time for you
to enter the fire!''

The arrogant god grins at me as he steps slowly forward and faces the enormous tower of flames. As he approaches the heat his confidence melts about him and he feels the great flames and he is afraid. He closes his eyes and takes a breath, rushing forward. He cries out as he nears the fire, but he can go no closer. All the gods rise indignantly. Tecuciztecatl roars like a hurricane and runs toward the fire again. Four times he runs and four times he cannot go into the fire.

Then again there is silence. The immense flames rise and dance and send the comets into darkness. The universe thrusts its body against its mother's womb, staggering to be born and crying out with an infernal scream that resounds endlessly around us. And again the gods speak: "Now it is time; it is the time for you to try, Nanautzin!"

The gods stand high against the raging fire and gradually turn their white eyes so they are looking at me. They say my name again: *"Nanautzin . . . it is time."*

In an instant all my fear pours out of me. I am sick. I begin to choke and I cannot breathe. But then the fear is gone.

Without waiting a moment I struggle to my feet . . . tearing off my mantle with a shout and showing my terrible body to the fire of creation.

The priests tried to hold me back but I would not let them restrain me any longer, and I wrestled free and hurtled toward the fire that leaped up from the temple platform. There was a violent explosion in the moonlit plaza of the gods, sending up ten thousand bolts of lightning, which burst and showered down upon the Earth as silver rain. The mountains fell upon themselves in heaps and the sky opened and took me into its mouth. Then it was very dark. I could see nothing and I could hear nothing. The great fire faded into the distant night. The sound of burning flesh was heard, crackling noisily.

In the darkest night the gods sat down exhausted, waiting for me to reappear. Their wait was very long. And then the sky began to turn luminous, as a crimson aura began to form. The gods gasped and knelt to await the rising of ugly Nanautzin. They looked everywhere, but they could not guess where I would appear. Only the god called Quetzalcoatl knew the place from which the Fifth Sun would rise. And so it was . . . I came into the sky flaming red and I faltered from side to side. No one was able to look upon me, my light was so brilliant and golden.

"But how shall we live?" the gods shout. "The Sun is still! It does not move through the sky and there is no night and day!"

I falter to and fro. I falter. My brow is burning and I am dizzy. Someone is chanting, someone far away. "The Fifth Sun is called the Sun of Movement for it follows its course; but you do not move, Nanautzin! You do not move!"

I could not move. I tried again and again to get up from the damp floor of the temple platform but I was too dizzy. I could not move!

"And the old people," someone was murmuring in the darkness, "and the very old ones, they say that there will be earthquakes and there will be hunger."

But I could not stand up. I tried again and again, but I could not get up. The Earth trembled beneath me and my head moved around in circles.

The gods cried out and plunged obsidian knives into their veins, letting blood pour into the sky. Then their blood became a great wind and it swept down upon me and I floated to my feet. I was as light as a man made of dust and I drifted past the priests who tried to restrain me and I tumbled toward the steps, going down headlong, escaping toward the horizon, which began to overflow with blood.

There was loud chanting everywhere. The words bounded back and forth before me as I hurtled down the steps toward a distant world that was gradually turning into white powder. *"Sssssun in which we live . . . this Sun in which we live is also the Sun of our prince of Tula, Quetzalcoatl!"*

Now I was screaming . . . plunging down . . . falling and falling over the steps that crumbled beneath me. Falling. Silver falling. Red and crimson and turquoise falling. One million bells! One million claps of thunder! And I, Nanautzin, collapse into the arms of a golden god with hair on his pale face and his mouth filled with the silk of the maize.

When I opened my eyes I saw an enormous Moon moving through a dark sky. It was the face of Montezuma. The Great Speaker gradually took shape over me. Then he leaned slightly forward and he whispered, "Woodcutter, what did you learn?"

Six

The pulverized charcoal of the broken Palace of Tula stirred in the breeze. The adobe dust of the ruined houses blew in the wind. Tula was a place of sorrow. A place that crushed the heart with its silence. And a place haunted by butterflies and visions.

I sat in the evening with Montezuma, recovering from the powerful revelations that had come to me atop the temple in my dreams. I lay back exhaustedly and listened to my Lord recite many tales of our people. To Montezuma time was a book in which he could read the names and acts of men.

"It was in the second year of the reign of Lord Ahuitzotl that the great temple of Tenochtitlan was finished at last," he said in a gentle voice as he gazed at the toppled landscape of Tula all around us.

For Montezuma the ancient city was a wilderness and a place of mourning. It was the burial ground of an unequaled civilization. For me Tula was a place of learning, for it was here that my Lord looked backward into his most precious visions and his voice was filled with the sounds of long-lost histories.

"A stone was erected on the great stairway of the temple of Tenochtitlan depicting the radiant Sun above two former Great Speakers of our nation—Tizoc, who began work on the temple, and my uncle Ahuitzotl, who completed it. It was an achievement of profound sacredness. Before ordering work to begin on the temple, Tizoc offered blood from wounds and the priests made many ritual prayers. My uncle Ahuitzotl was so awed by the completed temple that he became determined to make more blood offerings for its dedication than had ever been given to the Sun."

When Montezuma spoke these words he looked melancholy and dismayed. He nodded his proud head and then he murmured, "My uncle was a bold man. Perhaps he was too bold. He sent his armies into the mountains of Oaxaca to capture prisoners for the sacrifice. Again and again he sent out his warriors until at last they had caught every grown male of two entire Mixteca tribes. All of them were put in wooden cages and brought back to Tenochtitlan. And then two entire tribes were put to death. Even the bravest of our allies were appalled by my uncle's plan. Nezahualpilli, Lord of Texcoco, told my uncle that so great a sacrificial ceremony was wasteful and unholy. The good number of sacrifices, he told my uncle, was twenty, and that was the correct number of victims to be offered to the gods. But my uncle Ahuitzotl wanted to overwhelm the gods with his generosity. I was only a boy, but I recall that he dedicated the temple with countless sacrifices, with thousands upon thousands of victims, until I was certain that the gods were utterly drenched in blood. As the endless line of prisoners ascended to the sacrificial altar and their hearts were taken from them, I became frightened and I wanted to hide. The

A splendid sacrifice was being performed in one of the small temples of the Great Plaza of Tenochtitlan. *Codex Florentino.*

bodies became so numerous that they could no longer be fed
to the people and the dogs. I began to tremble, for I feared
that my uncle was creating a deep river of blood separating
men and heaven so we might never again be able to reach
the gods!"

Montezuma's face filled with fear, and then he glanced
at me and drew a regal expression about him like a mantle.
He looked like a god against the darkening sky as he
continued to speak. "At eight temples of Tenochtitlan the
priests slashed and sweated and slashed. The blood was
everywhere, running down the temple steps and pouring
over the Plaza . . . staining the precious white feet of
Quetzalcoatl, who abhorred sacrifices and cried out against
them. The skull rack was stacked high. The people could
eat no more of the flesh cut from arms and legs for them,
and the beasts were gorged on bone and muscle. But still
the bodies came tumbling down the steep steps of the
temples, making heaps of limbs and blank faces until my
uncle ordered the human carcasses to be thrown into the
lake just to be rid of them."

Then Montezuma smiled weakly and rubbed his
shoulder aimlessly with the gesture of a child. "All of this
happened long ago when I was a boy," he muttered. "Long
ago, when I had no power. I could say nothing. I could only
watch. Surely that immense sacrifice should have brought us
many blessings if the priests of Huitzilopochtli speak the
truth. But I have been very afraid, Woodcutter, ever since
the day of those sacrifices . . . and so are many of the
people. I have heard them speak of it. They still speak of the
excesses of my uncle with fear. They are afraid that he made
too bold a gesture and that the gods will punish us . . . to
remind us that we are only the creatures of the Last Sun,

which they will one day destroy with a little gesture of their hands."

All this Montezuma remembered and all this he told me while we sat alone at the end of a day among the ruins of Tula, watching long shadows crouch between broken walls and shattered stone images. Everything had died here except memories. Montezuma knew the story of our people better than any of the priests or teachers. In the books of his father's Palace he had found many things that no one else had found. He found the memories of our whole race, and he knew the history of the warriors of Tenochtitlan, and he knew the name of the place where they were born.

It is said that the mother of the gods spoke to a man such as me, a humble woodcutter, and she told him that a flood was coming to the Earth to destroy all the people, so he must therefore save himself by being sealed in a hollow tree trunk with only a female dog for company. That is what was written in the ancient books, and that is what the great Lord Montezuma told me. When the flood was ended, the man and the bitch came out of the tree and they lived in a cave. Then something strange happened. Since the wood-cutter knew he was the only surviving person on the Earth he was amazed each day when he came back to the cave to find hot tortillas and jars of fresh river water awaiting him. One day he hid near the cave and waited to see who was bringing him these good things. After a while he saw the dog take off her skin and reveal that under it she was a person. When she left the cave to go to the river for water, the woodcutter quickly grabbed the dogskin and set fire to it. At once he could hear the howl of the dog-woman's scream, for she could feel the fire on her shoulders, and large burns began to appear on her handsome body. The woodcutter threw water on her and saved her so she could become his woman. Their children became the people of the Valley of Mexico, the Chichimecs who inherited the Earth and made it their own.

"You must know all these tales," Montezuma told me patiently, "for these things are within you. These stories give us life and memory. They are the blood that keeps us alive and brings us dreams and visions in which we discover who we are!"

And so I always listened carefully when my great Lord sat among the ruins of Tula and told me stories in which I encountered the shadowy beings who live in our memories and dreams.

"We Mexicans came out of a cave on the island called Aztlan," Lord Montezuma told me. "We called ourselves Culhuas because we were the descendants of the mighty Toltec people who were the givers of art and knowledge. But we were a tribe without power and we could be crushed by any enemy. That is how we were in the beginning. We had four holy chieftains who understood all the signs and possessed a precious bundle in which an image of our tribal god Huitzilopochtli was carefully wrapped. They were our leaders in those long-ago days. And they brought us to this place, to the city called Tula, where we lived and multiplied."

Living in Tula in those days was an old widow who had a daughter and four hundred sons. One day this pious old lady found a little ball of feathers while she was sweeping the temple. She was fascinated by the downy ball and concealed it between her breasts. Not long afterward the children of the old woman were astonished to notice that she was pregnant. Their mother's impiety outraged them and they decided that she must be put to death. Her four hundred sons armed themselves and were about to attack their mother's home when the old woman heard a voice coming from inside her belly, and it said, "Do not be afraid, old woman." At once a fully grown, powerful son was born to her. He was a ferocious-looking man, strong, tall, and heavily armed. He carried the spear-thrower called *atlatl*, and he carried a sword. He also possessed a divine weapon that was called the Serpent of Fire, a bolt of lightning. With this matchless weapon he cut off his sister's head and dismembered her body, and he destroyed all of his many brothers.

"In this way," Montezuma told me, "we are the People of the Sun, for the great warrior born to the old widow was our great tribal god Huitzilopochtli; and her daughter was the Moon and her countless sons were the many Stars in the heavens. But the battle between these angry children of the old woman is never finished. That is the great burden of our nation, for only human blood can give Huitzilopochtli, the incarnation of the Sun, renewed strength for his endless battle against his brothers and sister, who would cast him from the sky if they could and bring the Fifth and Last Sun to a terrible end."

All these mysterious things were told to me among the ruins of Tula by my great Lord. And I was filled with fear for the desperate battle that we must help the Sun to fight. I was also filled with pride because I realized that the tribes of the Valley of Mexico were chosen to defend the greatest of the gods! We were his people. He had found us when we were weak and afraid. He had made us powerful so that all our enemies ran away before us. He had given us new ways in war and he promised to make us great among all men. All of this he promised and all of this he fulfilled.

In the old legend days, when we could not defend ourselves and ran away from every enemy like cowardly dogs, when we were sent into exile and had nowhere to go and had no place to build a temple to Huitzilopochtli, he pitied us and saw in our faces that we could be a people of flowers and spears. And so he called out to us and led us to the place where the eagle with a serpent in its claw was perched upon a rock in the middle of a lake. There, upon that water and among the marshes, he told us to build the greatest city on earth. And so it is that we built Tenochtitlan.

"Yes, Woodcutter," Montezuma told me as he beckoned to the litter bearers and turned his gaze toward the wrecked city of Tula one last time, "you have learned well. It is correct when you say that we are a great people. But you are wrong, Woodcutter, when you say that we are the greatest of all men. If you could read the messages of these broken stones and shattered houses you would know what I mean. There was once a greater people. . . . So great that it is impossible to speak of them. It was here, in once-supreme Tula, now rock and dust, that they lived and died. Everywhere are their memories, flying in the silence like butterflies and coming to haunt me when I am forlorn, when I am forlorn and frightened by what I read in the sky. Coming to haunt me when I feel weak and when the courage of battle is lost in me . . . and all that remains is some marvelous distant dream of Tula."

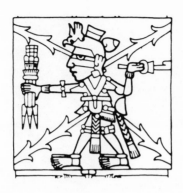

Seven

He sat upon his wicker throne and I sat beside him, wiser than I had been but still a woodcutter at heart. He spoke and I spoke. And sometimes he smiled when I spoke and I knew that I had been a fool. But he helped me by saying, "Thought is born of failure, Woodcutter."

I would listen to him and I would do what he said, for he was both a wise man and a god. And he treated me well though I was a woodcutter and a man of Tlaxcala, a city held in contempt by the people of my great Lord Montezuma. We had been beaten in battle by the people of Tenochtitlan called Mexicans. But they had refused to subjugate us and, instead, they had made us the "enemy" of their military games called Flowery Wars, which provided them with prisoners for sacrifices. My people were the food of the gods. I did not understand why it should be so. I did not try. But I could see reasons in the eyes of Montezuma, which were so misty and remote that I could not grasp them.

Now our Lord and War Chief, Montezuma, sat silently on his wicker throne in the coolness of the Council Chamber. His face was swept by strong winds. He was

The council of the court of Montezuma II. *Codex Florentino*.

planning an attack on the powerful people of Uexotzinco, who had broken their treaty and refused to pay tribute to Tenochtitlan. This was a very serious matter, for it had happened before and Uexotzinco was a very large and important city and might become a bad example for the other subjugated cities of Mexico.

So the clan leaders were beckoned. They gathered like fearsome eagles on the steps of the Palace, wearing helmets in the shape of the heads of jaguars, wolves, and birds of prey. Their armor of quilted cotton was brocaded in many colors and was embroidered with garish feathers. These ferocious chiefs with their glittering nose and lip ornaments of gold and jade marched ceremoniously through the great Palace door, while slaves and sentries stumbled out of their way. But when these greatest of Mexicans reached the silent anteroom of the Council Chamber they whispered like boys and dutifully shed their exquisite ornaments. They stripped off their rich mantles of elegantly embroidered cotton, and they removed their slender sandals. Wearing only loincloths, bareheaded and barefoot, with downcast eyes, they solemnly made their way toward the throne, where Montezuma sat in an implacable calm, dressed humbly except for the gold crown and jade earrings of his supreme office.

"Bid them be seated," my Lord told me very quietly.

Such powerful chiefs as these frightened me and I could not repeat the words of Montezuma. So the mighty clan chiefs remained standing in utter silence. And yet I could not produce the words that I knew I must say at once if I were not to appear ridiculous. Montezuma quickly glanced at me and I expected to see rage in his eyes, but his expression was so kind and reassuring that I found my voice at last.

"You will be seated," I proclaimed in my most eloquent manner. And the clan leaders sat down on the floor mats and small wicker seats of the Council Chamber.

The chiefs of the allied cities of Texcoco and Tlacopan had joined the warriors of Tenochtitlan at the war meeting. All these mighty leaders drew together around Montezuma, touching the ground with one hand while they covered their faces with the other, shading their eyes from his sublime radiance. And I sat beside the Great Speaker, I who spoke for him, and through me Lord Montezuma heard what his chiefs would have him do and from me they heard what he had learned from reading the heavens at night.

"Our Lord should be told that there are new problems," the chief of Texcoco said.

"My Lord," I repeated, "the chief of Texcoco says that there are new problems to be considered."

"Ask the chief of Texcoco what these problems are."

"Our Lord wishes to know the nature of these problems," I repeated.

"The city of Uexotzinco is powerful and will be a worthy enemy of the exalted warriors of Tenochtitlan, but now they have been joined by allies and this will require greater effort from our troops," the chief explained.

Montezuma wished to know who were these unexpected allies of Uexotzinco. The chief of Texcoco paused unexplainably for a moment and glanced nervously at the other clan leaders. Then Montezuma held his head a bit higher and very gradually turned toward the dumbfounded and silent chief.

"Nanautzin, you will ask the names of these allies of the city of Uexotzinco," my Lord told me sternly. But before I could repeat Montezuma's question the chief of Texcoco finally found his tongue.

"The allies of Uexotzinco are Atlixco . . . and also the city of Tlaxcala," he said, glaring at me.

Again there was a terrible stillness in the Council Chamber. In a voice which was barely a whisper, I began to repeat the remark to Montezuma. Then he interrupted me. "I need not be taught the names of our enemies. And I do not need to be told the names of our friends." Montezuma spoke directly to the assembled clan leaders in a grave voice as he slowly stood up. While still looking straight ahead into the averted faces of the chiefs, he placed just the tips of his fingers upon my shoulder. "So let us think and speak about our enemies and leave our friends in peace."

The rules of ceremony returned at once. The Great Speaker was seated, the clan leaders sat at his feet and each spoke in turn, and I repeated their words for Montezuma. It was quickly agreed to wage war against the offending cities. I looked into Montezuma's face when this decision was made, and for a moment I thought I could see the man and the god within him struggling against each other. But perhaps I was wrong, for almost at once an expression of arrogance came over his face, and within his eyes I could see fire and death and the shadow of Huitzilopochtli.

The combined armies of three cities were soon on the march. They set out in splendor when the Morning Star rose into the sky, announcing that they were envoys of Lord Quetzalcoatl, god-king of the Toltec ancestors of Montezuma who had made the rules of life. But in the faces of the warriors was not the sublime gentleness of Quetzalcoatl but the anger of the War God, Huitzilopochtli.

The people flocked to the roadsides to see the Great Speaker and his many allies pass before them. There were shouts of devotion and songs of joy. The people fell to their knees as the splendid war procession approached, dazzled by the glory of great Montezuma. And I walked beside his litter and I was filled with the sunlight of his splendor.

The Great Speaker was carried in a lavish palanquin, surrounded by an array of golden ornaments and brilliant feathers. He was magnificent in his most sumptuous wardrobe. His turquoise mantle and crown were bluer than the mountain lake, and his earplugs and bracelets were wrought of finest gold. Even his delicate sandals were made of solid gold. His awesome headdress of precious quetzal feathers was in the shape of a bird with its wings swept back. But most majestic of all was the regal symbol of his high office—a crystal lip plug decorated with a single blue feather. He was a marvelous sight! He was truly divine! Surrounded by the mightiest of his war chiefs, Montezuma II looked like one of the sacred rulers of the ancient Toltecs, more splendid than any man who had ever been elected to sit on the throne of Tenochtitlan and rule all the world.

He marched off to war in glory. Gifts were heaped upon the warriors: food and entertainments for the soldiers, jewels and ornaments for the captains, and rich cloth for the Great Speaker. Hymns were sung to Huitzilopochtli, and drums resounded and conch-shell trumpets hooted again and again. These warriors of Mexico were never so beautiful as when they were marching to war. All the disciplines learned at the warriors' school blossomed into an elaborate art of blood. Rituals were carefully performed on the battlefield to discover the propitious days for victorious battle. Spies were sent out to explore the enemy defenses. The members of this stealthy advance guard were called the Ocelot Warriors. The Eagle Warriors were reserved for the main attack. Hundreds of boys also accompanied the warriors, acting as carriers of war clubs, sandals, food, and other supplies.

Uexotzinco, the hill town of the enemy, was reached after several days of jogtrotting along the dusty paths of the high plateau. On the final day of the march we traveled slowly, allowing the Ocelot Warriors to make their way secretly among the boulders where they could spy upon the enemy. Then the daylight began to grow very dim, and we made camp for the night. Montezuma was always surrounded by his war leaders during these days, and he did not call me "Woodcutter," and he did not smile or look into my eyes. Instead he spoke his words quickly, and he ignored me when I repeated them unless I was slow in expressing some complex military strategy, and then he would coax me on with an impatient gesture of his hand. He was mightier than I had ever known him to be, but he was also somehow less divine.

In the night I shivered on my mat, for I could hear in the distance the muted voices of the boys of my own city, Tlaxcala. And so I could not sleep. There was no Moon, and the Stars had hidden themselves in the darkness like Ocelot Warriors. All was peaceful as Tenochtitlan's lads quietly prepared the armaments of the warriors. I lay on my mat in the darkness. Now and again the whispers of the Tlaxcalan

69

soldiers floated through the blackness. I was haunted by the sound, for I knew the cadence of their speech and I knew the cruelty it could express. When I had been a wretched boy, they had whispered about my scars. The boys had made up names to call me. And the girls . . . they had mocked my ugliness by calling me Tlemaitl, which is the name we use for an incense burner and which also means "hand of fire." So I knew these voices well as they drifted toward our encampment. Each night of my childhood these voices had been my sad lullaby. And tonight again, though I had been transformed and was no longer humble and hungry, that lullaby came back to me.

At dawn there was the howling of the Ocelot Warriors, who climbed to the hilltops where they welcomed the Sun. And after their wildcat chants, the Eagle Warriors stepped forward among us to dance in their feathered costumes. The Sun quickly grew ferocious and I could already smell the men's sweat. Everything around me was coming to life with excitement at the prospect of battle. I alone was fearful because I was torn in two. I loved the Lord Montezuma, but I could also hear from the distance the voices of my own people.

"You will stay close to me, for I will need you," Montezuma told me in a stern voice. "Now help me dress," he commanded.

I was nervous and my fingers faltered as I helped to tie Montezuma's panoply of painted paper banners and feathers. Then at last he was ready.

"Tell them it is time," the great Lord proclaimed.

My voice failed me for a moment, and then with a rattle I muttered, "Our Lord Montezuma Xocoyotzin says that we are ready and now is the time—"

Even before I had finished my speech the warriors marched solemnly forward . . . not like individual men but like a single massive being. I could not recognize any of them. Even the boys had changed utterly into something I had never seen before in the body of a man. And in the eyes of Montezuma I found flames and embers.

I had to run to keep up with them, as they marched to the entrance of the city where the local war chief, a Tlaxcalan, came out to speak with us. Anger filled his face when he saw me at the side of his enemy Montezuma, and for a moment I could not look at him. But then the Great Speaker said, "This is Nanautzin, my voice who speaks for me," and I was filled with an overwhelming sense of hatred for those warriors of my people who had degraded and abused me. I glared at the chief, a man whose daughter I had watched with a broken heart when I had been a boy. And I stood tall and drew my magnificent mantle over my shoulder and stepped closer to Montezuma.

The Great Speaker demanded that the tribute that had not been paid be presented at once, and that the leader of Uexotzinco resign and be replaced by a Mexican overlord appointed by Montezuma. He also demanded that the allies of Uexotzinco—Tlaxcala and Atlixco—return to their own cities at once. Furthermore, the offenders were to send to Tenochtitlan twenty young men each year for sacrifice to the gods of Mexico.

During all of this the leaders listened; then their chief bowed to Montezuma and said courteously that the people of Uexotzinco had their own leaders and would not subject themselves to the will of any other rulers. "Tell Lord Montezuma that we wish to be the friends of Tenochtitlan, but *none* of the men of our city will be sent to be sacrificed!"

No more was said. The chiefs on both sides drew up to their full height and turned back to their troops. And the war began.

The warriors of Uexotzinco came out at noon. They moved into two divisions at a jogtrot, holding their obsidian-edged clubs threateningly as they followed the lead of their battle chiefs, who wore on their backs large, brilliant Sun emblems made of extraordinary plumage. They yelled and shouted as they trotted into formation, trying to intimidate the warriors of Montezuma, who steadfastly closed in on them. The Mexicans were clever and they advanced in a very tight group, making their enemies think that they were few in number. But when the two armies were quite close to one another the signal was given—the howl of the ocelot—and suddenly the scouts who had been hidden came out shouting from behind the flanks of the enemy. The horrendous roar of the warriors resounded among the boulders as the battle began, and men leaped at one another and battered each other's shields with their murderous clubs.

I ran frantically among the wrestling men to keep pace with Montezuma, who was utterly possessed by the furor of the battle. An enemy stumbled in front of me and fell. At once he was seized and bound with leather thongs. His captors looked jubilant, for the unwounded enemy was a perfect prisoner for sacrifice. No matter how furious the battle, the greatest care was always taken not to kill enemies but to take them prisoner.

I rushed past the bound captives who were being

dragged away, afraid that I might be separated from the great Lord. By leaping over wrestling bodies, I caught up with him. Then suddenly a very tall man swung wildly first at me and then at Montezuma. My Lord pushed me aside and confronted the enemy. For a moment the two men leaped and danced around each other. Then the tall man took a tremendous swing with his blade-bristling club. Montezuma dodged the blow just in time. Then he lifted his shield to deflect the second blow and quickly struck his opponent's ribs. As the warrior groanded and doubled up in agony, Montezuma brought him down with the blunt side of his club.

Montezuma glowed with glory and his face was filled with exuberance and tremendous energy as he wiped the blood from his face and quickly tied the hands and feet of his unconscious prisoner. Almost at the same instant, he let out a roar of triumph.

I laughed with dizzy delight, and I was about to echo his triumphant shout when a limp body fell heavily at my feet and lay there twitching. It was a boy of my city. His eyes stared up at me. Suddenly there was no spirit left in me. I looked into the deathly face of that boy and watched as his bloody saliva made a fragile little bubble between his lips. Then it burst and suddenly the light went out in his frightened eyes.

The clubs slashed and chopped as the battle became so ferocious that blood splattered into the air like rain. I stumbled after the crimson figure of Montezuma as enemies lunged at him with bitter screams of rage. But the warriors of Tenochtitlan broke their skulls and cleared a path of blood for our great Lord. When a young enemy managed to

leap just in front of Montezuma, a warrior quickly slashed at
his legs and downed him with a single blow, but the club
had severed his leg at the ankle and his life was quickly
pouring out of him. He would be of no use for sacrifice. And
I saw Montezuma lean down and slash the young man's
throat, and then he cut off his ears as trophies. I remember
the grin on the face of Montezuma when he waved those
pathetic ears in the air. It was the last thing I recall about
that war.

Tenochtitlan was victorious and Montezuma was
radiant with his deeds.

I sat silently while the sounds of battle faded slowly
and the grass all around me turned red. The chiefs held a
council. Montezuma demanded that all those guilty of
thwarting his will must die. The chief of the city begged for
their lives in the customary manner, and finally he offered
tribute. Then for a long time both sides haggled until the
amount of the tribute was settled.

The Mexicans marched through the battlefield, hunt-
ing the prisoners they had bound and left there. After
passing a pole through the thongs with which the enemies
were bound, they shouldered their burdens and carried them
to the corral where the prisoners were kept. These captive
warriors quietly submitted to the slave poles that were tied
around their shoulders, and they made no effort to escape as
a point of honor. Though some of them whimpered, most
accepted the fact that they were to be given the glorious fate
of captives.

The victorious return to Tenochtitlan was more tumultuous than the departure. Montezuma was triumphant and
the Warrior God, Huitzilopochtli, had been well served.

Eight

Montezuma sat among the broken dreams of Tula and he brooded and he wept. As a boy and as a man it had always been his hope that the blood of the Toltecs that pulsed through his body would help him to restore the glories of the city of Quetzalcoatl and bring to his people a golden era more sublime than any day that had dawned upon the world. But such a dream was difficult even for great Montezuma, whose horoscope told him that he was precariously balanced between two realms, as a warrior of Huitzilopochtli and a priest of gentle Quetzalcoatl. And there were also bad signs in all those mysterious places where the gods conceal the destinies of men.

Montezuma wept and he cried out for help, but he did not want me to come to him. Nor did he accept the comfort of the priests of the temple of Tula who moaned for him. Montezuma wept the tears of Quetzalcoatl, the lost god and lost king whose great city had been devoured by time and whose carved bones had been spit upon the ground, making this sorrowful ruin called Tula. Montezuma wept for Quetzalcoatl, but the god would not look upon him because his hands were bloody with his gifts to Huitzilopochtli. The brave warrior in Montezuma was the enemy of gentle Quetzalcoatl. The bloody sacrifices made by Montezuma to glorify Huitzilopochtli also drowned Quetzalcoatl in remorse. This battle between two jealous gods was the same shattering discord that had brought Tula to its tragic end.

Montezuma cried out for Quetzalcoatl, but the great Lord of Tula shunned him and left him just as he had left the people of Tula many generations earlier. All these events were found among the books of the Palace of Montezuma's father . . . beautifully painted books bound in wood and set with jade. The secrets of one of these books were the secrets of Quetzalcoatl. It told the history of the mighty god and of his coming to the Earth and of the founding of Tula. On the other side of this same precious book was painted the entire history of the Mixteca tribe. It was Montezuma's uncle, Montezuma I, who had captured this marvelous book from the Mixtec and hidden it away in his Palace, where the young Montezuma had found it. And so my Lord knew more of his people's long story than any other living person.

"Tell me how our world was given to us," I begged Montezuma, but for a long time he wept and would not look at me. "Tell me about the god and king called Quetzalcoatl. Who is this gentle god who shuns the blood on your hands? Tell me about that gentle king who gave us the gifts of art."

Montezuma nodded sorrowfully. "I serve two gods, Woodcutter. The one enters me like a ferocious animal and makes my blood beat like the drum atop the pyramid, but the other comes and goes whimsically like a lover. Just when I think I have captured his heart, he vanishes and leaves me speechless and sullen. The one fills my body with power while the other fills me with love. I reach out for both, but I can reach neither. That is how it is now and that is how it was long ago when the Fifth Sun was made and our race of people came into existence. That is how it was in the legend days when Quetzalcoatl brought us to life with a drop of blood from his groin." After these mysterious words Montezuma became silent.

"My Lord," I begged, hoping his stories might cheer him, "tell me of the making of the Fifth Sun and tell me about the beginning of the people of Tenochtitlan, called Mexicans."

These questions seemed to awaken a flood of marvelous images in the memory of Montezuma, and gradually he sat up and gazed all around as if he could see each thing he described to me. In a soft voice he recited the most important history of all the histories of our people. He spoke on and on until it was evening, and I listened to his eloquent voice rise and fall against the chanting of the priests in the darkness.

During the age of the Fifth Sun, when the young Sun had just come into existence in the city of Teotihuacan, the gods wished to create a new race of people on the Earth. They decided to entrust the final restoration of mankind to the god whose name was Quetzalcoatl. And so he went at once to Mictlan, the Region of the Dead, in search of the bones of the last race which had been destroyed, for he needed these bones in order to create a new race of men.

"I have come for the bones that you guard here," Quetzalcoatl told Mictlantecuhtli, Lord of the Dead.

And the keeper of the bones said, "What would you do with them?"

And Quetzalcoatl answered, "The gods wish that some

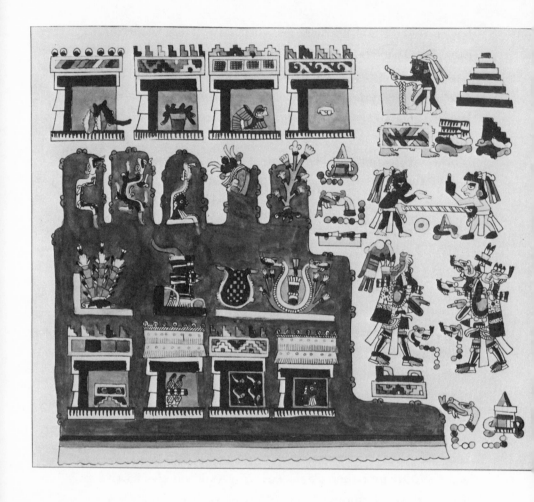

The last of the Toltec empire under Huemac, ca. A.D. 980;
painted by Mexican artists about A.D. 1350. *Codex Vindobonensis.*

people shall live on the Earth. And these bones are needed to make them."

But Mictlantecuhtli did not wish to give up the bones and tried to prevent Quetzalcoatl from carrying them away. With the assistance of his spiritual double, his *nahual,* Quetzalcoatl tricked the guardian of the Dead and succeeded in stealing the precious bones and carrying them to the place of our origin called Tamoanchan. There, in the silence of the holy day and night, with the help of the goddess called Quilaztli, he ground up the bones and made a powder of them and he placed this powder in an earthen bowl. Then Quetzalcoatl put his hands upon his groin and drew blood from himself, and this blood fell upon the bones and infused them with new life. And so it was that all the people called Toltecs came into being.

The Toltecs were the people of Quetzalcoatl, and they were nimble and wise; nothing was difficult for them. They knew how to cut precious stones and how to work in gold; they made many great things and they made many marvelous ornaments of feathers. All the arts of the great Toltecs, their knowledge and skill, came from Quetzalcoatl, who was their loving father. And so these fortunate Toltecs were very rich in all things. It is said that the squash of their fields were very big and heavy; that the ears of maize in their fields were as large as a grinding stone; and the blades of amaranth were as large as palm leaves. All this good harvest came to the Toltecs, and much more. They also grew cotton of many different colors: red, yellow, pink, purple, green, bluish green, blue, light green, orange, brown, and dark gold! These were the colors of the cotton itself, and it grew that way from the Earth. And so the Toltecs were very rich and they were very happy. There was no poverty among them and no sadness.

It is said that when Quetzalcoatl was still in the sky and did not yet live among men, he searched a very long time for a special food he could give to his people. One day he discovered the precious maize that the ants had carefully hidden away inside the core of a mountain. So much did the god Quetzalcoatl love the new people he had created that he changed himself into a tiny ant and stole a single grain of maize, which he gave to men. And from this one grain of maize has come all of the crops that feed Tenochtitlan today! And when Quetzalcoatl came down to live among the people he had created he taught them how to make beautiful mosaics with quetzal plumes and with the feathers of the bluebird, the hummingbird, and the parrot. But above all he taught men many profound secrets: how to measure time and how to study the movement of the Stars. He showed them the mystic calendar. And he also taught them love, for he was a life-giving god whose power was found in his gentleness.

So holy and so good was our Lord Quetzalcoatl that evil men loathed him. He was not like other men, for his skin was very pale and he had hair upon his face. He was tall and noble and more handsome than the greatest princes and kings. He did not love the life of warriors, and he disdained blood and refused to send prisoners to nourish the gods. This outraged the priests, for Quetzalcoatl was opposed to the sacrifice of his own children. He used to tell the angry priests that he wanted only snakes and butterflies to be offered in sacrifice. But there were those who hated his heretical ideas, and they would not embrace the new religion of Quetzalcoatl and were still faithful to the Warrior God, Huitzilopochtli. And so those who called themselves Tezcatlipoca, Ihuimecatl, and Toltecatl said, "This heretic Quetzalcoatl must leave our city, for here is where we live and we cannot live with a man whose ideas are abominations!" And then they said, "We will make pulque, and we will make him drink it so he loses his senses and has no power left against us!"

And they say that this evil wished upon Quetzalcoatl did not hurt him, for his goodness was so great that it protected him from harm. And still he would not permit his people to be sacrificed, and this greatly angered the wizards, the priests, and the magicians, so that they began to scoff at Quetzalcoatl. The magicians and the wizards said they wished to torment him so he would leave Tula forever. And Tezcatlipoca said, "I say that we should give him his body."

And so Tezcatlipoca—who is the shadow of Huitzilopochtli—came to Quetzalcoatl with a double mirror the size of an open palm, which he carefully wrapped so it could not be seen. When he reached the place where Quetzalcoatl lived he told the acolytes that guarded the great Lord, "Go and tell your master that a youth has come to show him his body and to give it to him."

When Quetzalcoatl was given this strange message he said, "What fool is this who sends me messages? What thing is my 'body'? Look carefully and see what this wizard has brought and then let him enter my chamber."

But Tezcatlipoca did not wish to show anyone the mirror, and he said, "Go tell your Lord that I myself must show it to him alone."

And so Quetzalcoatl let the scheming magician enter.

Tezcatlipoca gave the great Lord the mirror, saying, "Look and know yourself, for if you will peer into this object you will see your body."

When Quetzalcoatl saw himself he was very frightened and he turned away from the mysterious mirror with a groan as if he had been terribly wounded by the sight of himself.

"What is your trouble?" the magician slyly asked. And Quetzalcoatl told him that he was very ill and that his body was filled with pain. So Tezcatlipoca offered the Lord a strange medicine unknown to him. After much insistence the magician succeeded in persuading Quetzalcoatl to drink the liquid. It was the inebriating drink called pulque, which was forbidden to all but old men. And with much of this drink, the great Lord became so delirious and so passionate that he slept with a forbidden priestess who was thrown at him by the evil ones.

At dawn Quetzalcoatl awakened, and he was forlorn and his heart was filled with remorse as he cried out in pain. Many terrible things came to his people after he had been given his body. There were epidemics and fires and thunderbolts that fell to the Earth like stone axes. The mortified Quetzalcoatl burned his palaces, buried his treasuries, and left Tula behind him forever. He sang the sorrowful song he had made for the time of his departure: "This is an evil tale of a day when I left my home in great Tula. May those who despise me be softened by my hard and perilous journey. Let the one whose body is the Earth live on here and thrive. But may the rest of these wicked ones perish!"

Then, with a small group of the faithful, Quetzalcoatl traveled into exile and journeyed throughout the central valley and stayed for a time in Cholula. It is said that, on reaching the celestial shore where the world ends, he wept and brooded. Then he put on his glorious garments, his insignia of feathers, and his green mask and stepped upon a raft made of the entwined bodies of many serpents, and he sailed away to the land called Yucatan. Before his departure Lord Quetzalcoatl embraced his followers whom he was leaving behind, and he promised to return to Tula someday. He would come, he said, from the East in the year One Reed, which falls every fifty-two years in the Toltec calendar. He would recapture his land and his throne, and he would rule forever in peace.

And so he set off and was carried away by the sea. The rest is forgotten, for no one survives who knows if Lord Quetzalcoatl ever reached Yucatan.

All this Montezuma told me while we sat among the broken dreams of Tula. All this he had read in the book of his father's Palace. So Montezuma wept and he cried out but did not want me to comfort him. "Which am I?" he groaned. "Am I the faithful who follow after Quetzalcoatl or am I one of those blood-drenched wizards who destroyed him?"

Before I could respond, Montezuma waved me away despondently and beckoned for his carriers. "This is the fate of the Mexicans," he muttered. "We had everything, but we have lost it and cannot find it again! Now everything is a dream. And truth cannot exist here. It must be sought farther on, beyond the visible things and beyond the Region of the Dead where secrets linger out of reach of our eyes."

The War Chief whose daring and ferocity I had seen in battle had vanished from the face of Montezuma. As his litter was lifted into the air and we began our solemn march back to Tenochtitlan, the tumultuous cheers of war faded and a cloud of butterflies cast a perpetual shade upon my Lord as he rode silently above our heads.

I felt a chill in my heart as the shadow came over us. I could hear the whispers of the wizards in the tall grass, and I dreaded the dark creatures hidden in the trees who watched after us. It is said that the destruction of Lord Quetzalcoatl was the scheme of the witch-goddess called Tlazolteotl, and I could feel her power everywhere in the ruins of Tula. These feelings terrified me, but how much more terrified I would have been that sorrowful day long ago if I had known that in the little village of Soconusco lived a girl-child who was dedicated by the day of her birth to that same cunning goddess who had destroyed Quetzalcoatl. This infant was named Ce Malinalli: and one day she was destined to become a Nusta, a "Chosen Woman," whose dreadful mission it was to bring down the last of the Toltec dynasties and to overthrow the Sun himself!

Nine

The land of Tenochtitlan choked on soot and could not catch its breath. The clumps of maize withered in the Sun. There were no shadows on the parched ground. There was no rain. And all the signs were bad.

Even the lizards panted and perished, leaving their stiff, dry skins among the gleaming rocks. The soil turned to sand and was lifted into the air by hot winds that carried it away. Dust devils danced in frantic little circles and entranced the feeble crops, which could not resist their dervishes. There were many bad signs, and Montezuma and his hungry people wept.

"It is like the time of Nezahualcoyotl's son," the great Lord murmured as he waved aside his wise men and slumped down on his throne. "In those days there appeared a great splendor in the sky, born in the east and climbing high into the heavens until it formed a pyramid on the top of which were many tongues of fire. And the great men told their Lord that such signs meant that the times were approaching when the things Quetzalcoatl foretold would come to pass. I have told you this story many times, for you are my priests; and I have asked you many times if Quetzalcoatl will let us live when he returns, but you have no answers."

Montezuma sat silently for a long time while his wizards and wise men crouched fearfully on the floor.

"Get out!" the Great Speaker shouted, getting up abruptly and turning his back on them.

Everyone in the Council Chamber bowed repeatedly as they hurried out of the deep shade that surrounded Montezuma. They gasped and groaned as they withdrew, escaping as quickly as they dared. I was about to follow after the others, feeling confused and mortified by the rancor and suspiciousness of our Lord, when he muttered under his breath, "Not you, Woodcutter! Stay with me."

I crept back into the large, empty room and crouched on a mat in the corner, clenching my knees and feeling cold and ill. I watched him, but he did not move and he would not look at me. He seemed so old, sitting on his throne with stooped shoulders and a drawn, dazed expression on his face. All the strength had left his limbs. He seemed fragile and naked. And yet I could not utter a sound or move, because I sensed in his terrible melancholy something volatile and explosive. I dared not provoke him, and so I sat more humbly and wretched than I had ever been in the days when I was hungry and poor.

The Stars turned slowly. Then over the damp floor a breeze made its way coyly, like a flirtation. In the distance . . . a sound. Then silence and the heavy, motionless air. I whispered my thoughts to myself and tried to stay awake. My Lord had not moved, but stared at nothing and wrinkled his brow and nodded aimlessly. The Stars made their way through the appalling darkness, and the Earth ached with its barren fields and arid gardens. But then a breeze once again faltered past me. The sound in the sky came closer. This noise roused my Lord from his terrible dream and he looked at me intently.

"Is my Lord . . ." I began, but he frantically motioned for me to be still, and he listened carefully. There was a vast stillness. I held my breath and strained to hear what my Lord wanted me to hear, but there was nothing. His face began to settle back into its dismal frown, then suddenly a deep growl reverberated through the chamber. The growl became a roar as thunder fell upon us unexpectedly. The fainthearted breeze whirled into a gusty wind. Montezuma slowly arose from his throne, astonished by the sounds all around us, and hurried past the guards and ministers to the gates of the Palace. I tried to keep pace with him as he sent people scurrying out of his way. The wind flew through the Palace, and all around us was the stampede of thunder. When I caught up with Montezuma and stood dumbfounded in the doorway, a strong gust of wind swept against us. It brought a shower of large, heavy drops of rain.

"Rain!" Lord Montezuma exclaimed with such majesty that to all of us standing watching the downpour splash upon the parched ground it seemed as though he had commanded it.

"Rain!" we cried with joy. "Rain!"

And so for a time the signs were good, and my Lord came out from among the shadows and went to the temples, where he offered sacrifices of his blood and prayers and the hearts of many prisoners. And even when rats and mice in uncountable numbers invaded our flourishing crops it was a blessing to us, for rat meat is a delight and a delicacy.

The gods took pity on us and loved us once again. The warriors went into the field with confidence and courage, and our merchants extended their trading routes far beyond the horizon. All of these things pleased Montezuma. They were good omens that promised a year of fortune. And to the Great Speaker such omens were truly welcomed because it was the year 1 One Reed (1506), which marked the end of one bundle of time that passes every fifty-two years and, it is hoped, the beginning of another. One age was dying and another would begin with the year 2 One Reed if the gods would permit it. For in these last days, time grew stingy and the moments passed slowly and painfully while we awaited the ceremony called the New Fire.

Our days told us nothing, the night sky showed us nothing, and we could find no wizard or astrologer who could tell us if the world would be renewed by the gods for another cycle of fifty-two years or if it would be destroyed forever. Only on the night of the New Fire could such answers be found.

Then the *nemontemi* arrived—those useless days which lie between the end of one time cycle and the beginning of another. The best men of each household guarded their thresholds day and night against the intrusion of the dark powers who wait for the Sun to fall so they can shake down the world and destroy it utterly. It was a time of humility and penance. All ornaments were put aside and mantles of rude materials were worn by all. Blood was drawn from legs, arms, and earlobes. And we were miserable before the gods. The fasting began and the chants grew louder as the end of the world drew closer. All of the pottery was shattered on the hearths. The mats and wicker stools were burned. All our worldly possessions were destroyed, leaving us with nothing but our empty houses and our empty stomachs. Pregnant women hid in the huge baskets in which grain was stored, fearful that they would be turned into ferocious beasts during these dangerous days. All the adolescent boys spent each night walking to and fro with the crying young children of each house to prevent them from turning into rats at this fatal time of the New Fire.

The end of the final day came slowly and the great Sun cringed as he descended toward the hills where the darkness hid in waiting for him, its terrible claws longing for his golden throat. Night began to drive away the daylight, beating its luminous head until there was blood upon the horizon. Then it was night. The priests began the ascent of the Hill of the Star, a volcanic hulk that rises high above the entire valley. At the summit was a very ancient temple to the Fire God, which was the place of the ritual of the New Fire. At sunset all the fires were allowed to go out . . . even the sacred flames of the temples. Many people surged toward the sacred mountain where stargazers watched hopefully for the signs that foretold whether or not the Sun would be triumphant and rise again to give his people another day and another bundle of time. Great flotillas of canoes crossed the dark lake, and everyone peered upward into the mysterious blackness of the sky.

Now we were sitting under the massive sky of lights, which turned slowly and spoke to Montezuma and his priests. But we could not read the messages with which the gods emblazon the heavens, and we had to await the words of the wizards who knew these things. It was silent and windy. The Fire Priest sat in front of the dark altar where the fire had gone out, his sunburst headdress lightless and cold. The priests moved among us, painted black except for their faces, which were marked with the images of red and yellow flames. The Star-writing in the heavens moved to the highest place in the sky as we watched in silence and dismay. If the gods hated us as they had the four prior worlds, then it would be the end of us. The Stars would falter and stop moving across the Earth, the Sun would not rise again, and the Ollin Tonatiuh, the Sun of Earthquakes, would tremble, bend, and shatter, and then everything would be destroyed. For that is what was foretold long ago, and that is the destiny—sooner or later—of our world.

> Now our Father the Sun is thinking of departing
> with his thoughts, with his words, and with our lives.
> When he is above us, he thinks about us and our world,
> but when he approaches the place beyond the world
> he thinks of nothing.
> The flower, my heart, has opened
> to the Lord of Midnight.
> Will he celebrate the feast of dawning?
> Will he think of us and remember his world?
> Or has he descended forever,
> and vanished with all our words?

The singing begins softly in the distance. The lament of the children begins. I can hear nothing but the lament. It is an immense shadow where nothing grows. How helpless we are among these Stars. Who are we and why do we weep? Come away from the window, child, for the Sun has forgotten us and will not shine again.

90

The dreams and the omens. *Codex Florentino*.

The song moves along the valley, from one dark house to another. The chanting of the priests begins. I can hear nothing but their forlorn prayers. Words that are very small in the enormous night. I tremble and squeeze drops of blood from my ears. The blood flows down my shoulders.

The Pleiades pass over our heads. Now suddenly it is silent. No one moves or breathes. It is the time for Aldebaran to come upon the center of the sky. There is a gasp that rolls out of the throats of the hundreds of people transfixed upon the mountaintop. Then there is a shout.

It is good! We live again!

At the very moment when these powerful Stars passed the highest point in the heavens the sign was given. We would live again! The gods had consented to our continued existence. At once a cry of joy went up and the priests pushed a young prisoner back against the altar and quickly cut him open, tearing out his heart and throwing it to the Fire God. Another shout resounded across the entire valley as the priests quickly kindled the New Fire in the open breast of the prisoner. The joyous songs began and the tears of happiness fell in streams down the faces of women and children and men. The dancing began in the villages and in the Great Plaza of Tenochtitlan and in the Palace and in the houses of the lords. Young men lit their torches from the New Fire and hastily rekindled the altars in the temples of every town and village, from which the people took a bit of flame for their hearths. Like a shower of new Stars flashing through the darkness, the torchbearers spread the fire. Wherever the flame of life went, it brought laughter and singing. Children came out of hiding and pregnant women crept cautiously from storage baskets. At once the men began to make new utensils and furnishings for their houses and temples. Drums accompanied the great Sun as he marched victoriously back to us. And for a while our world was promised life and light.

Ten

Montezuma descended the steps of the temple of the Warrior God with a look of confidence. In his eyes the shadows of Quetzalcoatl had faded and the fires of Huitzilopochtli glowed. Now he did not often speak to me when we were in private but called for the dwarfs and acrobats to entertain him. He laughed during these days of the New Fire. But behind his laughter I could hear the growl of an angry animal.

"What do you think of the power of our ally, the Lord of Texcoco?" he asked his councilmen, who muttered among themselves but did not answer. "Ah," Montezuma said with a smirk and pulled me closer so he could whisper into my ear. "Ask them if the Lord of Texcoco has been Lord for too long. Ask them, Woodcutter!"

When I repeated the question for those assembled before Montezuma in the Council Chamber, everyone smiled the same smile that the Great Speaker had upon his face. And so the next day Montezuma secretly sent his ambassadors to the lords of Tlaxcala, telling them that their trusted ally, the Lord of Texcoco, had been gathering his mightiest warriors not for military exercises and sacrifices to the gods but with the intention of destroying the land of the Tlaxcalans. Montezuma did not speak aloud about this trick he played upon the "friends of the house," as he called my people of Tlaxcala, but a servant who attended my Lord overheard the plan and told me about it. I had no love for my people but I greatly feared the fires in Montezuma that were transforming him into a man with a divided head.

Next the alliance of Tlaxcala and Uexotzinco was broken. The Great Speaker sat with his war chiefs and planned to attack Tlaxcala. My Lord did not concern himself with my loyalties any longer, for he had forgotten me and only glared impatiently if I stumbled when I repeated his words. They were words like the bitterest weed and the hardest stone. They were not the words of a man but those of a god from the dark place.

The Tlaxcalans suffered a terrible defeat, for Montezuma had cleverly driven their allies from them before the battles began. The land was not taken from the people of Tlaxcala, but many men were carried off to be sacrificed in Tenochtitlan. I did not have the courage to go to the temples where my tribesmen were being dragged to the altar; since I could be punished with death for refusing to witness the sacrifices, I stayed with my Lord in the Palace, and when he did not need me I told him that I was ill. I did not want to see men die a bad death. They had been taken prisoner in a battle won by the lies of Montezuma and not by bravery and daring. I could not see deaths such as these, for the sacrificed prisoners would not go to the proud place of warriors and live in joy forever with the Sun. Instead they would become butterflies and haunt the evil hearts that sent them to an ignoble death.

Great Tlalhuicol, the mightiest leader of Tlaxcala, had

been captured and was one of the prisoners awaiting sacrifice to the Sun. When this great warrior of my tribe was brought before Montezuma I wanted to tell him the truth about his captors so he would demand his freedom and denounce the treacherous way in which his people had been defeated. But the Great Speaker would not let me near Tlalhuicol and made me sit in the corner while one of the elders served as orator. I crouched on the floor, saddened by the way my Lord treated me and angered that he had tricked my people with a terrible betrayal. I could not look at him when he spoke, nor could I listen to the stammering of the old man who tried to serve in my place. Soon, as my Lord spoke, it became clear that Montezuma so greatly admired Tlalhuicol that he wished to take him into his own service.

The great general of Tlaxcala turned his back on Montezuma and would not look at him. "You are my city's enemy. I do not serve with enemies!" he exclaimed.

For a moment the silence in the Council Chamber was fearful. Then Montezuma ordered that Tlalhuicol be sent back to his people.

"I will not go back to my people!" the warrior shouted. "And I will not be dishonored by being set free! I am a prisoner and I demand that along with all the other prisoners of Tlaxcala I be sacrificed on the warrior's stone, reserved for only the bravest men!"

And so it was. I recall even now that Montezuma smiled when great Tlalhuicol died on the altar with a look of victory in his eyes, with visions of the dancing warriors he would join forever in their glorious, golden circle around the Sun. And I remember seeing at the sacrifice, hidden in a special seat camouflaged with hundreds of flowers and disguised as people from Tenochtitlan, five foreigners I could not recognize at first. But then I knew them. They were five of the mightiest lords of Tlaxcala!

I could not believe what I had seen and I tried to deny it. The thought of such betrayal frightened me, and the possibility that the highest of the lords were capable of such violation of custom and divine law horrified me. But finally I had to accept this incredible treachery as the truth, for soon the great lords of Tlaxcala cautiously arrived at the Palace of Montezuma, only moments after the solemn ceremonies honoring the death of Tlalhuicol. And in the dining room, while I shuddered with dismay, the leaders of two enemy cities dined amicably and exchanged precious gifts and laughed about their monstrous deceptions.

My heart was cold and tears fell from my eyes when I recalled the gentle face of Lord Montezuma in the days when we sat in dusty Tula and dreamed.

After Tlaxcala had been subdued, Montezuma then made a prosperous peace with the people of Uexotzinco and Cholula. The nobles of the Palace were joyful, and everywhere in the domain of Tenochtitlan there were celebrations among the victors and a silent resentment and rage among those who had been defeated. And in my own heart there was a shadow that would not open itself to the sunlight. I no longer followed anxiously after my Lord and I no longer listened attentively to his every word. When he smiled at me and called me "Woodcutter" I did not believe what I saw in his face. I bowed more humbly to him than ever, but in my heart he was no longer a great man.

Then one day when I climbed to the gardens that flourished on the Palace rooftop, a terrifying thing happened. The deep, glowing heat of the Sun withdrew very slowly. A wind flew across my body and I was cold. I threw my hand up and covered my eyes. Then fearfully I glanced into the sky. A dense darkness was gradually devouring the Sun. It was the fantastic omen I had heard about since I was a child . . . the Sun was disappearing from the sky and darkness came down upon us until at last only the fiery shoots of the Sun could be seen, leaping out from within the black monster that had swallowed him.

Everywhere in the Great Plaza people were running for their lives and shouting warnings. I spun around in desperation and tried to escape the vision in the sky. I threw myself into a small room and rushed through a door and down a long corridor. Just as I burst into the Council Chamber I was suddenly thrown to the floor. My belly collapsed with fear as the stone floor undulated like a serpent and the walls swayed sickeningly. The Earth trembled and twisted again and again until I was certain the great stone building would come down upon me.

Then it was silent.

The Earth was still. Dust and sand sifted through the air. And very gradually the sunlight reappeared on the walls and in the windows. The voices of people gradually arose from the silence, timidly at first and then louder and louder until there were cries of joy and relief.

I did not get up from the floor of the Council Chamber where I had been thrown by the anger of the Earth. I lay there for a long time, feeling sick and frightened. Just in front of me, tumbled to its side by the rage of the earthquake, was the throne of the great Lord Montezuma II.

I was not a wizard and I could not read the signs in the sky, but I was filled with foreboding and I knew that a bad time was coming to the people of the Great Valley. First there was the large army that was overtaken in the rugged headwaters of the river Atoyac by a terrible storm, killing eighteen hundred men and sending floods into the valleys. Then three summers later a light was seen in the eastern sky. Every night it came: a great fire in the darkness. For three years this powerful mystery made its nightly appearance. The people called to Montezuma, but he could do nothing. He offered blood and he fasted, but still the fires did not leave the eastern sky.

The priests conducted many ceremonies and many prisoners were sacrificed, but the omen did not vanish. The holy men begged Montezuma to command a remarkable piety from his people, and he sent out such commandments. But then he beckoned me and we went into the Council Chamber, where he planned to attack the people of Zulantlaca, who had rebelled against the collectors of tribute. In the midst of his pious efforts my Lord turned to war. Within a few weeks the entire town of Zulantlaca was annihilated. Then, suddenly, Montezuma wiped the blood from his war club and turned into a priest and returned to the temple to pray. I lagged farther and farther behind him as he rushed toward some terrible place I could see vaguely in all the bad signs before us.

Three years later there were earthquakes. I could see in the eyes of the people in the Plaza and in the antechamber a fear that would not go away and could not be comforted. It was in that terrible year that Lord Tzompantecuctli of Cuitlahuac and all his sons were killed. Their murderers were the nobles of Cuitlahuac themselves, who did it at the secret order of Montezuma. I knew every detail of the assassination, for I heard the plans that were whispered in the Council Chamber.

Tzompantecuctli was murdered because of his words . . . for he had committed no offense other than sending Montezuma an explanation for the omen which terrified all of us. Montezuma asked Tzompantecuctli to send him a messenger with an explanation of our bad days. And so a messenger was sent and he addressed these words to my Lord: "I bring the good wishes of Tzompantecuctli. He bids me to tell you this: Our King and Master, what you have done is not correct. The way you honor the gods will hasten the ruin of your people. For the god we shall soon serve, my Lord, is not the same god we now serve. He is coming who will be the Lord over all and the maker of all creatures."

Hearing this, the enraged Montezuma sent word to Tzompantecuctli: "May your words stick in your throat!" Soon thereafter Tzompantecuctli and all his sons were strangled.

The gloom collected in the Palace until everyone was afraid to speak in the silence of the empty chambers. Even old friends of the Great Speaker were not safe from his anger. Nezahualpilli, Lord of Texcoco, from whom Montezuma had learned much about the art of poetry when he was a young man and whose city was a trusted military ally of Tenochtitlan, roused the ill will of the Great Speaker. One day the two rulers were arguing about the wisdom of their astrologers and their abilities to foretell the future. Montezuma scoffed at the wizards of the palace of

Nezahualpilli, for they had said that strangers would one day rule the land of Mexico. "Admit that your wizards are fools," Montezuma coaxed.

"No," the lord of Texcoco said flatly, "they are not fools, and I know that what they say is so. There are omens everywhere which tell us that we will soon face a holocaust." So certain was Nezahualpilli of the wisdom of his sooth-sayers that he challenged Montezuma to a wager: his whole kingdom against three turkeys, with the results decided by a ritualistic ball game.

When the day of the game came, all the nobles and priests of Tenochtitlan assembled at the sacred ball court in the Plaza and waited for the gods to speak to us through the luck of the game. Montezuma won the first two games, and his priests whispered to each other with reassurance and pleasure. But then Nezahualpilli took the last three games, and the Great Lord of Tenochtitlan lost the wager.

The wizards and magicians surrounded Montezuma and begged him not to listen to the false prophets of Texcoco, but he sent them away in anger and sat brooding on his throne while everywhere there were whispers and distant sounds and terrible apparitions that came down upon him, wave by wave, like a flood tide.

"Come here to me," he called out in a dry voice, gesturing to me like a palsied old man. "Come close and stop pouting or I will send you away."

Unwillingly I drew near, and when the immense room was empty except for Montezuma and me, he leaned down and whispered into my ear, wheezing as he spoke and trembling with fear. "My sister . . . my younger sister Papantzin," he told me in a quick, anxious murmur. "Do

you know what became of my sister? It is a terrible story and
I do not like to think of it, but now I must think of it again
and again. I must sit up in the night and think about it, and
when I try to eat and when I try to laugh I can only
remember what my sister Papantzin said and how it was the
day she died so young and handsome. She was gone before
the middle of the day though she had been laughing in the
morning. By night they had placed her poor body under the
cloak where it awaited cremation, and then when the priests
came to carry her away they found a terrible thing that they
could not believe, for my sister Papantzin was sitting up in
her grave and was alive again though she had been cold
and lifeless for many days. And they shouted the news and
came running to me with my sister, who looked as if she
might be mad and would not stop weeping until I knelt by
her mat and listened to her tales of the awesome things she
had seen in the Land of the Dead from which she had
returned!"

Montezuma panted for breath and his eyes were filled
with terrible remembrances as he gasped and moistened his
lips. "I will tell you what it was my sister saw," he
continued in a whisper, forgetting me entirely and slouch-
ing down to the floor, where he sat listlessly rocking to and
fro, to and fro, as he spoke. "She saw creatures she had never
seen before; she saw strange beings who dressed their bodies
with gray stone and whose craggy flint faces were covered
with hair. She saw these moving rocks, these men of stone
come from the sea. My sister saw them come up from the
waves, and then like an avalanche they tumbled down upon
all our armies and they threw themselves upon the cities like
molten stones heaved from volcanoes! And Tenochtitlan was

burning! The Palace of Montezuma was burning! And the land of the Mexicans was buried alive in the thundering landslide of the stone armies! This is what my sister saw in the Land of the Dead!"

"My Lord . . ." I stammered, trying to escape his gloomy mood. But he did not hear me and he sat rocking to and fro, saying nothing but only gazing into the air. I waited for him to give me permission to leave, but he did not see me anymore. The darkness came and I heard the night birds and the Sun came again and I heard the shuffling of servants lighting the cooking fires. But still Montezuma did not tell me I could leave him.

Then the nobles who served the Great Speaker came for him and led him away like an old dog on the end of a rope. I began to fear that, like his sister, my Lord would leave the world soon. But by the afternoon he was laughing with his advisers and he called for the dwarfs. And everything was agreeable to Montezuma. Fruits and tortillas dipped in honey and spices were brought to him on platters when he dined. He sat in solitary magnificence, separated from his servants and the four great men who attended him and from me by the tall wooden screen behind which he ate his meals. He was in so good a mood that he offered his councilors a dish of delicious fruits from the mountains. These great men who attended my Lord came humbly toward him and, without looking at his face, they ate what he had given them and bowed many times as they returned to their proper side of the wooden screen.

It was during this meal that two messengers were led into the chamber, interrupting the Great Speaker's meal and causing him to frown in anger. "We beg forgiveness for coming at this time and disturbing our Lord when he is at his dinner, but we have grave news which our noble lords have sent us to tell you. And so urgent is this news that we have been told that we must relate it to you at once, Great Speaker, even if we should have to shake you in your sleep and call you from your dreams."

"Yes, yes, enough of these empty words. Have them tell me at once what news is so urgent that it must come before my meal is done!" Montezuma muttered with annoyance, coming out from behind the screen and standing before us.

The messengers did not wait for me to repeat Montezuma's words. They glanced nervously at one another and then the taller of them began to speak in a voice so timid that his words trembled upon his lips. "We have run to your Palace and we have run for many days, for we come from the divine water where the Earth ends and the sea begins. We have been sent to tell you what we have seen and what many people who live by the water have seen since the Sun almost died in the mouth of a monster."

"Well, tell me! What have you seen? What have you seen?"

"We have seen islands that float and we have seen wooden houses that are carried on the water in the claws of immense white birds that flap their wings and stir the air and make the sound of the wind rising high into the sky. We have seen these things coming from out of the distance upon the water!"

Everyone was dumbfounded and Montezuma's face turned black.

"We have seen all these things," the messenger

The sky mirror in the head of a curious bird. *Codex Florentino.*

repeated in a murmur. "And all we have told you is true. We do not know what these floating houses are or from what place they have come, but this we do know: when we crept to the shore and watched carefully we could see some kind of men, some kind of fantastic people riding on the backs of these terrifying floating apparitions. We swear it, Montezuma!"

Montezuma raised his trembling hand and his eyes fluttered. Then suddenly he fell to the floor and moaned.

The great Sun arose each morning, but in the Palace there was no sunlight. The good days were gone. The priests whispered and the farmers murmured about the strange things that many people had seen. These visions did not only haunt lone supplicants who were half crazy from fasting and bloodletting, but were also seen by groups of common people and by sober noblemen.

The days passed and each day more stories of strange visions came to Montezuma's threshold. And each day the Great Speaker became more grave and solitary. Now we rarely spoke and he did not even realize that I crouched at his feet, awaiting his words. I was afraid of him. As the stories were told to him and the look in his eyes became more frantic, I became afraid of him, for I no longer knew him and I could not guess when rage would suddenly pour from him and drown everyone in his presence. He was like a wounded beast who was mad with pain and charged blindly in one direction and then in another.

"What has happened, what has happened?" he stammered in dread every time a messenger hurried breathlessly into his Council Chamber.

One man told of seeing a wailing woman whose face was stripped of flesh so that her eyes dangled from their sockets. She was one of those who died in childbirth and came back to bring warnings of misfortune. She appeared to a young girl who had gone to the well for water. She found a woman with long, beautiful hair sitting there. This strange woman slowly turned toward the girl, who screamed when she saw a bloody skull instead of a face.

From everywhere, from villages and cities all over the domain, came stories of fearful visions. Dreadful people came out of the darkness: humpbacks and deformed children and men with numerous limbs. Monsters with two heads appeared and disappeared suddenly and unexplainably. And sometimes these apparitions lingered. One group of deformities was surrounded by the warriors of a village and they were captured and brought to Montezuma. They were placed in a guarded hall and the Great Speaker was called to come see them. Montezuma shouted for me to accompany him and I hurried after his fleeting figure. The guards stepped aside and we entered the room prepared to see a terrible collection of human oddities. But what we saw instead were five brightly glowing creatures who hovered briefly in the air and then faded away and were gone. Montezuma was appalled.

These apparitions continued to appear. There were fires that could not be extinguished, comets raced through the sky for many days, and flocks of human deformities roamed the countryside. Montezuma was terrified because the day of Quetzalcoatl was coming soon and he believed the omens were warnings that that important day—9 *tecpatl* in the year One Reed (1518)—would not only be the time of the great god Quetzalcoatl but might also be the end of the world.

In those bad days there was a great wizard who lived hidden among the ruins of Tula, where he conversed with the Dead and repeated their wisdom to those who would listen. His name was Huemac and he was the Lord of the Land of the Dead, a magician of immense knowledge and power. Montezuma sent emissaries laden with rich gifts and the skins of many flayed men to Huemac, begging him to hide the Great Speaker from the derangement of the world that was crumbling all around him. But Huemac sent back word that he would not allow Montezuma to enter the Land of the Dead. When the Great Speaker heard the message that had been sent to him, he raged uncontrollably and sent the emissaries away to be killed.

"I do not accept his answer!" Montezuma shouted. "It was brought to me by fools and I do not accept it!"

Other messengers were then sent to beg Huemac to protect the Lord of Tenochtitlan by hiding him, but they were chased away by the Lord of the Land of the Dead and sent back to Montezuma with the message that his destiny had been forfeited because of bad conduct . . . because of excessive pride and cruelty.

"He sends word to the Great Speaker that you must perform the ceremonies of purification," the messenger stammered fearfully as he knelt before Montezuma.

"Take these liars and fools away and kill them!" my Lord shouted.

And then, out of fear or perhaps out of confusion, my Lord submitted to a twenty-four-day fast, until his cheeks were hollow and the flesh around his eyes turned soft and purple. But this penance did not save him, for only two days after his fast ended there came news that a shepherd had been carried away by an eagle to a glistening grotto where he had been received by a person of great beauty and power. When the shepherd returned, he proclaimed fearlessly, "The Lord of the grotto was so great that by comparison Montezuma is nothing."

The Great Speaker spun around and shouted a curse. Then he grabbed my arm and pulled me after him so quickly and violently that I could barely stay on my feet. "Call for my litter! Call at once for men and carriers!" he exclaimed. "At once! At once!" he yelped.

I hurried off to find my Lord's chief bearer and his carriers. When I told them that they were wanted they instantly felt my anxiety and hurriedly presented themselves at the door of the Council Chamber.

We set out at once, traveling at first by road and then by a small boat that carried us to a secluded island. There we remained for several days, trembling and hiding like fugitives, until one of Montezuma's ministers discovered where we were and came to convince the Great Speaker that he must return to his throne in Tenochtitlan no matter how dreadful the prophecies were for the future.

I watched as Montezuma shook his head defiantly and backed away from the old minister like a frightened child. At first my Lord would not consider leaving his hiding place, but the minister urged him to perform his duty and promised in a whisper not to say anything about his desertion if Montezuma would return quietly to his Palace.

Hopeless and overwhelmed by bitterness, my Lord sat on his litter as we bore him back to Tenochtitlan.

At night, from the garden rooftops of the Palace, I could hear the voice of a woman crying, "My children, we are lost." But when the guards went in search of this woman, they found no one. Then one morning some hunters came to the royal antechamber and brought with them a mysterious bird they had captured. This bird had a mirror in its skull, revealing all the heavens even when the sky was bright and there were no Stars or Moon. The ministers carried the bird into the Council Chamber and showed it to Montezuma, who at first refused to come near it. When at last the Great Speaker was convinced that he must examine the strange creature, he gazed horrified into the mirror and saw the sky imprisoned there. And when he peered at it a second time he could see an army of men coming toward him.

Montezuma cried out in terror and shouted for his astrologers. But when the soothsayers and magicians hurried into the chamber, the bird flew away and was never seen again.

For the domain of the great Lord Montezuma all the signs were bad. Nezahualpilli, Lord of Texcoco, and a strong ally of Tenochtitlan and a trusted and old friend of my Lord, suddenly died. Therefore the council of Texcoco named Ixtlilxochitl, a young noble of great virtue, to be the new Speaker of the city. But Montezuma rejected the decision and asked the Texcoco council to elect his friend Cacama instead. The councilmen complied reluctantly, and the enraged Ixtlilxochitl, with a large band of defiant young men of the city, took to the hills and lived in exile. In this way Montezuma's enemies grew more numerous, and in every subjugated town of his domain there were people who frowned and muttered angrily when they paid tribute. In many remote forests and rocky canyons were young men like Ixtlilxochitl who awaited the time when Montezuma would stumble and they could victoriously return to their homes.

My Lord Montezuma was no longer divine. I dreaded him, for his fear made him mad. His greatness was smothered. His head was split in two and he spoke in two voices and could not make up his mind, for one part was contrary to the other part. I watched as he gathered all the sorcerers and wise men of his Palace and begged them to reveal the dreadful secret that lay behind the countless omens. Each time they spoke, Montezuma raged at their replies and sent them away to be killed.

Men who had seen strange things were brought to the Palace and commanded to tell every detail of their visions, only to be thrown to the floor by the guards and dragged away. Even the astrologers, whom Montezuma revered, were accused of treason and heresy because they could not understand the signs in the sky. So they too were killed.

The people were afraid of my Lord. The Great Plaza was deserted. The nobles who served Montezuma were silent and pensive. The acrobats and dwarfs were solemn, and even the perpetual whispers that had once come from the apartments of the wives of the Great Speaker were silent. Anyone who had an extraordinary dream was required to come before Montezuma and describe what had been seen. But finding nothing that served as an answer to the riddles that plagued him, my Lord had hundreds of people put to death. And so it was that the dreamers were massacred in the Great Valley where the Toltecs had forged the mighty dream wheel and set it into motion.

From that day there were no more dreams. The world of powers and spirits was dark. No one said what he meant to say and every man bowed low to Montezuma with the reverence that is given to the teeth of the jaguar. The councilmen stayed away. The princes and the judges; the high priests, the warriors, and the masters of the youths; the keepers of the gods, the singers, the servants, and the jugglers did not approach Montezuma's throne but hurried past it. Montezuma sat alone with his anguish, and I sat beside him.

Then the Great Speaker, who could no longer bear the crushing silence, shouted to his war chiefs and sent them to faraway lands to bring the holiest of holy men to the Palace, by force if necessary. When these old wise men came before the Great Speaker and did not tell him something comforting, he became fierce and black and full of hornets and sent them away to be slaughtered. One by one they crept before the throne and one by one they whispered a prophecy, only to be angrily waved away and strangled in an adjoining chamber, where their withered bodies were piled.

"And you, what will you say?" Montezuma demanded in a voice so dry and choked that we could barely understand him.

A trembling old man fell to his knees before my Lord and murmured sadly, "From the water. . . . Very soon what must come will come."

Montezuma groaned. Everyone in the Council Chamber was abject and still, fearful of arousing the great Lord's anger. He sat hunched and stupefied, nodding to himself wearily and slowly rubbing his thumbs together. For a very long time there were no words, and I sat at my

Lord's feet so overwhelmed by his enormous despair that I could no longer feel anything. I watched Montezuma the way I watch an airborne hawk whose wide, floating circles seem remote and harmless until suddenly he plunges to the Earth and takes his victim in his claws.

Then I was startled by his voice. "You . . . Woodcutter! . . . Come here," he muttered. "You . . . Woodcutter . . . do you see how it is for me here? Or have you become as false and callow as the rest of these fools?" He seemed to await an answer, but his eyes defied me to respond. I desperately wanted to run away, but I knew I must not move. I waited silently. I could not look at him anymore. I could not look into his eyes where the Warrior God had once lighted two hundred fires. Where the gentle priest of Quetzalcoatl had once smiled peacefully. I waited fearfully.

"If you are not false and if you are still the same man who stole firewood from my forest, then I have a task for you."

I glanced anxiously at him.

"Since it has never bothered you to tell me the truth even when it angered me," he said, "I will send you to the place where the land becomes the water. Do you know this place, Woodcutter?"

I said that I did not know it.

"Then I will send three men with you—two to carry supplies and one to guide you to the sea. And when you return you will tell me what it is that I must fear."

"But I know nothing of these things . . ." I stammered. He turned his head and waved me away.

"Do not worry about what you do not know, Woodcutter! Worry about your life . . . for if you steal the truth from me I will not be as generous as I was when you stole my firewood!"

With this, Montezuma left the room and I gazed fearfully around me. I wanted to complain to those still assembled there that I was not suitable to carry out such a difficult reconnaissance, but the guards and the councilmen ignored me and turned their backs on me and hurriedly left, until at last I was standing alone in the deserted chamber. I had no choice. I would have to go to the very place where the most terrible omens had been seen.

Early the next day we left, crossing the lake as the Sun made his scorching summer ascent into the sky. We sailed to the opposite shore, where Chalco is located—a route familiar to me since I had taken it long ago when I had first come this way from my home near Tlaxcala. Then I had been a frightened boy. Now I was older but I was also afraid.

From Chalco we made our way along a narrow valley that twisted between the high mountains surrounding Tlaxcala. Our road led into a hilly region where every narrow ridge of soil had been transformed into precious vegetable garden. We crossed a wide ravine and passed among many little villages where the heat was so intense that not a single person was out of doors. Soon we came upon the walls of Tlaxcala and traveled secretly among the houses of our enemies, where festoons of flowers and vines, roses and honeysuckle filled the air with bright colors and lavish fragrances. My people regarded me either with fear or with disdain for sitting at the feet of Montezuma. And even the great men would not approach me, for I was Nanautzin, the Ugly One, who had been transformed by magic into the Chief Orator of the great Lord of loathsome Tenochtitlan.

I had no wish to remain in Tlaxcala and was glad when we finally resumed our journey to the sea. Now the land was entirely new to me, for I had never ventured this way before. We came upon a deep river where dwellings made an unbroken line on both banks and where many people hurried past us. A fortress loomed over this sprawling village, which I had never known existed though it lies only six or seven leagues from where I was born.

"The power of Tenochtitlan is immense," my guide told me. And so it seemed, for I could not imagine a domain that was wider or richer. Everywhere around us as we traveled to the sea was the land of Montezuma; and all the thousands of people we encountered were the people of Montezuma. Surely so great and mighty a ruler had nothing to fear, not even from omens and bewitchments, for nothing could possibly challenge the might of Tenochtitlan except the gods themselves.

Our route now opened upon a wide and fertile valley, watered by streams that rushed and leaped over their rocky banks even at the height of summer. The rich patches of soil were protected by stands of timber that cut the broad plateau into fertile gardens. Never had I seen such a vast and excellent farmland. Maize rose in thick patches that spread outward in every direction like a green, wind-tossed lake. At the end of this sumptuous country we came to the crest of a wild circle of mountains that abruptly fell away at our feet, descending so steeply and so far down that at the bottom we could see huge clumps of tropical vegetation choking the mouths of gaping ravines. These plants, which love the humidity and heat of the jungle, gradually took possession of the land as we made the difficult descent. For three days we stumbled over broken little paths that wound along the spur of the great volcano, on the summit of which balanced a rock shaped like a coffer. The glossy, dark-leaved banana trees threw up a dense green shadow around us, finally enclosing us entirely in a skyless world where water dripped slowly from one leaf to the next and made the jungle reverberate with ceaseless music. Behind us were the ragged flanks of the mountains with their gullies filled with dark pines. And beyond, to the south, stood the great Lord of the mountains, with his white robe of snow descending far down his magnificent sides, towering in volcanic solitary grandeur, the giant of the countryside beneath which everything else seemed small.

The pathways had been made nearly impassable by the summer rains, and we had to stop often and rest among the flowers and trees. The fragrances lulled us while the birds flashed through the foliage and dazzled us with their plumage and songs. Among the rotting logs and grasses on the jungle floor huge insects whose enameled wings glistened in the fluttering sunlight made their tireless way amid the thick, musky humus. We had come very far, to a strange land that I did not know. I did not recognize the blossoms, and all the animals also were strangers to me. This was the place where the Earth fell into the water, a region of peculiar sounds and fearful powers—things that rustled in the thick underbrush just out of sight, yet close enough so we could feel their warm breath upon our bodies.

Then the scent of salty water became strong and we came to the village of the man who had sent Montezuma a message, saying that he had seen the worst omen of all the bad signs that had appeared during the last ten summers. I had been sent in search of this town chief so I could question him and verify with my own eyes the visions he claimed to have seen.

This old chief was a humble fellow, ignorant and ill-mannered, who lived in a mud house surrounded by his destitute people. They had always feared his cruelty more than anything in the world. Yet now they would not obey him when he sent them out into the jungle to collect roots and fruits. They would not go to the big water to hunt the sea creatures. For they feared something they had seen on the water even more than they feared their chief.

"What is this terrible thing they have seen?" I demanded at once.

The leader would not answer, but wiped the sweat from his coarse face and squatted in his hut, shaking his head willfully.

"I came for the Great Speaker himself, and I ask in his name again: What have your people seen that has made you send terrifying stories to Tenochtitlan?" I commanded.

This lowly chief placed a very great value on his life and that kept him silent, for he had heard that all the dreamers had been massacred by Montezuma and that magicians and wise men had also been put to death for telling the Great Speaker what they knew.

"I have nothing to tell," he mumbled into his hands, afraid to look at me.

"I am Nanautzin, the Chief Orator of our great Lord, and I have been sent for your words! If you will not speak, you will surely die, but if you tell me what you and your people have seen by the water, then I promise you that you will not be harmed. But you must first tell me truly what you know and then you must show me whatever it is that frightens you. Then, and only then, can I return to our Lord and tell him what it is that we have found here by the water."

The chief grunted suspiciously and wiped his nose. He studied my face dubiously for a long time and then he sighed helplessly. "I am not a great man, and I have not been instructed at the temple, but I believe in all the ancient ways of our fathers . . ."

"Yes, yes," I said impatiently.

". . . and what I am going to tell you is the truth, for I am still too young to drink pulque and I am not a holy man. I only know about the vanilla, the cochineal, and the cacao, and I know nothing of strange things and magic," the chief whispered with dread, glancing out the door of his hut as if he feared that at any moment some unspeakably terrible creature would leap from the darkness.

"What have you seen?" I demanded nervously.

The chief paused for a long time, rubbing his hands together apprehensively and staring me in the eye. *"Itistheuggglyoness,"* he whispered in such a dread-filled voice that I could not understand him.

"Speak up!" I exclaimed. "Speak clearly!"

"Ah," he groaned, terrified that the loudness of my voice might bring something evil down upon us. Then he whimpered. "I will tell you . . . I will tell . . . but we must not make trouble because we are only humble people who cannot defend ourselves against these enchantments . . . these *ugly ones* . . ."

"*Ugly ones?*" I whispered.

I don't think I had ever before heard these words

spoken in quite that way, and for some reason the expression on the wretched man's face and the rattle in his voice terrified me. Now even I glanced toward the dark doorway of the hut and squinted my eyes, trying to see what might be out there in the night.

"It is in the water," the chief murmured as I leaned breathlessly forward to hear his words, "a mountain that goes from side to side. It is here and I have seen it. A mountain that does not touch the shore . . . an island that swims . . . that is what has come out of the water."

No one spoke. The little cooking fire popped in the silence and the frail trail of smoke rose through the hole in the ceiling.

"And the *ugly ones,*" I gasped, "what are these *ugly ones?*"

"I have seen them," the chief murmured. "They come out of the mountain when it is near the shore. These *ugly ones* come out of the floating mountain."

I gazed into this man's eyes, for I was not certain that I could trust him. "Is all that you tell me true?" I asked.

"It is true," he said quietly. "You will see for yourself. . . . . Come."

I hurried after him as he picked up his club and silently led us outside his hut, where he gestured for his headmen to follow quietly. We crept along little paths that circled down through the jungle and opened upon a narrow beach where the mysterious great water stretched out ceaselessly into the moonlight . . . a vaster lake than any I had ever seen. There we hid behind the foliage and watched.

"Ah," the chief whispered urgently and gestured for all of us to duck down into the leaves.

For a moment there was no sound except the turning of

the waves. Then I began to hear, at a distance, a sound unlike any I had ever heard, a babble, a low chatter that sounded as if it were the language of monkeys or some strange animal unknown to us. Very cautiously I raised my head and carefully peeked out between the leaves.

Galloping from the sea itself were massive four-legged, snorting monsters with grotesque human bodies growing out of their backs. The faces of these awesome creatures were as pale as the belly of a serpent, and they were covered with shells like the hard wings of beetles. Upon their pallid faces were many hairs, and from the hairiest part, where the mouth should have been, came the unintelligible babble that we had heard earlier in the silence of the night.

I could not speak, but stared at this unbelievable scene at the edge of the water. A rush of ideas battered inside my head but nothing made any sense. I could not understand what we were seeing, though it was right there before my eyes. But I knew that, whatever this vision might be, its discovery was urgent. So we did not remain even a day, but started at once on our way back to Tenochtitlan.

When I rushed into the Council Chamber and Montezuma saw the expression on my face, he immediately ordered everyone to leave and would not allow me to speak until the doors had been closed.

"Now," he said tremblingly, "tell me everything."

I collected myself and began to recount my astounding adventures. After I had finished telling all I had seen and heard, Montezuma sat silently for a long time. Gradually the panic in his face dissipated and he looked strangely calm, so utterly calm and resigned that I feared perhaps he were going to die or had gone mad. Then, as his shoulders sagged and his arms dangled at his sides, he slowly arose and a deadly smile came over his face. He winced uncontrollably and carefully backed away from his throne. He turned pale and swayed on his feet. And then very slowly he looked me in the eyes and said in a very faint voice, "It is the year One Reed . . . and as it was prophesied long ago he has come. Lord Quetzalcoatl has come."

II

In the Days of the Darkness

Confronting the strangers called Españoles. *Codex Florentino.*

Eleven

"There are no more than fifteen or perhaps sixteen of them, my Lord."

"One among them is surely a god, for all the others revere and obey him, and he wears the black mantle of Quetzalcoatl."

"The other beings are four-legged creatures. They have blue mantles or red. On their heads they wear something small that is scarlet in color, and they have very pale skin, much lighter than our own."

"Below the nose, their faces are hidden behind much hair, but the hair on their heads comes only to their ears."

Montezuma learned this startling information from his Ocelot Warriors, whom he sent out to spy on the strangers. He also sent Cuitlalpitoc, a trusted nobleman, to meet with Pinotl, the leader of the little coastal town where the ugly ones had been seen. Cuitalpitoc and Pinotl cautiously climbed high into a tree and spied on the peculiar beings who walked about on their floating island.

"They have a little boat on their sailing house, and this they lowered into the water, and then they climbed into it and sat motionlessly tugging at strings which they dropped into the sea. Now and again they quickly pulled back and brought a fish out of the deep."

Montezuma was forlorn when he heard these reports, and he did not speak a word.

Now he understood all the omens that had mystified his wise men for more than ten summers. Now he was completely resigned. It was exactly as it had always been foretold. Lord Quetzalcoatl had been driven out of his land by the evil magic of the wizards of the Warrior God Huitzilopochtli. Now these ugly strangers were bringing the god back. They were the same creatures who had accompanied Quetzalcoatl into exile. Among all his followers only the deformed and dwarfed, the humpbacked, had remained loyal to the defeated god. Some of these faithful creatures had perished from the cold in the mountain passes during the escape to the sea, and some were slain by the powerful wind that cast the trees down upon them, and others had plummeted into the deep ravines. Lord Quetzalcoatl wept for these humble creatures who died for him. His lament was heard in the highest places of the sky as he stepped upon his raft of entwined serpents and sailed toward the place where the Morning Star lives. And now, on the dawning of the new year, One Reed, Quetzalcoatl had returned as he had promised with renewed power to drive Huitzilopochtli from the temples and from the land. Surely the battle of these sublime gods would bring down the whole world and split the Tree of Life!

"And that is how it has always been foretold," Montezuma said after a long silence, ". . . that our world, the Fifth Sun, will end when the exhausted Sun cannot rise and earthquakes pound upon the rocks until they fall into the sea and all of us are swallowed up by the hurricane of fire."

No one in the Council Chamber spoke. My Lord gestured for me to come close, and then through my voice he addressed the trusted nobles he had called to the council. "You are the chiefs of my house and of my Palace. You are the strong walls of my life that support the roof above my head. I trust you, but hear what I say to you now, and should you speak a word of my plan, I will bury you under the foundations of my house, and your wives and children will go with you, and all that is yours will be taken away forever. Hear carefully what I command: Bring me in secret two of the finest silversmiths, and two lapidaries who are well skilled in the art of working emeralds. Bring me what I have asked quickly and silently."

When the artisans were found and were brought to the antechamber of Montezuma's Palace, they were told to enter, and they crawled into the presence of my great Lord and put dust upon their heads and covered their eyes. "Come to me," Montezuma bade me tell them. "I want you to make splendid objects. But do not reveal this to anyone or you will cause the ruin of your families. All shall die if a word is spoken of what I will now ask of you. Take care and listen to me well. You, old father," Montezuma ordered one craftsman, "you will bring your tools here to the Palace and in secret, behind a closed door, you will make a serpent mask of the finest turquoise mosaic, a massive shield of gold with bands of seashells and quetzal plumes springing from the bottom. And you," my Lord instructed another artisan, "you will make a quetzal-feather head fan, a plaited neckband of green stone beads, in the midst of which will lie a golden disk. And you will also make a turquoise spear-thrower, and obsidian sandals. And all of you shall assist in the making of these precious things so they may be completed in great haste but with great care. That is all I say to you."

Then Montezuma sent the craftsmen away and called upon his advisers and war chiefs. I spoke his words to them: "Come to my side and listen. It is said that our Lord Quetzalcoatl has at last returned to our land. Go to where he is and meet him. Listen carefully and watch everything. The Ocelot Warriors will be hidden away in the foliage and will be my eyes and my ears. And five messengers will make themselves known to the strangers and take them many precious gifts. The whole treasure I send must be well guarded, for if anything is lost your children will be slaughtered and your hoses will be burned. So guard the treasure of Quetzalcoatl well!" Montezuma proclaimed fiercely. Then he gazed at the noblemen who sat at his feet. I spoke these words for him: "Which of you will go to the strangers as my messengers?"

No one spoke. And as my Lord arose and slowly walked among the prostrate nobles they cringed and trembled. "You, priest!" he exclaimed directly to one of the frightened men. "You are the guardian of the sanctuary of Yohualichan and you will lead the other messengers to the strangers. The second shall be from Tepoztlan, while the third is from Tizatlan and the fourth from Huehuetlan. That accounts for all the messengers but one. Come forward, my Jaguar Knights, and let me look at you!" The men reluctantly stood up and approached Montezuma. He looked at them proudly, and then smirked and a cruel glint came into his eyes. He ignored me and spoke for himself in a strange voice. "Who shall be the fifth and last messenger?" he said teasingly. He looked around the room mockingly, like a child pretending to search for an imaginary person. And then he smiled directly into my face and nodded his head. "Perhaps I shall send the Woodcutter," he muttered. "Yes, perhaps I will send Nanautzin . . . because he is from Tlaxcala and, as everyone knows, his people are barbarians who do not believe in the gods. Therefore he has nothing to fear."

Someone laughed momentarily and then stifled the sound. In the silence everyone smiled. Montezuma nodded once again and came very close to me. "Isn't that true, Woodcutter? You Tlaxcalans do not believe in the gods. . . ."

I could not look at him and I could say nothing. Then my Lord stood over me as I crouched on the floor, and he slowly placed the toe of his sandal upon my fingers and very gradually pressed his weight down upon them. When I could no longer bear the pain I cried out with a whimper, and Montezuma stepped back and laughed, saying, "What is that you say, Woodcutter? Does that barbaric squeal mean that you volunteer? Ah, how very good for you!"

I was abashed but I would not display my shame. Among the titters of these arrogant men I stood up solemnly and took my place beside the frightened messengers. Whatever love I had ever felt for my Lord was now gone. I feared the strangers from the water far less than I feared Montezuma, for I thought his wits had flown out of his head and he was broken in two by the collision of Quetzalcoatl and Huitzilopochtli.

"Here is what you shall take to the shore," Montezuma told us. "Here is the treasure of Quetzalcoatl. These glorious things you will give to the god. Here also is the finery of Tezcatlipoca, and here the riches of Tlaloc. These many precious objects will be placed in baskets which you will take to the sea. And all of these splendid things which are called the array of the gods you will give to the strangers. You will welcome them humbly. But you will not invite them to Tenochtitlan. You will be gentle with them. But you will suggest that having visited us they will wish to leave our land forever. All this you will do! So go! Do not linger anywhere along the road! Pray to our Lord Quetzalcoatl and say to him, 'Your deputy Montezuma has sent us to you. And here is what he sends to celebrate your return to your homeland.'"

Twelve

The evening was filled with warm rain and distant thunder as we left Montezuma and went to the House of the Eagle Warriors to plan our journey to the water's edge. We found a secluded corner where we could speak privately, but there was no purpose in trying to keep our mission secret. Everyone had heard rumors. Many stories elaborately wound their way throughout the domain of Montezuma. Tales of terrible invaders also came to our ears from the distant tribes of great artisans living far to the south, where the floating islands had been seen by fishermen many days before we had seen them on our shores. The Eagle Warriors came to us and shook their heads. They were reverent men but they were also skeptical soldiers, these proud brothers of the most elite clan of Tenochtitlan's fighting men, and so they wanted us to spy on the strangers and discover what weapons they brought with them.

"We must be ready to destroy them," a young warrior whispered in earnest, "before they trick us with their magic!"

"But the gods would not trick us," exclaimed an old

priest who had joined the circle of excited men gathered around us. "The gods," he said, "are our fathers and they love us. Of all men we alone were chosen to be the people of the Sun, to nourish him and to bask in his golden glory! To be the greatest of his warriors and to win from weak men this mighty land of which Lord Montezuma is the absolute ruler! All this the gods gave to us. Why would they now take it from us?"

"But I tell you these strangers cannot be gods!" a soldier barked at the priest impatiently. "So stop trembling like an old woman!"

"I think perhaps they are sorcerers," squealed a little merchant who had slipped between the soldiers so he could peer at the five messengers who were to be the first to approach the gods.

"These strangers are the carriers of our Lord Quetzal-coatl," murmured a young priest, his eyes filled with tears that ran down his brown face, where they left silver trails.

"No, no, not gods," exclaimed another soldier, who bore many scars of battle and was much admired by his fellows, "Listen to what I am telling you. They are not gods, my friends. Believe me, they cannot be gods, for if they were truly gods they would come forward—would they not?—and they would call upon their priests to bring them the blood and the heroic hearts that nourish them. What they are I do not know . . . but they are not gods!"

Now everyone was talking at once and the uproar brought more and more curious soldiers and priests until it was impossible for us to plan our journey to the water. We quickly decided to return to our houses and to meet again at the *tzompantli,* the skull rack near the ball court, when the treasure of Quetzalcoatl had been placed in baskets and was awaiting our departure. So we left the crowd of angry men to their relentless debate and slipped away into the darkness.

Soon I was alone . . . looking into the clear night without fear or dismay. Though I had seen the intruders and their mysterious islands, and had more reason to be terrified than those priestly messengers picked by Montezuma, I felt no terror. And though these four renowned and powerful holy men were proud to have been chosen to speak to the gods, I felt no honor. For Montezuma had not wished to honor me but to humiliate me as a barbarian. I had seen the malice in his eyes. And I knew that he had come to loathe me. I had seen the naked little man behind his godly array and I had seen the coward within him. I had smelled the sweat of fear coming from his perfumed body. And in his evasive glances I had seen the squalor of his heart. Now he loathed me the way we disdain lost lovers to whom we have confided deep secrets.

I gazed up at the immense pyramid dedicated to Huitzilopochtli and Tlaloc and I put my foot on the first step of the great double stairway. Then I began aimlessly climbing to the temples at the top of the gleaming mound of cut white stones.

I had come a very long way from the marshes of Tlaxcala. I was the Chief Orator of the Great Speaker of Tenochtitlan. I could go where I wished to go. I could climb the most sacred pyramid of the realm and the guards and priests bowed and opened the way to me. I was a nobleman in a noble city, and yet I was a barbarian to my Lord. And to myself . . . I was even less. Every day I

awakened to find the woodcutter in my bed. Nanautzin
could not change. He was still as deformed and ugly as he
had been one evening many years ago in a lordly forest
where he had stolen a bit of firewood from the gods.

> This is the song I give to the wind
>> that tells how I am afflicted.
>
> It angers me that never again can I be born
>> and must leave the songs and flowers behind me
>> and depart forever, destroyed in my house
>> and forgotten.
>
> I am miserable on Earth.
>
> I unwind the jewels, the blue blossoms
>> woven over the yellow blooms,
>> and I suffocate on their intoxicating fragrance
>> and can live no more.

This is the lament I sang as I climbed the one hundred
and fourteen steps to the blue and white temple of Huitzilopochtli and the white and red temple of Tlaloc. This is
the song I sang as I stood at the top of the world where the
sacred fires burn for fifty-two years. And all around me was
Tenochtitlan, a place of unimaginable splendor.

I could see the three great causeways—Ixtapalapa,
Tacuba, and Tepeaquilla—and I could see the canals and
the bridges and the many temples that rose from each of the
twenty districts of the vast city. Below were the Great
Plaza, the ball court, the raised dais where the warriors
contended in war games, the House of the Priests and the
House of the Eagle Warriors, the skull rack, and the
rippling succession of houses . . . white, glistening white
in the moonlight and surrounded by the blue lake upon

which eternal Tenochtitlan floated in an imperfect sea of time.

And then everything before me began to dissolve into nothing. I could feel the Earth move and I could no longer stand upon my feet. I fell into a place where I had never been before, and when I awakened from my dream I knew that the world could be no more. The stones remember, and only men forget. We have lost our little dreams and have awakened together into a reality that destroys us.

At dawn the messengers came for me. Silently we departed for the edge of the world where the gods beckoned us.

While the Moon still lingered in the sky we came upon the desolate beach. It was a wide, blustery place except where the restless sand had been piled into hillocks by the perpetual motion of the wind. We crept through the low brush and cautiously surveyed the landscape, which had changed greatly since I had first seen the strangers. Here and there were peculiar objects perched on the sandhills: complex mechanisms supporting some kind of hollowed log made not of wood but of stone or metal. There were several of these strange contrivances and all of them seemed to be pointed at us in a threatening way, as if they were placed strategically to keep us away from the beach, but by what magical means I could not guess. Branch-covered shelters had also been put up, but there were no people. The gulls screamed into the gray horizon and the waves flowed high upon the strand, but there were no people and no voices. The floating island had come to rest in the sea, and the north wind had paused momentarily, but there were no signs of life. We did not make a sound or show ourselves. The crimson glare that accompanied the Sun as he battled the night from the sky cast a fearsome glow upon the beach. The wind whirled back into motion and howled. And we cringed and waited in the underbrush until the world was bright and the Sun had ascended to his supreme position in the center of the heavens.

I could not sleep. I lay motionless and gazed into the brightening sky and felt the sand around me slowly scorch with heat.

Then I heard them.

I pressed myself to the Earth and did not breathe. After a moment I summoned my courage and peered through the grass and roots. There were several beings coming out of the shelters. They were too distant for me to see them very well, but I could make out their spongy faces tangled with hair. And I could see that they were entirely covered, so I could not be certain if their bodies were pale and colorless or if perhaps their faces above the mass of hair were painted white to make them look frightening.

They had the faces of fish. Even their lips, as they jabbered, undulated like the mouths of fish. And when they walked their steps were stiff and heavy, like the movements of crippled men. They were certainly terrible enough to be gods, but I could not believe in them. I could not accept them as deities because their movements were awkward and not eloquent like those of gods. And from this gracelessness I knew that we had reason to fear them.

Then suddenly six four-legged monsters appeared, dashing out of one of the shelters and snorting and bucking with their long legs while the top half of the creatures bobbed back and forth senselessly. I was about to cry out to my fellows that we must run for our lives when unexpectedly the top half of the monsters divided from the bottom half. I stared at them in astonishment and could not believe what I had seen. For now the four-legged monsters walked about by themselves and twitched their long ears, while the top half turned into warriors just like the other gods.

"Ah!" I muttered uncontrollably. "Perhaps these men are really gods after all!" For the animals I had mistaken for monsters were some curious kind of huge deer upon which the warrior gods could ride by some marvelous magic!

These were not the only fearsome animals brought by the gods. Tied to the doorposts of the shelters were massive wolves that howled, barked, drooled, and frothed at the mouth. If the gods released these beasts they would surely pick up our scent and tear us apart. I buried my face in the sand and trembled, afraid to breathe for fear that the wolves would hear me! Their barking grew more and more ferocious and I did not know whether to flee or to play dead. By now the barking had grown so terrible that I simply had to peek out and see if the animals were coming.

Fortunately the wolves were not barking at me but at a little group of local villagers who were cautiously coming down to the beach from the direction opposite our hiding place. They approached hesitantly, stopping again and again and turning back in fear, only to resummon their courage and approach once again. These fishermen and farmers carried baskets of fruit and vegetables, bundles of flowers, choice cuts of freshly killed game, and many rustic little trinkets of gold with which they hoped to welcome the gods. The bravest of them crept as close to the encampment

By the great water was the most fantastic vision
ever seen in the land of Mexico. *Codex Florentino.*

of the strangers as they dared, reaching out with their offerings and quickly putting them on the ground before dashing away—throwing dirt on their heads and sobbing hysterically as they fled.

The strangers shouted at the people, but their words said nothing to us. We could not understand. So the pale ones called into their shelters and soon someone came out. I was amazed to see that this person was not one of their own kind but one of us—a brown woman of our land wearing strange things upon her body and speaking in strange words.

I watched very carefully from my hiding place as one of the gods spoke to a pale young deity who then spoke in another very peculiar tongue to the brown girl. Then the girl approached the frightened villagers and exclaimed in the language of our land, "Do not be afraid. My name is Ce Malinalli and I am from Painalla in the province of Coatzacualco. Listen to me and do not be afraid. I have been chosen to speak for these great ones who have come to our shores."

Gradually the terrified villagers began to creep toward the camp, trembling and cowering and throwing dirt on their heads. "Do not be frightened," Ce Malinalli said again and again. "If you do as they bid, you will not be harmed. So do not be afraid. Come and bring the offerings you have prepared. The strangers will thank you through my voice, for I speak the language of the south. One of these pale men was thrown into the sea, and he saved himself and lived for many summers in the land of the south where he learned our way of speaking. He can tell me what the strangers say and I can repeat their words to you in the language of our land. So bring the gifts and do not be frightened."

The village people approached the brown girl called Ce Malinalli and they sniffed suspiciously and then they cautiously touched her skin and the alien trinkets she wore around her wrists and neck. Soon they summoned enough courage to circle each of the pale ones. They shook their heads in astonishment as they gazed at these gods who looked like nothing that had ever existed in their lives or in the long history of their land.

I carefully crept among the peacefully dozing messengers and awakened them, gesturing for them to be silent while we spied on the curious activities in the strangers' camp. The gods appeared friendly to our people and did not seem to intend to harm them. We quietly assembled the gifts we had brought, and on a signal we stood up bravely and faced the great gods as elegantly as our fear allowed. The villagers dropped silently to their knees when they saw that we came dressed in the mantles of the noblemen of Tenochtitlan, great city of the Valley of Mexico. In the stillness we walked forward to greet Quetzalcoatl in behalf of our Lord Montezuma.

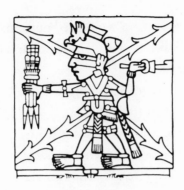

Thirteen

"It is the wish of my master," Ce Malinalli said to us as we approached, "to know who you are and from where you come."

"We have come from the city of Tenochtitlan," I said to her. "We have come as the messengers of our Lord Montezuma."

One of the strangers spat on the ground. Then he said through the girl, Ce Malinalli, "Maybe you do and maybe you don't."

We did not understand this remark and did not know if perhaps the god were mocking us. So we knelt on the ground, covered our eyes, and put dirt on our heads. Then we were asked, "What have you brought in the baskets?"

"It is the gift Montezuma sends to the great Lord among you," I answered, standing and facing the gods and seeing that they were no longer displeased but wanted to inspect our offerings.

After they were certain that we were truly the voice of Montezuma, we were well greeted by the strangers. Then Ce Malinalli said, "The Lord of these strangers awaits you. He asks you to come to him where he lives—in the floating houses he calls *buques.*" She pointed out into the water where the immense islands of wood tipped to and fro in the waves. And we were afraid.

The fishermen of the village were called, and when they came with their little canoes, everything we had carried fromTenochtitlan was placed in them and we floated out into the water and approached one of the buques. This wooden island was a fearful enough sight from a distance, but as we drew closer it loomed larger and larger; it grunted and growled every time it swayed, and its tall, naked tree trunks tilted dangerously back and forth above us. We were so terrified we could not speak.

Then a long metallic tentacle reached out for us, grasping our boat and pulling it against the heaving side of the creaking water monster. We waited silently without moving. Then something was dropped down on us. We kept our courage and realized that the ropes that had fallen over the side of the buque were intended as a ladder by which we could climb to the top of the floating island.

I was to be the first to take the ropes into his hands and climb, but I could not gather the courage to do it. I had seen prisoners proudly climb the temple steps to the altars where they were fed to the gods. I understood that the gods must be nourished. But I did not want to climb the ropes to the top of the buque and I did not wish to be eaten by the gods. Perhaps Montezuma was right and all the people of Tlaxcala were barbarians, but whatever I might be, I was certain that every throb of my heart begged me to run away and save myself.

The messengers pressed against me and urgently whispered, but still I could not move.

142

"No one will harm you," Ce Malinalli said.

Hearing the reassurance in my own language gave me courage, and I blindly climbed the ropes as quickly as possible and did not open my eyes again until I felt hands take hold of me and put me down on solid ground.

But it was not ground that I discovered when I opened my eyes. I was standing on top of the wooden island under its tall leafless trees, which were imprisoned in many strong ropes dangling high in the air and snapping loudly against the wooden trunks like the lash of many whips. When all of the messengers had come up and the baskets were also brought to the top of the island, then suddenly the god Quetzalcoatl appeared in a doorway, coming out of the bowels of the floating house. The priests who had accompanied me from Tenochtitlan moaned and crumbled to the floor, covering their heads and offering ecstatic prayers and salutations. I stood absolutely motionless, unable to bow or kneel as the god came toward me, bristling with black hair that curved around his large mouth and hung from his ears and nose. His legs and feet were black and his chest was enveloped in a glistening shell marked like the back of a tortoise. On his head he wore something I had never seen before, and in his eyes there was nothing . . . nothing at all. No rage or power, no compassion or wisdom. There was only an empty sky in his eyes like the eyes of the mountain goat in which nothing is written. But when he glanced at the baskets filled with the array of the gods I saw something come into Quetzalcoatl's eyes. I did not know exactly what the expression meant, for I had never seen such a look except in the faces of very old men who have seen the belly of a beautiful girl-child.

The god stood before me and put his fists on his hips and held his head high.

"My master wishes to know," Ce Malinalli asked me, "who you are and from where you come."

"It is from far away in the great city called Tenochtitlan that we have come," I answered.

"If that is true and you are really from Tenochtitlan, who is your lord?"

"Our Lord, he is called Montezuma, and we come as his messengers."

"These are the gifts we bring to the god from his deputy Montezuma," the priest of Yohualichan said.

"And what are these black-robed men who have come with you?" Ce Malinalli asked me. "Are they priests who have come with you?"

"Yes," I said, "those who come with me are priests, and I am Nanautzin, the Chief Orator of my Lord Montezuma."

"And are these priests also the subjects of your Lord Montezuma?" Ce Malinalli asked in behalf of Lord Quetzalcoatl.

"Yes, all people are the subjects of Montezuma; there is no other above him on Earth."

When Ce Malinalli related this comment to Quetzalcoatl, he laughed and waved me aside as he stepped forward and peered into the baskets we had brought to him.

"These are the ornaments of Quetzalcoatl," I explained as I hastened out of the god's path and bowed to him. "We wish to attire Quetzalcoatl in his precious garments."

This request was not understood by the god, who repeatedly questioned Ce Malinalli until he seemed contented with her explanations. Then he stood confidently and smiled as we approached him.

Solemnly we arrayed Quetzalcoatl. With reverent care we fastened the turquoise mask in place, the face of the god with its bands of quetzal feathers, and its serpent earrings of green stone hanging from the lobes. The god's empty eyes stared through the eyeholes at us and made us tremble. Then we dressed him in the lavish vest and the necklace made of green stone in the midst of which was set a bright golden disk. Next we fastened to his hips the mirror of smoking glass, and dressed him in the cape called *tzitzilli*—"ringing bell." And we placed on his arm the shield with fringe and festoons of quetzal plumes. And about the calf of his leg we wrapped the green stone band with the golden shells. And finally we laid before him the sandals of obsidian.

The other adornments that we had brought from Montezuma were carefully placed in rows on the floor in front of the god. And when all this was done, Quetzalcoatl gazed skeptically at what we had presented to him and he awkwardly stooped down and peered at one of the objects and he turned another over with the tip of his foot. Then he looked at me squarely and asked, "This is all? Is this all that you bring to me?"

I stammered as I glanced in confusion at the priests. They trembled and nodded to me, and I whispered, "This is all, O our Lord."

The god was very angry at my reply, and he shouted so loudly and quickly that Ce Malinalli could not speak for him and we could not understand what he said. The priests groaned and murmured that we had surely committed some

145

The ambassadors were chained and then the thunder roared
and fire burst from the magic stick. *Codex Florentino.*

terrible heresy that endangered our whole world. But we did not know what we had done to offend our Lord Quetzal-coatl. Yet his anger stormed over us. We fell to the floor in the torrents of his rage, as many of his warriors came running out from the belly of the buque. They seized us, and on our ankles and necks they fastened pieces of metal. They bound us together and would not let us go.

Then a fat warrior came toward us with a stick in his hand, which he waved threateningly as he laughed. I did not know what it was he had in his hand, but I feared perhaps it was their sacrificial knife. Before it could touch our hearts, however, the warrior suddenly held the metal stick high in the air and it made a terrifying roar of thunder. I cried out as it spouted smoke and fire and so deafened me that I thought I was surely dead.

I could hear the gods laughing, but I could see noth-ing. I was dizzy and ill, and I fell into a heap with the other messengers, who had also fainted.

When I opened my eyes I found myself sitting up and leaning against the others while warriors forced a sour red liquid down our throats, which looked like blood but did not taste like it. Then they offered us food and they unbound us. They smiled and told us not to be afraid. But I could not understand these gods. I did not know why they had been so enraged, and now I could not grasp the reason for their smiles.

Quetzalcoatl stepped forward and motioned to us to rise. When our heads cleared and we were once again on our feet, he said to us through Ce Malinalli, "I have been told by the fishermen that they greatly fear the warriors of Montezuma. It is said that his soldiers are very strong, very brave, very great. They tell me that if there were only one soldier of Montezuma, still he would conquer all opponents. That is what I have heard from many of the people who fear you. But these are only stories, and I am not convinced," the god said with a smile. "So I have decided to test you and see just how strong you really are."

We were given spears and swords and leather shields though we were not warriors and did not know the proper use of such weapons. And while we looked at each other in confusion, Quetzalcoatl told us, "When it is dawn we shall fight each other in pairs, and then we will discover if the stories told about the soldiers of Montezuma are true or false. We shall see who among us fall to the ground!"

My heart pounded and I bowed repeatedly as I turned to Ce Malinalli and exclaimed, "Please tell the god that we do not come as warriors but as messengers. Montezuma would not permit us to make combat with the gods. We have come only to salute the Lord Quetzalcoatl, and should we do what he has commanded, Montezuma would be wrathful and he would destroy us!"

But Quetzalcoatl did not listen to me. He waved me away and I dared not say another word.

"No," the god barked, "the combat must take place! I want to see for myself what kind of warriors you are! Therefore, eat before the first light, when I also will have a hearty meal. But then at dawn be prepared to defend yourselves!"

Just at that moment a magical bell sounded which, though it had no effect upon us, caused all the warriors of the god to throw themselves to their knees as they offered up their orisons to a very large wooden cross planted in the sandy beach. We gazed with curious surprise as one of Quetzalcoatl's black-clad priests came forward and officiated over rites entirely alien to us. This priest, whom Ce Malinalli called *padre,* spoke to us through her words, but at first we could not grasp what he was saying. He showed us the woman god with her little baby and the man god on the wooden cross. And when we said that these were not the gods we knew from our forefathers, the priest assured us that he had come with the intention of giving us the true gods and destroying all of our ancient deities. He then put into our hands a little image of the woman god and the baby and told us that when we returned to our cities we must place this icon in our temples instead of our own gods.

I looked first at Quetzalcoatl and then at his priest. And I asked, "Then it is true that you have come to bring down Huitzilopochtli and the magicians who tricked our Lord Quetzalcoatl and sent him into exile?"

The padre did not give any attention to my question, but smiled in a peculiar way and said, "All your idols and all your gods must come down. None will remain."

Then we were sent away to sleep on the beach and to prepare for the combat the next morning. We muttered to each other as we withdrew. The warriors of the god smiled at us and gave us little strings of crude beads, but we did not wish to have anything from them and we did not want to touch them or to be near them, for they had spoken of the gods and of the world as evil men speak. We were scarcely in our canoes when we began to paddle frantically for the shore, anxious to make our escape and return to Montezuma with our horrifying stories of the strangers. We were so frightened that we used both our hands and the paddles in order to reach the beach more quickly. "O my friends, we must paddle with all our might!" the priest beside me groaned. "Faster, faster! Let nothing evil happen to us here! Let nothing happen . . .!"

In the darkest night we slipped away and started our frenzied journey back to Tenochtitlan.

Fourteen

It was night, and the Great Plaza floated in a tide of shadows. Many temple fires glowed in midair atop the pyramids, and Tenochtitlan was asleep except for the sentries who ceaselessly peered into the darkness, watching for omens and strangers.

"Who is there?" a voice commanded as we neared the Palace of Montezuma.

"I am Nanautzin, the Voice of our Lord, and I have come from the water where he sent me."

"Ah!" came several voices. "They are back!"

"The messengers have come back from the sea!"

The voices reverberated through the Plaza and into the halls, and soon a dozen guards had gathered around the little fire that lighted the grand entrance of the Palace.

"Come—come quickly." An elderly man beckoned to me. "Montezuma has ordered that you be brought to him even if it were deepest night when you returned and even if our Lord were sleeping. Come! Come quickly!"

When I hurried into the sleeping chamber of Montezuma, he hushed me and hissed, "No!—not here! You are not to speak of it here! I will hear you in the House of the Serpent. . . . Do you understand? But not here!"

Then Montezuma ignored me and spoke to the man who had conducted me into the apartments of my Lord. "You will take them to the House of the Serpent," he said. "Two captives will be adorned with the paint made of chalk. Go now, quickly!"

We bowed and withdrew while Montezuma, with only the aid of his humble house slave, began hastily to dress.

"We must fetch the priests who accompanied you to the water and then we must hurry to the House of the Serpent before our Lord arrives there," the old man murmured. "It is good that you have returned, for Montezuma has been mad with expectation since your departure. For him there has been no sleep or food, and no one dared speak to him . . . so grave was his face and so frantic the look in his eyes. He sighed. He sat listlessly. He lost himself in despair in the day, and at night he was filled with wild forebodings. Nothing could comfort him, nothing could calm him, nothing could please him. . . ."

"But did he say anything?" I asked in a whisper. "Did he console the nobles and the people?"

"He spoke to no one while you were gone. I was his voice in your absence, and I did not speak for him. Only once did he mutter something, and though I heard it I dared repeat it to no one."

"And what is it that our Lord said?" I urged.

"He said . . . '*Who is the great Lord here? Who now commands our land? Yesterday it was I . . . but now my heart burns and I know nothing. Where may we go to live contentedly? All the roads of the sky are sealed to me and I receive no answers!*'

Then our Lord was silent before he spoke again, saying, *'Who are they? What do they want? And will they dare come here to the holy city Tenochtitlan?'* That is what our Lord Montezuma said to himself in a wretched whisper while you were away, Nanautzin."

"And nothing more?"

"Nothing," the old man said solemnly.

We approached the House of the Serpent. We could hear the chanting of priests as they laid the chalk-painted captives upon the altar and opened their chests. The other emissaries who had accompanied me to the water hurried along behind me as I mounted the steps and entered the chamber of the Serpent. Those assembled there bowed as we entered and covered their eyes and sprinkled us with the blood of the sacrificed captives. Then Montezuma suddenly stepped out of the shadows, saying, "For this reason do we offer you blood, for you have gone to a perilous place and you have gone there to look into the faces of the gods and to know them . . . you have even spoken with the gods!"

And when the ceremony was finished, the priestly messengers recounted to our Lord all that had happened to us by the water. They told Montezuma how we had made our journey and all that we had seen when we arrived at the sea. And then I told him about the peculiar food of the strangers, who did not eat hearts and blood. "As for their food," I told him, "it is like the food we eat. It is like fasting food . . . white and big and not heavy like tortillas but flaky and light. It is like straw but with the taste of pith from the stalk of maize . . . and a little sweet. Yes, it is honeyed to eat; it was sweet to the tongue," I explained.

Montezuma listened intently and now and again

The prisoner was sacrificed and blood was sprinkled upon
the messengers, for they had spoken to the gods. *Codex Florentino*.

sighed in astonishment. He was especially amazed to hear about the stick that roared; to hear how the thunder had resounded and how it had made us faint. "This stick is powerful magic," one of the priest messengers muttered, "for it is a fearful thing. When it explodes it is a volcano—smoke swells out of it and it has a foul odor! Rocks burst forth from it—and fire and sparks!"

"Their weapons are made of black metal and even their bodies are metallic, like the shell of a tortoise with their black arms and legs coming out of holes in their shells."

"But their limbs are not truly black, for I saw that they are tightly covered with some kind of woven cloth; and I suspect that their entire body is unnaturally pale!"

Then I silenced the messengers with a gesture and I waited for Montezuma to respond to what we had told him. But he stood as if paralyzed with dismay. Finally he muttered, "Yes . . . yes . . . now go from me . . . ."

"But," one of the messengers exclaimed, "my Lord, we have not told you about the gigantic deer on whose backs they ride!"

"There is more?" Montezuma groaned.

"These deer are as tall as the rooftops of our houses! And the wolves that also came with these strangers are enormous, with flat long ears and dangling jowls from which saliva flows! The animals are angry and they pant and bark and jabber as if they were speaking the same language that is spoken by the gods."

"And the strangers' shields and swords and clubs are made of metal and cannot be broken by the strongest warrior. And the warriors are hairy and graceless and bold. Some of them are black-colored—some are soiled gods and have very kinky hair while others are yellow-headed and have golden hair on their faces like the silk of the maize."

Slowly Montezuma stepped back and raised his hand as if he wanted to push us away. Then he faltered and fell back into the shadows. We could hear his breathing but we could not see him. Then from the darkness came the sounds of his weeping. We timidly bowed and in mortification and misery we withdrew, leaving the sacrificed captives dangling over the altar stone. Their heads were twisted to the side and from their lightless eyes came tears of blood.

My Lord Montezuma sat alone on his throne in the Council Chamber, and I sat in a distant corner and clenched my knees and stared at him. Councilors came and went; noblemen visited and waited. Everyone waited, but Montezuma did not speak. Many came to the Palace in the Great Plaza of Tenochtitlan, but no one came away with any hope, for the great Lord of the land was silent. Many came to him for advice, but they came away with nothing but a memory of his forlorn face, which they peeked upon in secret, encouraged to defy custom by Montezuma's defenselessness.

"He is smaller than I thought," they whispered.

"He is less elegant. . . ."

No one came away from Lord Montezuma with anything good in his heart. And nothing came to Montezuma, for the tribute of the villages and cities had dried up like a barren field when the strangers arrived, and all the gifts due to my Lord were sent to these mysterious gods who did not act like gods and did not speak or move like gods.

"My Lord," the councilmen muttered fearfully as they crept to the feet of Montezuma, "what shall we do? What can we do? Must we wait for the world to end and do nothing but moan and die?"

"We must wait," Montezuma said in a dry voice.

"For what do we wait, my Lord?"

"We must see . . . we must discover if these strangers will leave us or if they will stay. We must find out what they want," Montezuma murmured so softly that I could hardly hear his words.

"My Lord," the councilmen asked, "will they come here? . . . Will they dare approach Tenochtitlan?"

"I do not know," the great Lord whispered, ". . . I do not know. . . ."

"And are these strangers truly gods or are they monsters?"

"I do not know. . . ."

"But we must discover their real faces and hearts!" the priests exclaimed.

"We must find out how to protect ourselves," a warrior declared in a stout voice.

When at last Montezuma arose, the assembled men of the Council Chamber dropped to their knees and were silent. The great Lord paced slowly across the room and then he returned to his throne and sat down.

"Now listen to what I say," he pronounced in a terrible, thick voice. "I want the filth men and I also want the evil ones. I want all of them . . . the sorcerers and magicians, the astrologers and the soothsayers. All of them. . . . I want every black one of them in this land . . . every evil person whose eye is crooked and whose mouth spits foul blood and venom. I want the singers of songs that kill children and whose hopping, twisted dances bring drought and vermin and sickness. I want the tellers of bad enchantments and those half-human deformities who dream of their enemies and put worms into their bellies and hearts.

These monstrosities and fiends I want by the hundreds! And from them I will choose the most terrible and send them to the strangers!"

And so the evil ones were summoned. Montezuma also sent for the elders who were not obsessed with life and could look fearlessly at the gods and see what was really before them rather than seeing what they fear. And he sent for strong warriors and instructed them to provide all food the strangers might require. He sent these warriors to provide for the gods so their hearts might be satisfied and contented. He also sent captives so that they might be offered if the strangers asked to drink their blood. All these things Montezuma sent to them. But before these messengers left the Palace, the great Lord called the wizards and magicians to his chamber, and he took me by the shoulder and he drew me close to him and he whispered into my ear, "Tell them that they must find out something. . . . Tell them they must discover who these strangers are. . . . Tell them that they are to sing and they are to dance but no one is to know. They are to speak to the wind and bid it crush the strangers, and they must bring sores and sickness to them, to break their bones and turn their food into poison so they fall ill and die or become fearful of the magic of our land and leave us forever! Now tell them! . . . Tell them these things!"

But the magicians had no power against gods, and their enchantments and dances were harmless. The strangers were divine, and no evil came to them. They ate the food brought to them and they talked to the villagers through Ce Malinalli, and nothing bad came to them. So the magicians hurried back to the city, to tell Montezuma that the strangers were invulnerable and that magic was helpless against them.

"We are not equal to them!" the wizards exclaimed. "Compared to them we are nothing!"

Montezuma abruptly turned away from the wizards and dragged me after him as he hurried into the antechamber, where he confronted the astonished warriors and noblemen waiting there. Montezuma gave them this order: all the captains and chiefs and nobles, under threat of death, were to take the utmost care of the strangers and to provide them with their every need lest they become angry and bring the world down before hearing the pleading of the priests of the Temple of Quetzalcoatl.

Then Montezuma sat alone on his throne and waited, praying that the strangers would reward the generosity of the people of Tenochtitlan by turning back to the place from which they came. But the messages from the shore did not tell of the strangers' departure but of their preparations to march inland. And my Lord groaned loudly and shouted into the vacant rooms of his Palace.

"They are coming onto the land," the messengers reported; "they are coming into the countryside, and they are moving across the Earth where our forefathers were born. They are already on the move and they are well cared for by our own warriors, who will do nothing to displease them. They are under our own protection from our enemies and allies alike, and everything is done to honor them."

Montezuma cried out in rage, "Get out! Leave me! Leave me! You—you too, Woodcutter—get out!"

We crept away in confusion. Everywhere there was bewilderment. In the Plaza the people were terrified by the rumors. They stood together and talked about the news that came from many places, saying that the god Quetzalcoatl had returned to claim his throne and to throw down the Warrior God who had tricked him. In the streets there were arguments among the priests and the warriors, and the people listened and became more terrified by the confusion of the great men and the elders, the high priests and the war chiefs. And there was weeping, and in the air were countless songs of lamentation. But there were also those who did not fear the gods. There were mothers who said, "My beloved sons, how you will marvel at what is about to befall us!" And fathers said, "O my precious sons, you are the witnesses of an astonishing era!"

And the elders went before the gloomy Lord Montezuma and said to him, "It is not hopeless, our great Lord, for the strangers are accompanied by a girl of this land and she speaks in our language and she is called Ce Malinalli. She is from Painalla, and it was there that the strangers found her on the shore and took her into their floating island to speak for them and to serve Quetzalcoatl. The god puts his hands upon her in the presence of our warriors and makes her his wife."

And the messengers said, "The strangers have harmed no one but wish to know us and tell us about alien gods they bring. They also wish to know our Lord Montezuma."

Montezuma was tormented by this news. "What are you saying!" he exclaimed. "What do you mean? What have the strangers asked about me?"

"They wish to know many things. They ask many questions about the great Lord of our land."

"What? What?" Montezuma snapped impatiently,

staggering from his throne and confronting the messengers.

"They ask us what kind of man he is."

"They say, '*Is he a youth or is he a mature man? Is he old? Is he feeble?*' All these things the gods have asked of many people."

" '*Is he perchance an old and childless man?*' —that is what they inquire of the warriors and priests. '*Is he already white-headed?*' "

"And the noblemen told the gods that you were a mature man, neither young nor old, neither fat nor slender, but handsome and healthy and wise."

When Montezuma learned that the strangers were making many inquiries about him, he was ill with anguish. And when he was told that the gods expressed the determination to come to the city, to march to the gates of Tenochtitlan and to see Montezuma's face, our Lord was anguished and withdrew from his messengers. He said nothing and he ate nothing, and in his eyes was nothing but madness and despair. In his nervous eyes the warrior was gone, the man was also gone, and what remained was a frightened child.

When Montezuma realized that the strangers were advancing upon his Palace he wanted to run away. He whispered to me in the evening that he wished to escape and hide away in a cave. He asked me to bring his most trusted counselors, and when they came before him, he told them that he wished to flee. And though all of us who heard his plan were sworn to secrecy and threatened with death should anyone learn of his wish, the news went out into the streets and the people knew that our Lord was afraid. And so he could not run away. So he could not go into hiding and escape from the strangers. All hope was gone for Montezuma. All strength was gone. The soothsayers' words haunted him and overcame his heart and vanquished it. Nothing was left but confusion and remorse. And Montezuma could do nothing but wait. He sat very still on his throne and he lay sleepless upon his bed, and he waited for whatever would come down upon him.

In the night the birds were silent and only the sound of distant weeping came through the window. The Moon rose into the sky and danced with the shadows in the lake.

Fifteen

The anteroom and chambers were silent. The women's laughter was lost among the vacant apartments, and a last, long line of servants carried away Montezuma's possessions and closed all the doors of his Palace. I hesitated as I left my rooms, for they had been the only comforts I had ever known. Then I fastened the shutters and brushed the ashes from the hearth. My Lord had vacated his splendid Palace and left for his princely home, abandoning his throne in the deserted Council Chamber as if to give the gods a sign of resignation.

Perhaps the gods understood Montezuma's gesture, for news arrived that they were coming. They had begun their march toward us. The terrible suspense and uncertainty were over. Now perhaps Montezuma would call upon his war chiefs and prepare to resist and crush this small army of strangers. Perhaps at last Montezuma would sweep the aliens into the sea and annihilate them with the enormous force of Tenochtitlan and its many allies.

But Montezuma said nothing. And Montezuma did nothing.

Every day messengers ran breathlessly into the room where Montezuma heard their dreadful stories. "A man from Cempoala!" they panted as they crept to my Lord's feet. "The Chief of the House of Arrows, he is the first to bow to the gods!"

Montezuma gazed into the garden beyond the window and did not listen as I repeated each word the messengers muttered.

"This man from Cempoala helped the gods . . . he interpreted for them, he showed them the road to Tenochtitlan, and he advised them and guided them through the land, leading the way."

Still no word went out from Montezuma. The allies waited. The warriors waited. But Montezuma gave no commands. And the strangers were offered no resistance as they came toward us day by day. No one raised a weapon against them. No one stood in their path or told them to leave our land. But when they came to the place called Tecoac where the Otomi people live, the warriors of the region could not endure the mortification of these strangers overrunning their villages. At noon they came out in battle array, greeting the "gods" with their shields. They shouted defiantly and attacked the pale strangers and those treacherous people of the coast who were their allies and servants.

"These are not gods!" they shouted as they wielded their clubs. *"These are mortal enemies who have come to make us slaves!"*

The men of Tecoac were good fighters, but they could not defeat the strangers. The Otomi were courageous warriors, but the fire sticks called "cannons" were terrible and no one could stand before one of them and live. The

164

strangers destroyed every soldier. They annihilated them utterly. They trampled upon them and they struck them and broke their bodies with the thunder of the cannons. They shot them with "crossbows," and on the ground the men of Tecoac bled and died with their faces in the dirt. The women wept and cried out, but no one was listening. In Tenochtitlan my Lord Montezuma was not listening to the lamentation of the women of Tecoac. No one counted the dead and no one put ashes upon his head and moaned. Sorrow was overwhelmed by fear. No one spoke and no one stood in sunlit doorways. All the houses were closed. For the gods had broken the bodies of those who worshiped them. They had destroyed the army of the Otomi and left nothing in the road but broken spears and spilled blood.

My own people, the Tlaxcalans, were the allies of the Otomi, and though they were very numerous and strong, though they were feared as great warriors and had thus remained free from the domination of Tenochtitlan, it is said that they were afraid when they heard news of the defeat of the Otomi. The cannons and the big deer that the strangers rode and the wolves that fought for them terrified the Tlaxcalans, and it is said they were filled with foreboding. News came to us that they gathered together and took counsel. All the captains and chiefs met and talked, and this is what they said.

"How shall we be? Shall we go out to meet them? Do we dare? For the Otomi is a brave warrior but the strangers thought nothing of him and walked over him as if he were nothing. They can destroy a warrior with a glance of the eye! They are so powerful that their breath kills anyone who stands before them. So how shall we be?"

"Do we meet them in battle or do we go out to them with gifts?"

"We must greet them as friends! We must not resist them or they will destroy us as they destroyed the men of Tecoac! We must go over to their side!"

All these words were reported to Montezuma by his spies.

Therefore the rulers of Tlaxcala went out to meet the strangers and they carried many gifts and much food. They bowed humbly, though Tlaxcalans are a fierce people who do not bow to enemies, and they said to the strangers, "You are weary, our Lords."

Of all the people of this land the Tlaxcalans are the most hated, for they have resisted Tenochtitlan. And therefore when Montezuma learned that the Tlaxcalans had allied themselves with the strangers, he was horrified.

"They went out to meet the gods," the messengers told my Lord. "They brought them food and they paid them great honor and guided them into their city. They gave them houses in which to sleep and they sent their noblest daughters to them!"

Montezuma glared at me momentarily. For a long time he was silent, and then, when the messengers had crept from the room, he muttered, "Those barbarians who are your relatives are hungry for our riches and our lands! These savages of yours want to eat us alive, but all you will get are the scraps from the table of the strangers. Nothing more!" Then he put his foot against my side and pushed me to the floor. "Nothing—nothing more!" he raved as he stumbled from the room and fled from me, his shrill voice echoing through the corridors and the empty rooms of his house.

Now I was alone.

My own people of Tlaxcala despised me for my betrayal,
and Montezuma, who had raised me so high, had turned
away and thrown me down like a fool. And I stood alone,
more vulnerable . . . more naked than ever in my life.
Inside me was all the misery I had ever known, and it grew
strong in my loneliness. It suffocated me so that I could not
think. It turned me into nothing. And I was afraid.

Now it was evening, and the lingering sunlight spread
immense amber shadows across the Great Plaza where I
stood so small and ugly.

In the dimness of the yellow evening I sang softly to
give myself courage.

> Oh, you thief of pretty songs!
> Where will you find them when they are lost to you?
> Now you are needy and poor once again,
> > but perhaps one day you will discover
> > the black and red ink
> > of wisdom.
> Then, at last, you will be a beggar no longer.

Across the Great Plaza people, hurrying, passed me on
their way home. Then it was silent. Somewhere people were
eating together. But I am Nanautzin and I have no home.
Within my rooms there are no children. The woodcutter
does not have a wife to comfort him, and he is not a priest
for whom celibacy is a comfort. In the lean light of dusk the
heart feels its terrible emptiness. I cannot stand the sound of
my own groan, and I cannot bear the terror that grows
within me now that Lord Montezuma has laughed at me.

For a moment, all around me, the coming and going of

people, has ceased, and quite suddenly the streets are silent—occupied only by homeless dogs and homeless men.

I am such a man.

"I do not love my Lord," I whispered as I stood in the midst of the deserted Plaza. "I do not love him," I said.

A short, warm gust of wind rustled past me and vanished into the still and motionless world. From far away came the voices of boys: laughter and shouts, echoing from the House of Boys where the young warriors live.

The girls giggle as they run past me. Their bells resound and their feather ornaments flutter. When they enter the house a shout comes from the boys. Then there is much laughter. Another girl runs past me, but when I gaze at her she does not see me. I am too old to be a boy. I am too old to be unmarried. I am too old to be looking at Dirt-eating Girls. I am Nanautzin, the Ugly One, and girls do not notice me. I am not good to look upon, but the girls are very handsome.

> In the sky, a Moon;
> on your face, a mouth.
> In the sky, many Stars;
> on your face, two shining eyes.

These girls are the servants of Tlazolteotl, the witch goddess who eats the evil that pours out of men. They are pampered children, and they are trained to dance and sing. They massage musk from the deer into their thighs and between their breasts. Their bells reverberate when they move their legs. Their nipples are ebony and large. But the girls will not look at me. Even when I lived in the House of Boys, these girls would not look at me because my scars were ugly. I was hidden behind my ugliness, so they could not see me. I shouted out from behind my ugliness, but none of them could hear me. I loved their knees. I loved to watch them move as they danced in the House of Boys where they came to comfort us, smiling through the black circles painted upon their mouths, their yellow-stained faces lighting up the desire of the young men, their long black hair hanging loose and lustrous with sweet-smelling oil. I longed to touch them. I loved to reach out as they hurried past me and feel the warmth of them against my palms. Until, one by one, they slipped away with the boys and I alone remained. *In the sky, a Moon . . . only a Moon.*

Their beauty was false. In the eyes of these haughty Dirt-eating Girls was fire and smoke. Soon nothing remained but ashes. When they became feeble or sick, they were taken to a ceremonial place where suddenly, in the midst of their dancing, they were strangled and thrown to the ground in a heap. Now their bells were silent. Their smiles collapsed upon their lips. And because they had eaten much evil in their lives they could not be sent to the other worlds and they could not be buried or cremated. And so their bodies were taken away and thrown among the reeds where the vultures found them. Soon nothing remained. Around the decay of their lifeless bodies the lone and level land stretched far away.

When at last it was dawn I wearily returned to the house of Montezuma. I waited at his doorway, but he did not come. Though he was awake and the Sun was high in the sky, he did not come out of his bed. He did not ask for me and he did not send word to me.

After the annihilation of the Otomi people there was

fear everywhere in our land, and everyone hopelessly waited for the strangers to attack again. The priests waited, and the war chiefs, and the people waited.

"Nanautzin, listen to us!" the warriors told me. "You must go at once to the city of Cholula and tell the people there that we are their friends and we will protect them. You are still the Chief Orator of Montezuma and you are still a man of Tlaxcala; so you must also speak for us to the Tlaxcalans, who hate our allies of Cholula so much that they will surely incite the gods to attack and destroy them. They will say that the Cholulans are the allies of Tenochtitlan and that they are our spies. So you must tell your people, the Tlaxcalans, in the name of our Lord Montezuma to come away from the side of the strangers or all of us will perish. Though we have long been enemies, we must now be allies if we are to survive."

I did as I was told, but I was too late. When I arrived at Cholula the strangers and their Tlaxcalan allies were already at the city's gates. I sought out the lords of Cholula, but they were hiding. They had heard tales of the cannons that broke the bodies of all the Otomi warriors, and so they trembled. Before I could stop them, they had sent out their noblemen and priests to greet the strangers, and to beg them not to allow their enemies, the Tlaxcalans, into their city.

I walked beside the war chiefs who went to Ce Malinalli, the brown girl who speaks for the strangers. She bowed to them and then she gestured into the distance where the white leader with the black beard stood on a hilltop surrounded by his warriors.

"This man is called Cortes," she said solemnly, and we

repeated the peculiar name to one another. "He comes from a very distant land ruled by the mightiest of all lords," she said with a convincing expression on her face, though none of us believed her. Then she presented the padre-man I had already seen on the beach. He was called Olmedo, and he carried the god of the cross who had been sacrificed.

Then Ce Malinalli asked the war chiefs of Cholula many questions about me and she gestured for me to approach her, but I was determined to find my carriers and return to Tenochtitlan at once. I hurried away and did not look back. My possessions, however, were not yet ready for the journey home, and while I was urging my servants to complete their packing, Ce Malinalli came to me and bowed. Her manner was coy and she spoke like a Dirt-eating Girl of the House of Boys. When she looked at me she pretended not to see my ugliness, but her eyes said what her face did not say. And I distrusted her.

She said that she had come to tell me that her Lord, the man called Cortes, wished the Chief Orator of Montezuma to remain. I lied to her and said that I would not leave the city.

"Tell me, what are these bad signs in Cholula?" Ce Malinalli asked. I pretended that I did not understand her question. So then she asked, "Why is the city fearful and why are there barricades in the streets?"

"I do not know," I lied. But she did not believe me and told me to accompany her to the place where her Lord Cortes awaited me. I did not wish to go, but I had no choice.

The strangers were encamped in one of the palaces of Cholula. They had released their enormous deer in the courtyard, where the fearful people crept to get a glimpse of them. As we passed among these soldiers, an elderly woman greeted Ce Malinalli and asked her to come aside and speak to her. We followed this woman to her home, where she invited us to enter. Then the woman gazed at Ce Malinalli and murmured, "You are a woman of this land, Ce Malinalli, and in your face I see much nobility."

Ce Malinalli bowed very low, but in her face I saw cunning and not nobility; in her eyes I saw the blackness of wizards. The old woman nonetheless trusted Ce Malinalli and wanted to help her. "These strangers are not your people," the old woman murmured cautiously.

"They are pigs," Ce Malinalli said in a flat voice. I watched her as she spoke and I did not believe her words. "They are barbarians," she told us. "These white men will take away our children and eat them," she said.

The woman embraced Ce Malinalli and they wept together. Then the old one said, "You must listen to me. When you are given a sign you must leave the white men and come away quickly!—quickly! Do you understand, Ce Malinalli?"

An expression of cunning burst into the face of Ce Malinalli, and a girlish smile obscured her thoughts. "Ah," she murmured, "then it is true. There is a conspiracy!"

"Yes, it is true," the old woman explained confidently. "The conspiracy originated with Montezuma himself," she said. "He sent rich gifts to the greatest holy men of Cholula, to bribe them into attacking the strangers."

Ce Malinalli was silent for a moment, and then she whispered, "I am grateful for your warning and I shall run away as soon as I am given the sign. I want nothing more to do with these white barbarians!"

The Massacre at Cholula. *Codex Lienzo de Tlaxcala.*

With this, Ce Malinalli pulled at my arm and we hurried away toward the quarters of Cortes. But the streets and plazas were so filled with people that it was difficult to move. Hundreds of celebrants assembled in the temple patio for the lavish ceremony honoring the arrival of the strangers at Cholula, a city long honored as the home of the god Quetzalcoatl.

I wanted to escape, but Ce Malinalli watched me carefully and would not release my hand until we were at the side of her Lord Cortes. She immediately told him the secret confessed by the old woman. The man called Cortes was furious when he heard about the conspiracy of the Cholulans. At once the sobbing old woman was seized, and upon a signal from Cortes she was decapitated, her head falling so close to me that blood spattered on my legs. Then Cortes pushed me aside as he shouted for his soldiers and sent them in every direction as fast as they could run. In this confusion I had a chance to escape without Ce Malinalli's seeing me and I slipped into the crowd.

I carefully crept from the mob of excited people and made my way toward the Great Temple patio, where the carriers were awaiting our departure for Tenochtitlan. Once I had located them we cautiously headed for the city gates. It was very difficult to move through the crowds that had assembled in the Great Temple patio. The ceremonial music had already begun and throngs of lavishly dressed celebrants crowded the dance area. We staggered forward, squeezing through a wall of people, finally making our way through the last of the gates of the temple patio. Then I suddenly heard a fantastic clattering surrounding us. It was a prolonged clanging, which was so ferocious that I thought we were being overrun by an avalanche. I was thrown back against a wall with tremendous force as a group of the strangers charged past us and poured into the ceremonial plaza where the Cholulans were dancing in their splendid regalia.

My carriers screamed out in fear as they dropped their burdens and fled into the crowd. I shouted after them while I dodged the soldiers who hurtled and clattered past me in their suits of metal. For a moment I could not escape in any direction. I looked down into the frantic ceremonial patio in horror where the soldiers of Cortes were throwing themselves upon the worshipers. They barricaded all the gates so that no one might escape. Then they lunged into the unarmed multitude with their swords and knives slicing the air. They cut off the hands of those who played the instruments. They stabbed the priests and decapitated the young men, and blood ran in the sacred patio and the bodies were heaped in the corners and all the people were slaughtered. When the fighting ended, the temple patio was strewn with dismembered hands and feet and heads. The worshipers were broken and their bodies were tossed into the streets.

I ran as fast as I could, my tears blinding me as I stumbled and groaned. All around me the people of Cholula were shouting warnings to one another, and as their voices were heard throughout the city, the men became mad with grief and they became strong with sorrow. They cried out, "Get your weapons and kill them! Kill all of the strangers!" And behind these fierce voices of warriors came a great crowd of the common people, all armed, whose eyes were filled with horror and murder as they rushed toward the enemies in the Great Temple patio. As I fled through the gates of Cholula, there was nothing but the long, demented shout of battle all around me. My body was splattered with the blood of my people and in my eyes were a thousand tears.

"My Lord," I whispered to Montezuma, "Cholula is no more! It is finished and dead!"

Montezuma was silent, but his war chiefs stood up and they shouted, "They were slaughtered by the Tlaxcalans!"

"Six thousand throats were cut—six thousand!" they exclaimed.

"The lies of Tlaxcala have destroyed Cholula!"

When the people of Tenochtitlan heard the news they were torn by fear and rage. They did not know whether to fight or to run away. The elders went out into the streets to comfort the young men, for all the people rose up in revolt and demanded that Montezuma send his best warriors to destroy the strangers and drive them into the sea. Thousands of angry people marched into the Great Plaza, and they shouted into the air so that the Earth moved and the force of their rage made them dizzy.

Now Cholula was dead. Now there was blood in the Plaza and the limbs of dead men and women littered the streets. Now the invaders wiped their swords on the long black hair of the corpses and grimly set out on the road toward Tenochtitlan once again. The soldiers marched in their suits of metal and the dust rose from their feet in whirlwinds along the road. Their spears glinted in the Sun and their swords and suits clanged and clattered loudly as they marched. With them came their treacherous allies and the great wolves they called "dogs." And above their heads were many colored banners and the large wooden cross of their god in whose honor my people had been slaughtered.

Sixteen

The people of my land are brave and in their hearts is great daring. We swing our clubs as warriors and we pray to our gods as men, but these strangers, these *Españoles,* they fight like ants. They cling to one another so we cannot get at them and they shout commands to each other. They make war as if they were playing the sacred ball game. They plan each movement, transforming ten warriors into a single mad animal that kills everything in its way. And they do not take prisoners. They do not strive to capture their enemies for the sacrificial altar. They open every chest with their swords of metal and they sever arms and feet and heads with each swing of their terrible weapons. They trample us and break our bodies. They make sparks and thunder with their cannons, and trees and walls and people disappear in smoke and fire. Their magic has no pity. It only makes death. It spills the precious food of the gods upon the ground. It is a bad magic, but it is more powerful than any magic we know.

We are a people to whom the gods speak. And when a victory in a ball game or in a battle falls to one side rather than to another, we know that the gods have told us who will prevail. So the victory of the strangers at Cholula spoke to Montezuma and he understood that they must prevail. He could hide from them in the shadows, but he could not turn them back any more than he could bring life to those who had died at Cholula. And Montezuma waited.

Each day the people shouted in the Great Plaza of Tenochtitlan. They carried sticks and they argued; they carried offerings and they wept. They believed that the people of Cholula were not as good and brave as the people of Tenochtitlan, and they did not believe that the defeat of Cholula was a sign that the strangers were greater than all of us and therefore destined to rule over us. They shouted in the streets and they beat any person who didn't look like a native of Tenochtitlan. They cursed my people, the Tlaxcalans, and accused us of inciting the strangers to murder Montezuma's allies at Cholula. They loathed the people of Tlaxcala so much that I did not dare leave the house of my Lord. And though he, too, glared at me and would not permit me to come close to him anymore, he protected me and prevented the warriors from beating me.

"Your barbaric relatives are the dogs of these Españoles," he muttered to me from across the empty room in which we now spent all of our days. "Your shameful people are the lice of this stranger called Cortes! So you will go to them in my behalf, Woodcutter! And you will smile at them with your Tlaxcalan smiles, and you will lie to them with your Tlaxcalan lies and tell them you yourself are Montezuma Xocoyotzin . . the great Lord whose face these strangers wish to see. And once they have seen your face, which they think is the face of Montezuma, perhaps they will leave us and go away . . . so I can breathe . . . so I can live . . so I can lift this terrible sickness from my heart."

Then Montezuma sent me to his chamber, where his servants dressed me in his apparel. And he sent for his chiefs and selected among them those most gifted in diplomacy and deception. This scheme strengthened Montezuma. Though he was no longer one of the gods and though his wisdom had abandoned him and his courage had turned to chalk, his cunning bloomed more lavishly than ever. He became a spider that walks sideways and hides among the foliage until its prey is caught in its web. Thus it does not kill by its strength but by its cunning and its poison.

When I was dressed in the array of our Lord and the great men who would accompany me had been selected, the priests surrounded us with incantations and the keeper of the treasures brought baskets of precious feather streamers, golden banners, and necklaces of precious stones. When we left Tenochtitlan our procession was truly elegant, for Montezuma had spared nothing to disguise us as the supreme ruler and his entourage. Conch trumpets sounded and the drums resounded, and I, Nanautzin, the poor woodcutter from the marshes of Tlaxcala, was borne above the heads of the people, who covered their faces and dropped to their knees as my golden litter passed them.

When we came to the place of many volcanoes where the steep, twisting trail is called the Eagle Pass, we saw the strangers circling up the mountain toward us in long, curling rows. How small they looked against the wide, convulsive thighs of the smoking hill called Popocatepetl! There were perhaps six hundred of them, no more. More awesome than the small ranks of the white invaders were the sixteen gigantic deer on whose backs they rode. And more terrifying than the deer were the hundreds upon hundreds of Montezuma's enemies who had allied themselves with the man called Cortes.

Seeing that the strangers were approaching us, we laid down our burdens and waited. Though the great chiefs who accompanied me knew that I was not a nobleman but a humble woodcutter raised to the exalted position of Chief Orator, they did not make light of our royal charade, but bowed to me most reverently and covered their eyes even when the strangers were far away. They treated me as if I were truly the supreme ruler of our land.

When the strangers came upon us there was much wind and Popocatepetl groaned. Then the brown woman called Ce Malinalli bowed and approached us. She did not recognize me from our meeting at Cholula, for my costume was so wondrous that it transformed even ugly Nanautzin into a great Lord. She covered her face and averted her eyes, and I watched her carefully. I had been the lowest of men and I knew all the devices of underlings. Ce Malinalli's humility was not true and her modesty was not genuine. Though she moved timidly, her submissiveness was an utter lie. For within this deceitful brown woman was a heart like the heart of the strangers, full of greed and deception. It was a disease they had brought, and Ce Malinalli was sick with it.

Then the man called Cortes came toward me. His step was fanciful but awkward and his bow was as lavish and ridiculous as the prancing of a perfumed old woman. His skin was spongy and pale and his black beard was curly and coarse. He was a tall man with a large chest and an athletic

Dressed as Montezuma II, Nanautzin meets the strangers
in the place of the volcanoes. *Codex Florentino*.

build. His eyes had a grave expression, but when he spoke his face instantly belied his kindness and revealed a calculating mind and a pitiless heart. There was something in his expression that was both familiar and frightening to me. And as he stood up and gazed at me I tried to recall whom he reminded me of.

I did not speak and I did not stand. One of the great chiefs who accompanied me greeted Cortes and spoke to him through Ce Malinalli.

"Is this truly the great Lord Montezuma?" she asked.

But the chief who spoke for us did not answer the question. Instead he gave orders that the baskets laden with gifts be presented to Cortes and his war chiefs. No sooner had the Españoles seen this rich treasure than their mouths danced as if a spell had overcome them. Their little eyes glistened with pleasure and their faces burst into smiles. They were utterly delighted, and they ignored me entirely as they hovered over the baskets of gifts. It was the gold that most attracted their eyes. They picked it up exuberantly and they fingered it like monkeys. They were obsessed with its glitter and its weight, though they did not seem to see the graceful forms into which our great craftsmen had fashioned it. It was the gold itself that seemed to entrance them. Perhaps they needed gold just as our priests needed blood; perhaps it was gold instead of blood that they fed to their god who lived on the wooden cross.

Then I suddenly realized what it was that had been so familiar to me in the face of Cortes. It was the lust and the cunning hidden away behind his dark, sullen eyes. It was the arrogance and emptiness. All of these things I had also found in the eyes of another god—in the eyes of Montezuma. For the truth is this: Cortes longed and lusted for gold just as Montezuma in the service of the War God was swollen with a greed for power.

And so I sat silently and was filled with dread as I watched these aliens from the sea hunger like pigs for that gold. They snatched at it and they rubbed it and they even put it into their mouths and chewed upon it. They snatched up the golden ensigns and waved them in the air and held them up to the sunlight and smelled and licked them and put them between their legs while they giggled and laughed uproariously. And everything they said was said in their barbarous tongue and everything they did was done in their barbarous manner. Their greed frightened me more than their ferocity, and I quickly gestured to the carriers to prepare for our departure.

When the man called Cortes saw that we intended to leave, he beckoned the brown woman, Ce Malinalli, who was busily fastening a regal necklace around her neck. After they whispered to one another, the woman approached me and bowed, asking, "Is this Montezuma? Is this the great Lord whose gifts we have accepted?"

I did not wish to speak, but I had been given instructions by my Lord. I could not disobey his command. I glanced with revulsion at the necklace on her throat and at the golden ensigns clutched in the hands of Cortes, and then I muttered, "I am he."

But among the Tlaxcalan allies of Cortes were some of the warriors who knew me and had heard of my rise in the court of Montezuma. And these Tlaxcalans whispered to Ce Malinalli, "He is not Montezuma. He is his Chief Orator, Nanautzin. And he is a liar as well."

But Cortes was confused by the whispers of his Tlaxcalan warriors and instructed Ce Malinalli to ask me again, "Are you indeed the great Lord of Tenochtitlan called Montezuma?"

"Yes," I said, "I am your servant. I am Montezuma."

But the Tlaxcalans exclaimed, "You fool! You wood-cutter and liar! Why do you try to deceive us? What do you take us for? You cannot deceive us; you cannot make fools of us! You cannot blind our eyes or stare us down, for we will not look away! Your magic does not frighten us! You cannot bewitch us and you cannot make us faint or die!" And then they exclaimed, "For you are not Montezuma! He is there in his city. But he cannot hide from us. Where can he go? What hiding places are there for him? Can he fly like a bird? Can he dig deep into the Earth? Can he burrow into the mountains and hide inside? You go back to your great Lord and you tell him that we are coming to see him! We are coming to meet him face to face. We are coming to Tenochtitlan to hear his mighty words from his own lips! You tell him that!"

We were so frightened by their threats and by their taunting that we hurried away. The carriers burst into a run while the chiefs tried to retain their dignity. The bearers of my litter stumbled, and the Españoles laughed and mocked me as I tottered on the throne of Montezuma. Then we staggered across the plain until even the warriors among us lost all restraint and began to run.

Seventeen

When we entered the apartment of Montezuma he silently gestured for me to speak. I quickly recited all the curious events that I had witnessed, and what I could not recall of our meeting with the strangers the priests added stammeringly. We were so anxious to tell all that had happened to us that we spoke rapidly and all at once, interrupting each other until at last we had said all we had to say and a suffocating silence overtook us.

Montezuma listened to our report stoically, and then he bowed his head and did not say a word. For a very long time he was silent, and we stood at a respectful distance waiting. When at last he spoke, his voice was flat and dry and toneless: "Then there is no hope, my friends. Pity the old and the innocent. Pity the children of our land. What help is there for them? Whatever is coming to us and whenever it shall come upon us, all we can do now is wait. We can do nothing but wait. . . ."

And so we waited. I crouched in a corner of the empty room and waited while my Lord gazed into the air. Each day the messengers brought the news of the march of the strangers across our land. But Montezuma did not command that the warriors attack them or engage them in battle. No one was allowed to raise weapons against the soldiers of the man called Cortes. And everyone was commanded to provide for the invaders and to give them what they wanted. And when the words of Montezuma were known to the people in the streets and in the countryside, it was as if our whole land lay silent. No one went out of his house. Mothers no longer allowed their children to go into the streets. The plazas were silent and the roads were silent and no one ventured into the city. The peasant people peeked out of their windows, watching for Death to come down the deserted road . . . watching for the gods or monsters or men who wore white masks and bartered death for gold.

Then news came that Prince Ixtlilxochitl, Lord of Texcoco, the brother of Cacama, had gone out to the strangers and greeted them at the gates of Texcoco. And news also came that Prince Ixtlilxochitl had listened to the priest called padre and had come to love the god who lives on the wooden cross. He had come to love that god so dearly that he had asked to be made into one of his followers, who are called *Christians*.

"This sacrilege cannot be true," Montezuma muttered.

"It is true; all of it is true, my Lord," the messenger stammered.

Even before I could repeat what the messenger had said, my Lord Montezuma shuddered and turned his back on us.

Then the news came that Prince Ixtlilxochitl of Texcoco had gone before his mother, Yacotzin, and told her all that had happened to him and asked her to come before the priest called padre so he could sprinkle her with his water and make her into a Christian. But Yacotzin was a great woman, and she glared at her son and told him that he must be mad to allow such a despicable and unholy conversion by a handful of barbarians. She told her son that she would die before she would accept the superstitious ravings of a bunch of savages. And so her son, in a rage, left his mother and ordered that her rooms be set on fire.

"And so the great woman of Texcoco is dead by her own son's hand?" Montezuma whispered.

"Not so . . . my Lord," the messengers replied. "For she came out of the smoke and flames and saved herself. She went to the padre of the strangers and he named her Doña Marina because it is said that you cannot be one of these Christians if you have a name like Yacotzin! And after her, her four daughters, the princesses of Texcoco, were also sprinkled with the water of the padre, and though they did not feel anything and did not know anything, the man called Cortes told them that they were saved and would go to a good place when they were dead."

Montezuma said nothing. I released the messenger and crept to my Lord's feet, but he ignored me. Again I waited in silence.

The days passed, and nothing more. No one ventured out and no one came to the apartment of Montezuma. Nothing happened and no one spoke. And so we waited.

I was asleep when I heard Montezuma's voice. It was in the middle of the night and yet my Lord was pacing to and fro in his apartment. "Woodcutter!" he shouted when I did not awaken at once.

I leaped to my feet and bowed to him.

"Send messengers! Send them to bring my nephew

Cacama if he still has his sanity and has not also become a
heathen like his brother, Prince Ixtlilxochitl! Send for my
own brother Cuitlahuac! And call my chiefs to me at once!"

"My Lord," I whispered, "it is darkest night. . . ."

"Woodcutter! . . ." he shouted. And I fled to do his
biddings before he could say more.

Soon Cacama of Texcoco arrived. Next came Cuitlahuac, my Lord's younger brother. And finally the oldest
chiefs crept into the presence of Montezuma. My Lord
proposed a discussion of these strangers who called themselves Españoles and Christians. He asked his council to
debate the wisdom of welcoming the Christians as opposed
to driving them away.

Cuitlahuac did not await any discussion but stood up
at once and told his brother that the strangers must not be
welcomed and that they should not be allowed to advance
any farther into the heartland of Mexico. But Cacama
disagreed, insisting that it would be a craven display not to
allow the Christians to enter the gates of Tenochtitlan, for
the warriors of Anahuac—the vast region of the Valley of
Mexico—were so numerous and powerful that they had
nothing to fear from the strangers. Montezuma, he said,
could destroy all of them by simply lifting his hand and
giving the command to attack should the strangers' conduct
prove unfriendly.

"Coward and fool!" Cuitlahuac shouted at Cacama, the
Prince of Texcoco. "These barbarians are hungry for gold
and will stop at nothing to get it! They talk about their god
with their mouths while they steal our gold with their
fingers! They will destroy us! They will eat us alive!—just
as their god devours our gold!"

"I tell you, the gods have declared themselves against us!" Cacama replied.

"They are not gods but men—greedy men who wish to subjugate us and exact tribute from us!" Cuitlahuac said in a rage. Then he turned to his brother, Lord Montezuma, and he said with an urgent voice, "I pray to our gods that you will not allow these strangers into your house. I tell you, my brother, they will cast you out and they will take you from your throne, and when you try to resist them, it will already be too late and they will have come too far for us to drive them away! I pray to you, my brother Montezuma, do not listen to Cacama, for he is like his brother, Ixtlilxochitl, Prince of Texcoco; he is enchanted by the sinister magic of these Christians who promise many things but have given us nothing but death!"

Montezuma turned away from his brother. "It must be as Cacama has said . . ." my Lord stated slowly. "Whoever these strangers may be, gods or men, their coming was long foretold, and to resist them would be to resist the faith of our fathers."

"But, my brother!" Cuitlaluac exclaimed.

"No more from you, brother," Montezuma muttered without looking at him. "You are always anxious for the extremes of action. You are always ready for heresies. Enough of your objections. I have told you what I choose, and that is all there is for us to say to one another, Cuitlahuac."

A terrible gloom came over the council, for every chief and elder agreed with the militant opinion of Cuitlahuac and considered Cacama a traitor for urging Lord Montezuma to welcome the Christians. But my Lord dismissed them

with a gesture. And then he called me to his side to speak
for him to his nephew Cacama.

"Go out to these strangers and greet them for Montezuma and tell them that I will await them in my capital,"
he told him. Then, without looking at him, he turned
toward his brother Cuitlahuac and said, "You will wait for
them in the Palace at Ixtapalapa, where you can do no harm
with your uncontrollable rage."

And so again we waited.

In the time called *Noviembre* by the strangers, on the
eighth day of that time, and in the year that the strangers
count to be one thousand five hundred and nineteen, they
came to Tenochtitlan. Their trumpets came first, a long
grisly utterance that rebounded across the lakes. The feet of
the deer upon which they rode came next, clattering over
the causeway that stretches in a perfectly straight line across
the salt flats of Texcoco to the very gates of Tenochtitlan.
Then four men on their tall deer came into sight, leading
the others. They came hesitantly at first, looking in every
direction carefully, peering among the houses for enemies,
and glancing up at the roof terraces.

Then came their huge dogs, sniffing each thing in the
road and panting continually, the saliva coming down from
their large mouths. After the dogs came the one who carried
the banner of the strangers. He marched forward, shaking
the banner, making circles with it in the air, and waving it
from side to side. Then came many bearers of iron swords.
And each of the swords was flashing and glistening fear-
somely. After these soldiers came the men on the tall deer
whose bells resounded as they moved. These deer neighed
loudly and pranced and clattered on the causeway. And

190

these deer sweated so that their flanks glistened, and in their mouths was much foam. They made a pounding sound as they trotted toward Tenochtitlan, leaving holes in the ground where their hoofs landed.

Then came the warriors of the crossbow whose arrow-filled quivers hung down on their shoulders and whose stiff armor reached down to their knees and whose heads were covered with metal. And behind the crossbowmen were the warriors who carried the hollow rods that made thunder and the iron weapons called cannons that also made thunder. With these weapons they made a continual explosion. They thundered again and again into the air as they came forward, smoke spreading everywhere, making the people faint with fear.

Then came the warrior who is called Cortes, the war chief of the strangers. Around him were his bravest soldiers, and they surrounded him like a sheath. He walked boldly, and he did not look to the right or to the left. His face was covered with hair and his costume was black.

Finally, after Cortes, came the warriors of Tlaxcala, whom the people of Tenochtitlan abhorred and feared. They came arrayed for war, each in his cotton armor that protected him from arrows, each with his shield, his bow, and his club. The Tlaxcalans marched with their knees bent, whooping their war cries, shrieking with delight, and singing the songs of Tlaxcala, which they knew the people of Tenochtitlan loathed.

At Xoloco the strangers came across the wooden drawbridge and were greeted by the hundreds of chiefs who had been sent out to announce the approach of our Lord Montezuma, and to welcome the strangers to his capital.

They brought trays heaped with flowers, and they brought garlands and ornaments of gold, and necklaces of rich stones. Then the glistening entourage of our Lord Montezuma emerged from the great avenue that led through the heart of Tenochtitlan. Amid the rows of nobles were three soldiers bearing the golden wands, and behind them came the royal palanquin ablaze with burnished gold, and borne on the shoulders of our most elegant and worthy nobles. Over the litter of Montezuma was a canopy of elaborate feather work, speckled with jewels and fringed with silver filigree. He glowed in the Sun and he was truly magnificent. The greatest nobles of the land who carried him were barefoot and walked with a slow, measured pace, their eyes lowered to the ground. I walked by their side. And I was raised up by the grandness of the power and fear I felt.

Then we halted, and Montezuma, descending from his litter, stepped forward, leaning on the arms of the Lords of Texcoco. As Montezuma advanced under his canopy, the attendants covered the ground with cotton tapestries so his feet might not touch the soil. And throngs of people lined the path of our Lord and bowed to him and averted their eyes from his brilliance. His mantle sparkled with precious stones and pearls. The soles of his sandals were fashioned of gold. On his head he wore deep green plumes that floated down his back. The sight of him was overwhelming, for I had never seen my Lord Montezuma looking more elegant and majestic!

When the soldier called Cortes saw that the great Montezuma was coming, he got down from his tall deer, and in the company of his war chiefs he approached our great Lord. And when he drew near Montezuma they both paid great reverence to each other.

I stepped forward to speak for my Lord, but Cortes gestured for me to retreat and in my place the woman called Ce Malinalli stepped forward.

Then Cortes said, "Are you Montezuma? Are you the king of this land? Is it true that you are the one called King Montezuma?"

For a moment my Lord hesitated, and then he said, "Yes, I am Montezuma." After a long silence he continued, "I welcome you to this land. You are weary," Montezuma whispered, "you are weary . . . my Lord. The long journey has tired you, but now you have arrived on the Earth. You have come back to your city, Tenochtitlan. You have come here to sit on your ancient throne, to sit under the canopy of Anahuac." Then Montezuma bowed humbly as no Great Speaker of our land had ever bowed to another. "The Lords who have come before me," Montezuma said, "have guarded your land for you. The Lords Itzcoatl, Montezuma the Elder, Axayacatl, Tizoc, and Ahuitzotl ruled only for you in the city of Tenochtitlan. Your people of this land were protected by their mighty swords and sheltered under their wide shields. All this which has come upon us was foretold by the Lords who governed your city, and now it has taken place. You have come back to us. You have come down from the sky. If only the Lords of our land were watching now! If only they could see what I see, my Lord! For now I have met you face to face. I was in agony for five days, for ten days, with my eyes seeing nothing but the Region of the Dead where the Mysteries await me. And now you have come out of the clouds to sit on your throne again. Rest now, and take possession of your royal house! Welcome, great Lord, to your land!"

When Montezuma had completed this amazing

Ce Malinalli, center, acts as interpreter for Cortes and
Montezuma at the gates of Tenochtitlan. *Codex Florentino*.

speech, the woman Ce Malinalli spoke for him in the barbarous language of the strangers. Then Cortes responded and Ce Malinalli repeated his words: "Tell Montezuma that we are his friends. Tell him there is nothing to fear, now that we have seen his face and heard his words. Tell him that we love him and that our hearts are most contented, wanting nothing more than what we have been given."

Then Cortes stepped forward and brought out a sparkling chain of colored crystals, stones containing intricate patterns of many colors that were strung on gold cords rubbed with musk so that the necklace had a charming scent. This necklace Cortes placed around the neck of the great Montezuma. And when he had placed it there he was about to embrace our Lord, but the great nobles who accompanied Montezuma held back the arms of Cortes so that he should not embrace our Lord, for they considered it an indignity.

Then Montezuma appointed his younger brother, the warlike Cuitlahuac, to conduct the strangers to their residence in the city. And again he stepped into his litter and was borne away amid prostrate crowds of people. The Españoles quickly followed after him, with their banners flying and their music pouring out from every side. The strangers exclaimed over everything they saw before them, as if such things were new to them. They dismounted from their deer, and they mounted them again, and dismounted again, so as not to miss a single thing that interested them. They marched through the southern quarter of Tenochtitlan, among our handsome houses of red stone with their flat roofs covered with flowers. They came into the plazas and marketplaces that were located among our houses. They gazed at the pyramids upon which the temples rose against the sky. And they seemed to be amazed.

As they passed down the wide avenue, the strangers crossed the many bridges that span the canals where hundreds of people gazed up at them from their canoes. Finally they were brought to the Great Plaza in the center of Tenochtitlan, where the grandest pyramid rose high into the golden sunlight—the radiation of the supreme god to whom it was dedicated.

My Lord Montezuma awaited Cortes in the courtyard of the vast Palace built by Axayacatl, the father of Montezuma. This immense building of Tenochtitlan was to be the barracks of the strangers. Approaching Cortes, my Lord took from a bundle of flowers that I carried a massive necklace on which the figure of a crayfish was represented in pure gold. From this glorious necklace hung eight ornaments, also of gold, representing the same sacred shellfish. Montezuma hung this handsome collar around the neck of Cortes, saying, "This palace belongs to you, my Lord. Rest after your long journey, for you have much need to do so. And in a little while I shall visit you again."

Then Montezuma withdrew, bowing humbly to the leader of the strangers. But Cortes hardly noticed Montezuma's departure, so utterly was he captivated by the golden necklace that lay upon his shoulders.

Eighteen

When my Lord Montezuma was given word that the Españoles had eaten heartily and lay upon their mats in blissful sleep, he sent me to announce his approach.

"I come in behalf of my Lord," I informed the woman called Ce Malinalli, "to say that Montezuma is coming again to pay his respects to Cortes."

"Wha . . . wha . . . wha?" exclaimed the dozing white god when his brown woman tried to awaken him. They crouched and whispered together with a cunning that reminded me of two weasels about to ambush a dog. They chattered in that grotesque language of the strangers until at length they assumed a very ceremonial attitude.

"A moment," Ce Malinalli formally intoned. And so I waited politely, watching the sleepy Español attempt to pull his black skin over his bony white legs. I gazed incredulously at this exotic, pale hulk as it staggered and tipped and tilted while trying to encase itself in every kind of fabric and metal and even a peculiar little pillow that cushioned its groin. When this elaborate and artless ritual was completed, I bowed to the man whom my Lord called "god," and I conducted him to the chamber where Montezuma awaited him.

Cortes and my Lord received each other with much deference, and after they had exchanged greetings and taken their seats, a conversation between them began. The nobles of Montezuma stood on one side of the chamber while on the other side stood the war chiefs of Cortes. Ce Malinalli, who begged to be called by her new Christian name, Doña Marina, stayed close to the side of Cortes and repeated his words to us in the language of our land. I watched her carefully, for I had felt from the first instant I had seen her a revulsion so deep that I had no trust in her. She was artfully coy and she seemed to be the kind of woman who used being a woman only when it served her purposes. Her self-conscious elegance and falseness of heart made me disdain her. And her treachery against her own people made me detest her every word and gesture.

"Ce Malinalli," I said, watching her wince at my use of her native name, "my Lord wishes to ask certain questions about the land from which your masters come."

She glared at me momentarily and then an expression of gentility came over her face. She made a grand gesture as if opening the way between Montezuma and Cortes, and then she reluctantly stepped back so her master could see that it was I, Nanautzin, who spoke for the Lord of all Mexico. And I spoke truly and well, for I had no schemes hidden behind my smile, and I did not hope to win riches or power from my Lord. I was as fearful of the greatness of these lords as this woman Ce Malinalli, but I had given up nothing of myself in order to be raised up by them. For I was still Nanautzin, the Ugly One, and I was still a despised

Tlaxcalan, and I held my gods within my heart and would not abandon them as she had done. I had seen her walk in the blood of her own race of people at Cholula, and I had seen her turn away from their cries of agony. And though she was the mat woman of this stranger called Cortes, it was not love that filled her eyes with dreams. What blinded Ce Malinalli was her ambition. For it was said that she counseled Cortes to defer his landing on our shores of Mexico until the time of the predicted return of Quetzal-coatl. And it had also been said that she advised her pale lord to wear the black garments of Quetzalcoatl. These were her cunning treacheries against the faith of her own people. And all I say is true, for these blasphemies were known to many men, such as Cuitlahuac, the brother of Montezuma, who laughed at my Lord's belief that the strangers were gods.

All this came into my thoughts as I gazed at Ce Malinalli, and I was filled with rage. But in the chamber of Montezuma I dared not show the least expression of my true feelings.

My Lord made many inquiries concerning the country of the Españoles, their sovereign, the nature of his government, and especially their motives for visiting Mexico. When Cortes began to answer these questions, I found in the tone of his alien words and in the expression of his face an air of deception. And the words that came from the lips of Ce Malinalli in his behalf were dead before she uttered them.

Cortes explained that he had come a great distance simply to see so distinguished a king as Montezuma. Cortes said that he came not to take a single treasure from our land but to give us a treasure beyond compare: "It is the blessing of the true Faith which is called Christianity," he said.

Montezuma heard all of this without any expression on his face and he made no response to what had been said to him. Instead, my Lord pretended that he did not know that these were gods, and he asked in regard to their rank in their own land, questioning if they were truly kinsmen of their "great sovereign."

For a moment Cortes seemed taken by surprise. Then he smiled an unpleasant smile and tilted his head slightly to the side. "We are kinsmen of one another," he said, "and we are subjects of our great monarch who holds us all in his peculiar estimation."

"Ah . . ." Montezuma said with a deliberate trace of disappointment in his face. And before Cortes could counter with assurances, my Lord arose and prepared for his departure.

As Montezuma was conducted from the presence of the strangers and led back to his own apartments, the various war chiefs of Cortes boldly stepped forward to present themselves. Montezuma endured their glances but gave them no acknowledgment as he swept past them. Their curious names rang out in the halls as they uttered them in a sharp military cadence: *Alvarado . . . Sandoval . . . Ordaz . . .* unpronounceable, barbaric growls. My Lord Montezuma was oblivious to their insolence and did not seem to see them. Then a soldier stepped directly in front of Montezuma so that my Lord would be forced to take notice of him. My heart fluttered with fear, so impudent was the gesture. But my Lord seemed imperturbably calm as he stopped and slowly turned his gaze on this barbaric braggart. I had seen my Lord when he was divine and I had seen him when he was like a frightened child, but never had I seen in his wide, brown eyes the sublime dignity that now flowed into them.

The warrior stood erect and blurted out his name so that spittle flew into the air: *"Juan Velásquez de León!"*

"Yes"—Montezuma smiled faintly with an elegant turn of his head—"perhaps that is true." And then he looked directly into the eyes of the pale warrior until a terrible embarrassment overcame the young braggart and he self-consciously backed away from Montezuma. Then in a moment my Lord was gone.

When it was evening the people of Tenochtitlan hid behind the doors of their houses, dreading the darkness that held the Sun captive in the night where he could not protect his chosen people. In the Great Plaza, among the marketplaces, and along the canals and roadways there were no sounds or movements. But from the Palace of Axayacatl, where the Españoles were quartered, there came the echoes of drunken celebration and revelry. Then suddenly the thunder reverberated among all the buildings and shook them to their foundations, and the stench of sulfurous vapor rolled above the walls of the Palace. The strangers had ignited their cannons and the roar brought the people to their knees in fear. Men and women came dashing hysterically from their houses and scattered in every direction. They fled aimlessly, crashing into one another, stumbling, staggering, and falling to the ground. They rushed off as if they were being pursued by monsters. It was as if they had eaten the mushroom that confuses the mind and fills the eyes with colors and apparitions. They were overcome with dread as if the thunder resounded in their heads and would not cease. And as the darkness fell in the moonless sky, the terror and panic spread from house to house throughout the city, and the people of Tenochtitlan lay awake and trembling on their mats and held their babies to their breasts and were afraid to utter a sound while they desperately prayed for the dawn.

In the morning, a messenger awakened me. Cortes had sent him to request permission to visit Montezuma in his Palace. I quickly arose and crept to the closed door of my Lord's chamber, where I whispered the message. In a moment Montezuma appeared, fully dressed and radiant with energy and calm. He granted the request of Cortes and sent four of his nobles to conduct the Españoles into his presence.

When Cortes and his war chiefs arrived, accompanied by Ce Malinalli, Montezuma was quietly seated at the farthest end of his spacious Council Chamber, surrounded by his favorite advisers. My Lord received the strangers with great kindness and invited them to be seated. But no sooner had Cortes taken a seat than he unceremoniously opened a conversation through the voice of Ce Malinalli, about a subject that seemed uppermost in his thoughts.

"I wish to tell you about the true Church," he said solemnly. "I wish to tell you about the holy mysteries of the Trinity, the Incarnation, and the Atonement."

And as Montezuma looked at him with clear eyes and a patient smile, the stranger spoke about the origin of the world, the creation of the first people, paradise, and the fall of man. It was a most remarkable narration, so complex and amusing that I could not help wondering how Cortes managed to remember such an incredible assortment of delightful fantasies. In some of his myths he had even guessed some of the truths of our own faith.

When Cortes paused and my Lord thought perhaps he had finished his narration, he attempted to give some polite response. But Cortes interrupted and continued his elaborate sermon. He assured Montezuma that the gods of our fathers were various forms of someone called *Satan* . . . and this Satan was extremely evil, we were told. Since Cortes knew so little about our gods and had only the prior day entered our capital as an honored guest, I could not comprehend how he knew enough about our religion to instruct us in it, let alone to deplore it as evil. I was staggered as was my Lord by his rudeness.

"I have come to snatch your soul, and the souls of your people, from the flames of the eternal fire by opening to you a purer faith, *Christianity!*" Cortes exclaimed with a peculiar glint in his eyes. And then he earnestly begged Montezuma to secure his salvation by embracing the cross upon which the white god lived.

Montezuma listened to this astonishing recitation with respect and kindness, much as he would attend the imaginative stories of a child. When the rituals of something the Españoles called "the Mass" were described he winced at the notion of a people who feed on the flesh of their own creator! He listened with silent attention to every word Cortes had to say through the mouth of his mat woman, until at last the white man had concluded his long account.

Then Montezuma sat peacefully for a long time, smiling at Cortes. And finally he said, "I realize that you have often discussed these matters since you have arrived in our land. My people have brought reports of your religious fervor and it is very admirable. I do not doubt, as you have said, that your god is good. My gods, too, have been good to me. And many things that you have said of the creation of the world are also found in the teachings of my faith. But forgive me if I say that it seems unnecessary to discuss this subject any further. My ancestors were not the original people of this land. We have occupied it but for a few ages, and prior to that time we were led here by our great god who, after giving us laws and ruling over our nation for a time, withdrew to the regions where the Sun lives. He declared on his sad departure that he would again visit us and return to his throne. The wonderful deeds of your warriors, your fair complexions, and the place from which you came to us, all these things showed that you were the descendants of our great god who left us so long ago. And we greeted you as gods for these reasons. But I had heard accounts of your cruelties—that you sent the lightning to consume my people or crushed them under the feet of the ferocious beasts on which you ride. Now I have seen you. I have heard you speak. And I have listened to all you have said. I have thought upon you and your words. Now I am convinced that you are not gods but men of some different race."

Cortes looked at my Lord with astonishment, his expression revealing that he was somewhat distressed by Montezuma's confident appraisal of his guests. But before Cortes could speak, my Lord continued with a polite smile, "You, too, have been told, perhaps, that I am a god, and dwell in palaces of gold and silver. But now you see it is

In the Days of the Darkness

false. My houses, though large, are of stone and wood like those of other men; and as for my body," Montezuma said as he bared his tawny arm, "you see that it is indeed flesh like your own. So rest now. I will see that your wishes shall be obeyed in the same way as my own, for you are the ambassadors of your great sovereign beyond the waters, and though you are not gods you fulfill the prophecies and I believe that you are the beings destined to rule this land."

Then, in the utter silence of the chamber, Montezuma and his greatest chiefs and lords bowed humbly to Cortes. The priests, however, pressed themselves in horror against the walls and turned away from the intolerable sight of their great Lord prostrate before the barbarians.

Ce Malinalli told Montezuma what it was the Españoles needed: tortillas, fried chickens, hens' eggs, pure water, firewood, and charcoal. Then my Lord ordered that everything the strangers requested be sent to them. The priests moaned and the young chiefs clenched their jaws in rage. They no longer loved Montezuma, for he had betrayed his people. But they could not defy the commands of the Great Speaker, and so they did as he bid them do, providing the intruders with all that they desired.

All of our days were filled with pain and misgivings. The people murmured discontentedly. But they endured the strangers, for it was the wish of their Lord Montezuma. The priests wept and drew blood from their arms and legs. The warriors frowned and smothered their rage. The elders shook their heads in resignation and despair. But the brother of Montezuma, called Cuitlahuac, beat his fists against the walls of his chamber and declared that we were

205

being driven to our destruction by Montezuma's madness.

The days were filled with these sad things.

Then one morning a messenger came to Montezuma with the request from Cortes that he be allowed to visit our holiest sanctuary, the temples atop the Great Pyramid. The priests shrieked, but their outcry did not influence Montezuma. He sent back word to Cortes that he was welcome to come with the Great Speaker to the temples.

When Cortes arrived before the pyramid, two priests and several tribal leaders were waiting at Montezuma's command to bear the white man on their shoulders up the one hundred and fourteen steps of the massive monument of stone. Cortes, however, declined and said that he preferred to march up at the head of his select guard.

On reaching the summit, the white men gazed at the vast platform of paved stone and frowned at the large block of jasper upon which the offerings of blood were made to the gods. As each of the white warriors passed the altar they made a peculiar, rapid gesture across their chests and faces. After watching them repeat this gesture several times I decided it was some kind of barbarous magic by which they hoped to show themselves worthy to our gods.

Now Montezuma, attended by the chief priest, came forward to receive Cortes, Ce Malinalli, and his warriors. "You are weary," he said to the white men; "the ascent of our great temple has wearied you." But Cortes with a boyish grin assured my Lord that the Españoles were never weary.

Then Lord Montezuma directed his guests to the brink of the temple platform from which they looked out over Tenochtitlan.

The precious city lay spread like a mosaic of lovely

jewels and silver and gold. The terraces of the houses bloomed riotously with flowers. The sunlight glistened upon the canals where canoes by the hundreds brought food to the marketplaces. Our mighty city rolled into the distance, reaching the very feet of the immense mountains whose frosty peaks glittered in the golden illumination given by the Sun to his chosen realm. Long, dark wreaths of vapor rolled up from the towering summit of Popocatepetl, which stood powerful and rumbling above the vast Valley of Mexico.

This glorious vision brought tears to my eyes as I watched the strangers and saw greed overtake their faces. These few warriors from another land stood in the midst of an immense population that could crush them instantly with the slightest effort. And yet the strangers huddled together rapaciously, gazing at the treasures of our world, which our Great Speaker wished to thrust into their hands like a demented father who abandons his house and sends his children into slavery.

When Cortes spoke to Montezuma again he asked if he and the white man at his side called Padre Olmedo might enter the sanctuary and see the shrines of our gods. The priests pressed forward anxiously when they understood the request, but Montezuma quietly consented and led the strangers into the holiest of holy places.

When they had seen the place of ritual and the images of the gods, they turned away in disgust and hurried out into the open air, for the odor of the sacred blood repulsed them.

Cortes turned to Montezuma with a frown, and he said, "I do not understand how a great and wise king like

Montezuma II is taken prisoner and the treasury
is plundered. *Codex Florentino.*

you can put faith in such evil spirits as these terrible idols, which are the representatives of the devil himself! If you will but permit us to erect the true cross, and place the images of the blessed virgin and her son in your sanctuaries, you will soon see how your false gods shrink before them!"

Montezuma was greatly shocked by these sacrilegious statements. Indignantly he whispered among his priests and shook his head in dismay.

"These are the gods," he answered aloofly, "who have led my people to victory since the first days of our nation. These are the gods who have sent abundant harvests to our soil. These are the divinities in whose behalf we maintain the world and the holy fires. Had I thought you would offer them this outrage, I would not have admitted you into their presence!"

Cortes was visibly shaken by Montezuma's anger and made feeble efforts to apologize for wounding the great Lord's faith. But Montezuma would not listen to him and, with a gesture, he sent him away and remained, saying that he must expiate, if humanly possible, the serious crime of exposing the shrines of our divinities to such profanation by strangers.

For a moment I feared that the war chiefs of Cortes would seize my Lord or harm him, but the man called Padre Olmedo restrained them with his words. Then they silently withdrew, making their way down the steep descent of the stairway while great Montezuma stood in the wind and lifted his voice to those weakness-despising gods of our forefathers. The volcano belched smoke. The Sun rode across the sky. And beneath our feet the Earth trembled.

Nineteen

My Lord Montezuma sat gloomily among the flowers of his terrace and gazed toward the Palace where the strangers made their endless chatter. Abruptly, without announcement, my Lord's younger brother Cuitlahuac bounded onto the terrace and greeted Montezuma with the mixture of impatience, impudence, and affection that was typical of his passionate manner. "Now see where we are!" he exclaimed with a concerned expression.

"Where are we, my brother?" Montezuma murmured without taking his gaze from the encampment of the Españoles.

Cuitlahuac laughed with sarcasm and shook his head as if he pitied my Lord. "We are in the trap," he muttered with an ironic little gesture of his hand; "far within the trap." Then for a moment the brothers were silent. They seemed hardly to know each other. I had rarely seen Cuitlahuac in the Palace of Montezuma, for they were divided by ambition and also by philosophy. And until now they had not often talked to each other.

"It was your nephew Cacama, Lord of Texcoco, who

begged you to take in these barbarians as if they were gods! But, my brother, even you have long known that they are not gods!" Cuitlahuac said impatiently. "Now your priests groan with ceaseless lamentations for the blasphemies of that ignorant savage called Cortes! But you insisted upon hiding behind those sniveling priests—and you would not hear the warnings of your war chiefs—and you dreamed your dream of Quetzalcoatl come home again! Now even your priests realize their error. They opened the breast of Tenochtitlan to the knife of these rascals with their rude grunts and their swaggers and their ridiculous claim to a civilization greater than our own! The priests and you have given our whole world to these hairy brutes!"

Montezuma made a faint motion with his hand but did not take his gaze from the strangers' camp.

"Now what do you have to say, my brother?" Cuitlahuac snorted with annoyance as he paced across the terrace and muttered with deep concern. "The war chiefs, the priests, even the fanatical wizards have denounced these strangers and called them enemies and begged you to lift your hand and give the signal to destroy them. But still you hesitate. My brother, you *hesitate!*"

Again there was silence. Then in a hoarse whisper Montezuma spoke: "Through our holy books we know that neither I nor any living person in this land is really a native of it. All of us are strangers who came from very far away. And we have always known that those from whom the original great Lords of this land descended must one day come back to rule, and that we ourselves must be their vassals. All this we have long known. And it cannot be altered, not by the war chiefs or by the priests or by the wizards . . . and not even by you, my restless young brother. Just as the very heart of a man must be given up to the gods, so now our great city called Tenochtitlan must be delivered up to those who have come to claim it for the gods."

Cuitlahuac threw up his hands in dismay. Then he strode up to Montezuma and arrogantly stood over him. "On this very terrace," he cried, "you will die, great Montezuma! In this very city you will see the blood of your people and then you will tear your hair and weep for all your weak-kneed reverence! You will die, and many will die with you! But before you die you will see the calamity you have brought down upon your own people. Mexico will die in your mouth. The ants will crawl upon its corpse and our pyramids will be pounded into the ground and forgotten! All this I have seen in my dreams while you, Montezuma, you sit among the flowers and dream of destiny!" Then, in a rage, young Cuitlahuac turned and left.

Never had anyone spoken so impudently to the Great Speaker. I did not move for fear that he would vent his outraged feelings upon me. But my Lord did not shout or bellow, and he did not call for his guards or his priests or his ministers. He sat silently, rocking gently to and fro, his eyes fastened ceaselessly upon the place where the alien mumbling of the strangers mixed into the vast silence of the fearful city.

It was upon that same terrible day that the members of my Lord's family began slipping away from the royal apartments with their precious belongings. The corridors were silent. The looms were idle, and dust collected upon the stools of the ministers.

Then there was the clattering of the tall deer that the Españoles called "horses." In Montezuma's courtyard a large force of alien soldiers assembled. Stationed on all the roads leading to the royal house were many of the strangers in battle dress. Suddenly there was a loud knocking at the doors and I hastened to answer, for there seemed to be no attendants left in the house.

Cortes marched forward when I opened the doors, pressing me aside. "We have come to see your king," he announced.

Five of his mightiest war chiefs surrounded him. I pulled back and trembled, for their odor was over-whelming—like the stench of urine. Ce Malinalli smirked as she repeated the words of her master. Then she pressed the fingertips of her outstretched hand into my shoulder and said, "Move quickly, Ugly One, and tell your lord that he has visitors."

The entire group followed so closely behind me that they were upon Montezuma almost before I could announce them. Then abruptly their manner changed. Their grim faces were now smiling politely as my Lord received them. Soon a conversation began, and Montezuma called upon me to distribute presents of gold and jewels to his guests. There were no servants to assist me.

Gradually the royal chamber filled with many white soldiers who arrived in groups of two and three, as if by chance, but at such careful intervals that I became alarmed. Cortes carefully pronounced the names of his five chiefs as they arrived: "Pedro de Alvarado, Gonzalo de Sandoval, Francisco de Lujo, Alonso de Avila, Velásquez de León."

I looked into their death faces and saw blood flowing in little veins under their transparent skin. I could see the red sores upon their cheeks where the thick hairs sprouted from their pale, bluish flesh. All this I could see as I trembled and they snatched the gold trinkets from my hands. The one called Velásquez was the worst, for his eyes were colorless and his nostrils were filled with hair, and when he smiled his gums were white and his teeth were as sharp as the fangs of the jaguar.

"My Lord . . ." I stammered fearfully, but Montezuma paid no attention to me. He engaged the Españoles in polite conversation, bowing again and again to Cortes and finally offering him one of his own daughters as a wife. To this Cortes laughed nervously, glancing momentarily into the eyes of Ce Malinalli, and then explaining that he already had a wife in a place called Cuba and that his religion forbade him a second one. By the expression on her face I knew that Ce Malinalli, the woman of his mat, knew nothing of this wife of Cortes. She turned dark and a storm passed through her eyes. It was a moment before she was able to translate the words of her master. I saw a wound appear in her pride and the sight pleased me immensely. Though cunning was her own potent weapon she bled easily from the jabs of her master's guile.

When the chamber was filled with the warriors of Cortes, the conversation shifted abruptly.

"There has been treachery among your people," Cortes told Montezuma. "The chief called Quauhpopoca deceived us. He sent a message to Juan de Escalante, a faithful captain whom I left with one hundred and fifty soldiers at the shore, and he declared that he wished to go there in person to tender his allegiance to the Españoles."

"I know nothing of this . . ." Montezuma said weakly.

Cortes did not wait for Ce Malinalli to speak my Lord's words, but continued in a stern voice: "Your chief called Quauhpopoca requested that four of our soldiers be sent to protect him against unfriendly tribes he had to pass while going to visit Juan de Escalante." For a moment he paused and gazed around the room at his men with an expression of satisfaction. "The four soldiers were sent. And when they arrived two of them were murdered in cold blood by Quauhpopoca's warriors. The other two made their way back to their garrison and reported that this treachery was ordered by Lord Montezuma."

"I knew nothing . . ." my Lord stammered as his body went limp and his energy slipped away, leaving his eyes filled with fear and foreboding.

"I trust your word," Cortes said at length. "Therefore I will ask you to send for Quauhpopoca and his accomplices that they might be examined and the truth be learned and the guilty ones punished."

Montezuma made no objection. He sat motionless, staring from one of the white men to the next. But there seemed to be no courage left in my Lord, and he did not stir and he did not send away these strangers who had dared to impugn his word.

When the messenger had gone to summon Quauhpopoca, Cortes assured Montezuma that his prompt arrest of the wrongdoers convinced him of my Lord's innocence. With this assurance Montezuma seemed momentarily relieved. But then Cortes very slowly said, "Surely, my Lord, nothing would better attest the innocence of Montezuma than your willingness to transfer your residence from these apartments to the Palace that you have provided for our own quarters . . . just, you understand, my Lord, until the arrival of Quauhpopoca, when this unfortunate affair can be fully investigated."

Montezuma heard this scheme to imprison him with looks of utter astonishment. He became withered and small, but then in a moment his face flushed with resentment and he stood up with a dignity that was almost lost to him.

"When was it ever heard that a great Lord like myself voluntarily left his own residence to become a prisoner in the hands of strangers!" he exclaimed.

"I assure you, my Lord," Cortes murmured with false sincerity, "you would not go as a prisoner but as a guest. You will experience nothing but the most respectful treatment from my warriors and you will be in the company of your own loyal household, which shall come with you. You would simply be changing residences. . . ."

Montezuma would hear none of this deception. "Even if I should consent to such a degradation," he answered as he stood tall, "my people would not accept it!"

Cortes smiled unpleasantly and stepped slowly toward Montezuma. "What are you hoping to say with that remark, my Lord?"

"I am saying plainly," Montezuma answered with failing courage, "that if you wish to have hostages you must take one of my sons and one of my daughters, but you must spare me this disgrace or I cannot be responsible for the behavior of my people."

The warrior named Velásquez de León stepped forward impatiently and shouted, "*¿Que haze usted ya con tantas palabras? ¡Ó le llevemos preso, ó le dar'émos de estocadas, por esso tornadle á dezir, que si da vozes, ó haze alboroto, que le mataréis, porque mas vale que desta ves asseguremos nuestras vidas, ó las perdamos!*"

216

The great Lord Montezuma is put in chains. *Codex Florentino.*

The menacing faces all around him and the fierce tone of Velásquez's outcry alarmed Montezuma terribly, and he anxiously asked Ce Malinalli what the angry Español had said. She put on a sorrowful face that touched my Lord, and she urged him to accompany the white men to their quarters.

For a few moments my Lord looked around for some sign of pity or compassion from his captors, but as his eyes wandered over their stern faces and iron bodies he lost all hope, and with a voice scarcely audible he consented to accompany the strangers, to leave his home and his Palace, to close the doors upon the grand rooms in which he had once celebrated great victories. He bowed his head as he abandoned his dignity and embraced shame and humiliation, for he was willing to live in disgrace rather than to die.

No sooner had Cortes heard Montezuma's resignation than orders were given for the royal carriers. The nobles who bore and attended the litter were horrified when they realized that their Lord intended to surrender to the intruders. Montezuma, however, could not bear the infamy and he pretended that he was leaving his home of his own free will. But as the royal entourage marched through the streets under the close guard of the Españoles, the people assembled in silent crowds and rumors raced among them—their great Lord was being carried off by force to the quarters of the white men! Angry voices were heard in the crowd, until a wail of resentment echoed through the Great Plaza. But Montezuma himself called out to the people and begged them to disperse. He told them that he was visiting his friends of his own accord and that no harm would come to him. Glumly and reluctantly the people backed away and allowed the litter to pass. Then, when the entourage finally reached the quarters of the Españoles, my Lord sent away his nobles, telling them to return to their homes quietly. Then he gazed at me and after a moment he said, "And you, Woodcutter . . . what will you do? Will you go to your home among the Tlaxcalans or will you remain here with me?"

Though I did not answer I was not afraid. As humble as I had been in my unhappy life, I had never been as low and pitiful as my Lord Montezuma was now. I could not despise him for his cruelties or for his cunning and treachery. I could not rejoice in his misery, for I had come to love him. Not as a god and not as a great Lord; not even as a good man . . . but as a fellow creature whose brown skin was as easily broken and whose life ebbed as quickly as mine, whose eyes wept and whose heart ached like mine from the terrible brutality of the world.

"I stay," I murmured.

Montezuma was quickly installed in a vast suite of apartments and given every display of ostentatious respect in an effort to allay the suspicions and hostility of the people. From the strangers themselves he received a formal defer-ence, while his few noble attendants, wives, and servants offered him the silent and blank faces with which brown people express their most outraged sense of shame.

When Quauhpopoca was brought to Montezuma as a prisoner, my Lord received him coldly and turned him over to Cortes. He did not deny his part in the murders and he did not try to shelter himself by claiming that the Great Speaker had commanded the assassinations. When asked if he were a subject of Montezuma he replied haughtily, "What other sovereign could I serve?"

He remained resolute and brave until the sentence was passed, and then, as if he hoped to be saved by his Lord, he gave him a single, longing expression before he recoiled and announced that he had lied and that Montezuma had ordered the entire conspiracy.

Cortes quickly condemned Quauhpopoca to be burned alive in the small plaza in front of the Palace. Everyone fell silent and a terrible look passed between Quauhpopoca and Montezuma. The condemned chief would not turn his eyes away from my silent Lord even as he was dragged from the chamber and taken into the plaza where the slaves heaped his funeral pyre.

While a crowd assembled and the pyre was being built, Cortes entered Montezuma's apartment, followed by a young soldier carrying chains. He confronted the Great Speaker and charged him with being the contriver of the murders of the white soldiers. Without hesitation he ordered the soldier to fasten the fetters on Lord Montezuma's ankles. He coolly waited till this was done and then he turned his back and left the chamber.

The servants groaned and fled from the room, leaving me utterly alone with Montezuma. He sat listlessly, staring down at the chains. He made no sound or gesture. For a while it seemed as if he had gone mad and was unconscious.

I crept to his poor feet and I could hear his soft moans. I wept at the sound of his grief, for in his stifled sobs I could hear all my race of people crying. I took his feet into my hands and with shawls and mantles I tried to relieve the pressure of the irons upon his slender, blemishless ankles.

But I could not reach the cruelest cutting edge of the white man's iron, which had penetrated into his very heart. In his eyes I saw that he no longer felt that he was the Great Speaker.

The sound of the roaring fire came from the plaza as the execution of Quauhpopoca was carried out. The entire force of the Españoles was armed and posted everywhere to prevent any effort of the people to interrupt the punishment. But there was no attempt. The people of Tenochtitlan gazed in silent wonder, in quiet astonishment, as Quauhpopoca writhed in the flames, never making the slightest sound as his skin bubbled and split open and a shiny, boiling fluid poured over the crimson surface of his entire body.

When the flames completely enveloped him and his body dropped slowly into a simmering heap, Cortes reentered the royal chamber and removed the fetters from my Lord's ankles. But Montezuma did not stand up. He sat forever chained, his face blank and his delicate hands open and limp. Now his courage was dead.

When the Españoles demanded gold he made no objection. He guided them to it. He walked listlessly toward the treasury as the white men surrounded him closely and crowded around him with their weapons at the ready. They formed a tight circle all around him as he led them to the gold. And when they came to the treasure house called Teucalco, a rich feast of jewels and feathers and gold was spread out before them. The Españoles fell upon it drunkenly and immediately they began to snatch at the most magnificent objects of Mexico, stripping the feathers from the gold shields and pulling apart the necklaces and tossing the green stones away while they piled the gold into heaps on the floor. Everything else, regardless of its beauty and value, they burned. In the fires they melted down the gold into ingots. As for the precious green stones, these they threw on the floor where their allies from Tlaxcala snatched them up. I was ashamed and could not watch my own people behaving like savages. They crawled on the ground after the jewels like beaten dogs, while the Españoles fought one another, pushing and quarreling as they seized every trinket and object of gold.

But they were not contented. They barked furiously at my Lord, who staggered with fatigue and illness. They wanted to enter the royal storehouse of Montezuma in the place called Totocalco where his personal treasure was kept. And as they scrambled down the corridors after my Lord they grinned and shook with delight and chattered and chuckled. However capable they had previously been of giving an appearance of refinement, now they were themselves. When they entered the treasure chambers it was as if they had been blessed with the greatest joy. They sat down in the heaps of glorious relics and ornaments. They fell flat on their bellies and they embraced the gold as if it were a woman. They made love to the heaping treasure. They groaned and panted and convulsed with great shivers of ecstasy. All that belonged to Montezuma was spilled upon the floor and they seized these greatest of treasures as if they were their own, as if this plunder were simply a gift of good fortune. But still they were not contented. And after they had piled everything into the middle of the patio, Ce Malinalli climbed to the roof of the Palace and she called down to the nobles and ministers. "People of Tenochtitlan!"

she cried. "Come forward! The Españoles need your assistance! You must bring them food and pure water. You must bring them all that they need. Why do you not come forward? Are you afraid? Are you angry?"

The noble lords and the ministers were too frightened to approach. They were limp with terror and could not obey the command. They recoiled as if the strangers were ferocious beasts. But when Ce Malinalli told them that the Great Speaker himself commanded them to do what she ordered, they crept forward, bringing whatever was asked of them. With trembling hands they served the Españoles and emptied their fields and houses, leaving themselves nothing.

I sat opposite my Lord in a small room and I gazed at his bowed head and hunched shoulders. He rarely spoke, and when he did speak he always turned his face away from me. He could not bear my looking upon him. And in his shame he grew thinner and his face grew older. Then after many days we heard a commotion in the corridor and I was sent to discover its cause. I had listened to the jabberings of the Españoles long enough to learn some of their words, and by listening and watching their gestures I could often guess the content of their discussions. A messenger had just arrived from the great water where Cortes had established a village called Vera Cruz and left many white men to guard the shore. The message was the cause of the excitement, for it told of an enemy of Cortes, the Lord of the place they called Cuba. The Lord had sent an army to arrest Cortes and to take control of Tenochtitlan in the name of the Lord of Cuba. When I hurried back to Montezuma to tell him what

I had discovered he was amazed as I was, and for the first time in many days he was filled with hope. Could this mean the end of Cortes? Would his enemy crush him? Was it possible that Mexico would escape the white invaders, that they would destroy one another and leave no sign that they had ever desecrated our land?

Montezuma could not answer my questions, but in his eyes was a small rekindled fire. And when Cortes and many of his mightiest warriors left Tenochtitlan the trace of a smile crossed fleetingly over the weary face of Montezuma, for the strangers were leaving our city, bristling with their weapons, and they went to fight, not against our people, but against their own kind.

Twenty

In the streets of Tenochtitlan there were joyous whispers like the love songs of lovers. The retreating steps of the man called Cortes resounded expectantly in the heads of the people. And as he vanished beyond the causeways of the great city the whispers became louder and more jubilant. The hushed voices spoke of secret reveries in which two enemy tribes of white men met like angry bucks upon the strand beside the great water and ceaselessly battered one another, locking horns and drawing blood and throwing up dust in their furious battle. All these visions were carried in the whispers of Tenochtitlan when Cortes went out to meet his mysterious enemy at the place he called Vera Cruz. The war chiefs and the priests dreamed of the white men's broken bodies and of their splattered blood. They had come to loathe these pale barbarians so utterly that the daydreams of their dismemberment filled them with ecstasy. The anticipation of their cries of agony enthralled the people of Mexico. We ached to strangle them one by one, to shatter their ugly faces with stones, and to trample their bodies into the ground with our bare feet. So much did we despise the invaders.

The royal messengers came and went, whispering into Montezuma's ear. And my Lord smiled lavishly, a sweet malice flowing abundantly over his face. The messengers presented him with sheets of painted cotton depicting the great canoes that had brought new white soldiers to our shore. The paintings showed the anger that flew like arrows between those who had newly arrived and the soldiers that Cortes had left to guard the shore. Perhaps the newcomers had also smelled the gold, perhaps their bluish nostrils had picked up the yellow scent of the riches of Tenochtitlan that Cortes had stolen from us. Now they had come to take everything from those who had robbed our treasuries and our hearts. Perhaps now all of them would strangle on the gold they craved. Perhaps their greed would destroy them and set us free.

These were the secret thoughts that shimmered like sunlight throughout Tenochtitlan. We smiled poisonously at the Españoles who were left behind to watch us, and we bowed in mock humiliation to them as they swaggered among the monuments of our handsome city as if they were lords and we were their slaves. We whispered, and we dreamed of blood.

Then one day I was called to the great corridor where a soldier had come to request an audience with Lord Montezuma. His name was Pedro de Alvarado, and he said that Cortes had appointed him commander of the white soldiers left to guard our city. I bowed and watched him carefully as he spoke, for I had come to understand the traces in the strangers' pale faces that revealed their lies.

I had seen this soldier called Alvarado many times before. He was a dazzling color unlike any man I had known. His hair and beard shone like fine gold. He was as golden as the Sun. And he was a pretty man with a mouth that often smiled. He behaved like a woman who gazes at herself all day. He was so filled with himself that he became tempestuous and arrogant when his will was thwarted. Then he became like a mad dog, changing suddenly and unexpectedly. And yet when he passed we could not help marveling at his golden color and gleaming smile.

My Lord Montezuma greeted Pedro de Alvarado graciously, smiling and gracefully bowing with ease and confidence. "I am told," Montezuma said through Ce Malinalli, "that my people have given you a name."

"Yes, that is so," the golden warrior answered with a lavish smile.

"I am told that my people call you Tonatiuh, as if you were a child of the Sun."

"Yes, that is true, my Lord," Alvarado said. "That is the name by which your people sometimes call me. And I take it to be an honor."

"Then we are pleased," Montezuma said politely, turning away and grinning almost imperceptibly.

"I wish to inform Montezuma," Alvarado stated, "that while my commander, Fernando Cortes, is away I shall be in charge of the garrison and I will do everything possible for my Lord's comfort if he in return will keep the peace among his people."

"And where has my friend Cortes gone?" Montezuma asked with a subtle smile.

"No matter . . ." Alvarado said sweetly, "he shall return soon."

"Of course," my Lord murmured with an elegant nod of his head. "But they say that a great war rages between Cortes and another commander who is called Narváez," he said slowly and watched Alvarado's face to see the effect of his words.

The golden warrior smiled more lavishly than before and said, "Fernando Cortes is a great general, my Lord, and wherever he has gone and whomever he encounters he will return victorious!"

"Of course," Montezuma said quietly. Then, after a long silence during which the two men gazed at one another, with elaborately disguised contempt, my Lord arose and, walked slowly across the wide chamber. "It is now more than a year since the Españoles came to us," he said. "Now I am kept here among your soldiers and now the days move slowly from one to another. We have given much and we have asked little of you. Now, however, I must beg Pedro de Alvarado to listen to me. This is the time when the people of Mexico celebrate the festival of our great patron god. It is a ceremony that we call 'The Incensing of Huitzilopochtli,' and it is commemorated by songs and dances . . . and by a holy sacrifice. It is a ritual which is so important to us that the noblest men of our city don their richest regalia and come together in the court of the temple just in front of this Palace. There they honor the god who led us to the site of this city and began our great nation of which I, Montezuma II, am the ninth in a succession of Lords who have ruled over Tenochtitlan. It is a festival much loved by my people, and therefore I beg you to allow it to be celebrated."

Pedro de Alvarado nodded thoughtfully. "I will permit it," he said haughtily. "But there will be no sacrifice. Your priests and noblemen must agree not to offer human sacrifices and they must assemble without their weapons. Do you consent to these conditions?"

"Yes, I consent," Montezuma said wearily, walking toward the windows where the Sun made his triumphant light.

And so word went out to the city that the festival would be held on the day appointed by the priests, and that the celebrants would leave their weapons behind and come in peace. The women who had fasted for the whole year began to grind the seeds of the chicalote. For many days they labored in the patio of the temple where I could see them from the windows of the Palace. The Españoles were suspicious and afraid, so they went out into the patio and stalked among the women and peered at each one of them. But the women were simply grinding seeds and doing no harm, and so the Españoles grunted apprehensively and retreated back into the Palace.

On the evening before the festival began, the priests modeled the dough into the image of Huitzilopochtli. They gave this statue the appearance of a man and yet it was merely the paste made of chicalote seeds modeled over a framework of sticks. And when this idol was formed, they dressed it in feathers and painted crossbars on its face and gave it serpent earplugs of turquoise mosaic. In the nose they placed the ornament shaped like an arrow and made of gold and fine stones. On its head they placed the magic headdress of hummingbird feathers. Then the ornament of yellow parrot feathers was placed around its neck, and over this was fastened the cape of nettle leaves, which was painted black and decorated with five clusters of eagle feathers.

When dawn came and it was the feast day, Montezuma stood in the window and he said to the Sun, "Please hear me, my Lord. We beg your permission to begin the festival of our god."

And the Sun came into the sky and he replied to
Montezuma, "Let it begin. I shall be here to watch over it."

Then the war chiefs called out to their elder brothers,
saying, "You must celebrate the festival as grandly as
possible. You must amaze the strangers with your grandeur
and you must stir the god into love for his people!"

And the elder brothers replied, "We will dance with
all our might! We will dance as we have never danced
before!"

The face of the statue the women had made of
Huitzilopochtli was ceremonially uncovered by those who
had made vows to the god. Before the idol they offered
incense and gifts. And they lifted the statue, but they were
not allowed to carry it to its temple on top of the pyramid
because it had been forbidden by the strangers.

The young warriors came forward eagerly. They had
sworn to dance and sing with all their hearts that the
Españoles might marvel at the grandeur of the rituals.
Throngs of warriors came into the ceremonial patio, all the
greatest young noblemen of Tenochtitlan and even the
youthful lords of the allied cities. Six hundred magnificent
warriors elegantly stepped into the center of the patio,
dressed in their most cherished ceremonial costumes: graceful mantles with elaborate feather work; their necks, arms,
and legs ornamented with gleaming bands of gold and
precious stones. Never had the Lords of Mexico appeared in
such splendor and never had they seemed so brave, though
they were unarmed.

As the procession of the dancers began, I climbed
quickly to the terrace of the Palace. I hoped to find a better
view of the festivities than was afforded by the window of

the chamber where my Lord Montezuma was required to remain. The ornaments and feathers glistened in the bright sunlight. The song rose from the patio with such intensity of feeling that its sacred melody brought tears to my eyes. The Dance of the Serpent began slowly and majestically. It was the first in the cycle of holy dances dedicated to the patron god of our nation. The celebrants who had fasted for twenty days were honored, while those who had fasted for the entire year were much revered and given command of all the dancers, whom they kept in precise file with their pine wands. From every direction came the excited young men who wished to join the winding Dance of the Serpent.

The assembly of our great warriors was a glorious sight that we had not seen for many seasons. The power and beauty of the Brothers of Huitzilopochtli was awesome. And the great chiefs and brave young warriors who danced at the head of the lines made me rejoice at the renewed strength of our nation. I felt strong and righteous again. I could see my whole race of people before me once again, and I could feel pride instead of humiliation. I could remember how it had been in the days before the white men came, and I could recall the great tradition that flowed down through our years and lifted us with its ancient mystery and meaning.

"Come, my brothers!" I shouted jubilantly above the music. "Show us how brave you are! Dance with all your hearts, my brothers! Dance so that the whole Earth shakes and these barbarians can hear the hearts of our great gods beating frantically above the roof of the world!"

My spirit soared and I willingly plunged into a rare ecstasy, for it had been a time of much darkness and misery and I had not known such bliss for many seasons. Then, when the dance was loveliest and when the songs rolled over the terraces and all the people of Tenochtitlan had joy in their breasts again, something began to happen. I could not see exactly what it was, but I could tell from my position high above the ceremonial patio that something was wrong. One by one I noticed white soldiers appearing at the gates of the sacred patio. What did they want there? I could not understand what was happening below me, but gradually I could see that the Españoles were surrounding the patio. I could see many soldiers, and all of them carried swords and spears and shields though the celebrants had no weapons. These soldiers of Cortes were so numerous now that they stood one next to the other, and all of them were looking up at something. I quickly peered around the entranceways and passages that led into the patio, desperately trying to discover what the soldiers were staring at so intently. And then I saw him! At the top of the patio was a man. Above the patio where the defenseless people danced, above their heads, high above my people stood the golden Pedro de Alvarado! And his sword was raised. It was raised high in the air. And his eyes, they were filled with such terrible loathing and madness, they were so blinded by ugliness that I thought I was looking upon a monster rather than a man.

I shouted, but my shout was lost in the music and singing. Suddenly Alvarado lowered his sword. The white soldiers fell upon the celebrants. A wretched sob rose from six hundred throats. The groan surrounded us. We drowned in the horror that tumbled down from the sky. They blocked the gates and they struck down the old men. They raced among the astonished dancers. They smashed the faces of the young men and torrents of blood covered their mantles. The defenseless people ran sobbing while the soldiers stabbed them, speared them, shattering their heads, splintering their limbs. The necklaces and bracelets flew from dismembered bodies and clattered to the ground. The feathered mantles knotted into bloody rags while old men were battered as they begged on their knees for mercy. Boys stumbled blindly into the knives which pursued them. Heads resounded like melons cracking open as they struck the stone floor, and the screams were deafening.

I could not look away, but I could not bear to see the horror below me. I watched as a brave young boy fought desperately with his bare hands, trying to dodge the repeated and powerful slashes of the swords that bristled all around him. He leaped out of the way of a crashing blow and for a moment he seemed to spring to safety. Then he screamed. He leaped and froze in midair as a blade disappeared into one side of his belly and gradually tore out of the other side. He opened his mouth and his eyes bulged. He doubled over and clenched his sides in a pathetic effort to stay whole. But his intestines slowly began to spill out of him, and when he saw his insides falling to the ground, he threw back his head and choked for air. But he didn't die. He began to quiver and to vomit and to scream. He began to stagger as he tried to run. And he screamed. He screamed again and again. He tried to run away, but his feet tangled in his own bloody entrails. He fell into a heap. He collapsed into a heap, but still he did not die. He screamed and he screamed, and I will never forget the sound of that child's screaming.

The blood of the warriors poured down like water and it gathered in deep pools and the pools widened. The shouts faded. The screams ended. The outcries ended. And now only the moans remained among the piled bodies.

The Españoles murder the young warriors. *Codex Florentino.*

The Españoles ran like mad dogs and howled and barked and showed their fangs. When they heard the moans of the wounded they stabbed them repeatedly until at last there was only silence. Then they raced into the communal houses surrounding the sacred patio and they killed those who were hiding there. They ran in every direction, chasing those who tried to escape, and they broke their bodies and beat their heads until they burst open. They ran everywhere and they searched everywhere and they destroyed every person they found.

I sank to my knees and trembled. I waited with my eyes closed, knowing that at any moment a white soldier would burst onto the terrace and decapitate me or throw me to the ground below.

But then I heard it! From beyond the Palace walls there came a shout. First there was a single shout. It was not a cry for mercy. It was not a death rattle. It was a raving shout of anger. "My brothers!" the voice shouted. "Come running! Bring your spears! Bring your shields! The strangers have murdered the warriors!"

Then there was another voice. And another. "My brothers! Come quickly! They have massacred our young warriors!"

And another. "My brothers! Destroy them! Destroy every last one of them!"

Across the vast city the shouts resounded until there came one vast roar of grief that rose like a storm. Everywhere the people lifted their voices and shouted and shrieked and wailed. And they beat their palms against their mouths and made the sound of rage and grief.

I leaped to my feet and hurtled up the steps that led to the chamber where I had left Montezuma. I burst into the room and found him collapsed with shock by the window where he had witnessed the massacre. I embraced him and lifted him and carried him to a seat. As I splashed water on his face and fanned him and whispered desperately to him, the cannons began to explode. Running to the window, I could hear the outcries of my people. They picked up stones, clubs, and anything with which they could fight back, and they ran blindly into the torrent of iron arrows and cannon fire that the Españoles unleashed upon them. They fought with tears in their eyes. I could hear twenty thousand mouths shouting. I could feel twenty thousand fists pounding at the walls of the Palace behind which the strangers hid. And I began to laugh uncontrollably and I began to weep uncontrollably as I wrapped my Lord in a robe and dragged him toward the doorway where we could escape.

Then I was suddenly knocked to the ground. I clutched at Montezuma's hand but someone wrenched it from me. I opened my eyes momentarily and saw white soldiers shackling my Lord in chains. I reached toward him and then a foot came down upon my fingers and I heard them cracking. The floor turned soft beneath me and I heard my mother singing.

> Moving forward and back
> stumbling with open arms
> weeping
> as they gather
> the bodies of strong young boys
> the women clutch their breasts
> while their lullabies
> come back to us
> with the sounds of their tears.

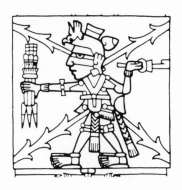

Twenty-one

The blue stones of his necklace were scattered upon the ground. Long welts appeared where his flesh had caught under the dirty nails of those who had chained him. He trembled senselessly as he lay with his head in my lap. He moaned. And while he grieved and moaned I sat hunched upon the floor and stared into the darkness of the tiny alcove where I had dragged his unconscious body.

The white soldiers ran in every direction and shouted to one another in panic. Now they were surrounded and they were frightened. All around us was the endless drumming of thousands upon thousands of fists, beating against the Palace where the Españoles had hidden themselves behind the thick stone walls. The frantic pounding did not cease, not even when the cannons burst with smoke and fire and blew terrible holes into the solid barrier of brown bodies that marched upon the Palace. The fists pounded and the cannons roared and bodies burst and bled and fell into heaps. Wave upon wave of enraged people swept down upon the strangers and then retreated with desperate injuries, leaving behind a vast field of mangled bodies that deepened with each attack.

When the Sun covered his eyes to the slaughter and could remain in the sky no longer, the dusk ignited with golden light the twisted rows of brown bodies that covered the entire landscape surrounding the Palace. I had fallen asleep over my Lord, and when I felt a hand upon my shoulder I awakened with a cry. It was Itzcuauhtzin, the nephew of Montezuma, who had gained entrance to the Palace.

"My Lord!" I exclaimed. "Are you wounded? How have you managed to come to us?"

Itzcuauhtzin ignored my questions and swept me aside with an urgent gesture. He crouched over Montezuma and gazed into his face and whispered insistently to him. But my Lord did not respond and he did not seem to recognize his nephew.

"Attend your Lord," Itzcuauhtzin ordered as he gloomily sat down on the floor and gazed into the air, shaking his head with the urgency of his thoughts.

Then, as the light was leaving the western sky, Lord Itzcuauhtzin climbed to the roof of the Palace and shouted to the throngs of people below. "O Mexicans! O men of Tenochtitlan! O men of Tlatelulco! Hear me! Your Lord, the Great Speaker Montezuma, speaks to you through my lips, and this is what he says to you: 'Do not die, my people! Your blood is wasted on this futile battle. You must not fight the strangers! We are not their equal in war and we can only die while they alone know the magic that lets them live. Hear me, my people, and lay down your shields. Weep in defeat but do not die needlessly!' All this your Lord Montezuma proclaims to you with courage though he is very low and though he groans. For they have put your Lord in chains."

Now there was a great clamor among the people. They jeered and made ugly noises and laughed bitterly. In their fury they shouted curses, saying, "Who cares what Montezuma says! He is not our Lord but the slave of the white strangers!"

Then there came a massive outcry that swept over Itzcuauhtzin like a fierce wind. Arrows flew wildly into the air and clattered upon the roof terrace. The Españoles reached out and pulled Itzcuauhtzin to safety though he struggled to remain on the roof, imploring the people to give up their siege of the Palace. The rioting continued for a long while, and then gradually, as the war chiefs and their captains circulated among the people, the sounds of rage faded and the pounding of fists ceased and we found ourselves alone in an appalling darkness and silence.

The Españoles whispered cautiously and were afraid to light a torch for fear of attracting the eye of a Mexican bowman. The people of Tenochtitlan carried away their dead and withdrew into the surrounding blackness, hiding behind the wrecks of the buildings and peering out from behind the broken façades of the roof terraces. The battle had ended, but the people had not withdrawn. They lay in wait.

The warriors and people of Tenochtitlan kept a close watch and did not allow anyone to enter or leave the Palace where we were held prisoners.

I sat alone, trembling and hungry, while in a corner of the dark chamber Itzcuauhtzin leaned over the deathly face of Montezuma and whispered to him.

In the city below there was a dreadful stillness. Only now and again was there a sound—a shout and running feet as the Mexicans captured someone attempting to deliver supplies to the Españoles. Then there was a shriek and silence. Some traitors tried to help the invaders. They hoped to win favor, but if the Mexicans discovered them they were killed at once. Their necks were broken. And if the sentinels caught sight of one of the servants of Montezuma, they killed him at once, shouting, "He was trying to bring food to Montezuma!"

They seized anyone who was dressed in the manner of the servants of Montezuma's Palace. "We have caught another traitor!" they would exclaim. "He was trying to bring news to Montezuma!" The prisoners would try to save their lives by pleading with the guards. "What are you doing, my brother? I am not a traitor! I am one of the people, too!" But the guards threw the captives to the ground and said, "You are a traitor! We know who you are! You are one of the servants of that dog Montezuma!" And they would kill them.

These were the reports of the clever messengers of Montezuma who managed to elude the guards and to bring news of the rebellion in the city and information about the exploits of Cortes and the band of soldiers he had taken with him to the coast. Though Montezuma was barely able to grasp the pictures painted on the cotton that the messengers brought, his nephew Itzcuauhtzin gravely studied the drawings and whispered fearfully to my Lord. I was so terrified by the expression on their faces that I crept toward them so I could hear what was being said. The news was disastrous. There had been a fierce battle at the place called Cempoala in which Cortes and his soldiers had met the much larger force led by Narváez, but somehow Cortes had defeated Narváez in a single battle. Now Cortes was victoriously marching back toward Tenochtitlan with three times as many soldiers as he had taken, for he had convinced the defeated troops of Narváez to join him in the battle against Mexico by promising them a handsome share of the gold he had stolen from us.

The messengers also brought news from our embattled city. The Great Council of the nation was meeting with the purpose of deposing Montezuma as Great Speaker and electing a warrior in his place. "No . . . no," Itzcuauhtzin sadly whispered to the messengers, "say nothing of this to our Lord. It will surely break his heart."

And then we waited in the darkness and the silence. After the people had trapped the Españoles in the Palace, there was no way for us to escape. Itzcuauhtzin and Montezuma huddled together and cringed each time the wrathful white soldiers berated them for allowing their subjects to starve the garrison. For seven days the people attacked the Palace, and for twenty-one days they blockaded the Españoles so cleverly that not one of them managed to escape. During these days all the causeways of the city were closed. The people destroyed the bridges and opened wide gaps in the pavements. They constructed high barricades, and they did everything possible to make the causeways that led out of the city impassable. The white victors were sealed alive in the city they had conquered. They were buried alive in the thick stone walls of the Palace, and we were buried there with them.

During these bad days Pedro de Alvarado was never silent. He angrily shouted orders to the hungry soldiers who knew that the attack upon the sacred patio was the cause of their predicament. They knew that the slaughter of the warriors had been the scheme of Alvarado, the temperamental officer Cortes had left in charge of the garrison. And Alvarado realized that the soldiers blamed him for the uprising that now threatened to destroy all of them. So there were dark looks in their eyes. This angered and frightened Alvarado, and he could never sleep and he was never silent. He drove the men with his orders: doubling the guard and taking extraordinary precautions against spies and messengers. Anyone who managed to slip into the Palace to bring news to Montezuma was secretly killed when leaving the royal chamber, so no one could carry the words of my Lord or his nephew Itzcuauhtzin back to the people and the warriors of Tenochtitlan. Alvarado was mad with his power, but he was also horrified by the results of his commands. He gazed dementedly at my Lord Montezuma as if he might strangle him at any moment, and we were afraid.

Then news of Cortes arrived. He was advancing upon the city. He brought many Españoles with him, many Tlaxcalans, and many Cempoalans. They were coming with the wide stride of warriors. They came arrayed for war, each with shield, obsidian-bladed sword, and hand staff. The Españoles came in clouds of dust that their feet sent into the air. Their faces were ashen with dust and they were very white and fearsome. They came running, shouting, "Hurry along, Tlaxcalans! Faster, Cempoalans! We go to kill the dogs of Tenochtitlan!"

The sound of their voices could be heard across the lake as they approached the city. Their feet thundered and their many cannons announced their arrival with smoke and flames. The war chiefs of Tenochtitlan came together in the Great Plaza, and they spoke to one another and decided to abandon the fierce warfare of their ancestors and to become foxes instead; to use cunning to trick the invaders, to blind them with cleverness rather than meet them in ferocious hand-to-hand combat.

And as the sound of the soldiers of Cortes became louder, the people of Tenochtitlan vanished. They slipped into ancient hiding places and secret niches. And then it was as if the whole city were stretched out dead. It was as if Tenochtitlan were a corpse. No one spoke aloud. No one moved. But many eyes watched.

There were no canoes upon the lake. The causeways were silent and shattered. The timber bridges were torn away. The marketplaces were deserted. No one stood on the rooftops. No smoke rose from the temples. There were no priests in the plazas, and in the streets the dust made tireless circles.

I crept to a window and peered out on the deserted Plaza. In only a moment the troops of Cortes suddenly streamed into the vast open space and then hurried into the doorways of the Palace where the Españoles were garrisoned. Then there were jubilant cries as the besieged soldiers embraced the reinforcements brought by Cortes. The reunion of old friends was the first time the white men had smiled in many days. But there were no smiles between Pedro de Alvarado and Fernando Cortes. They glared at each other silently, and finally Alvarado backed away when he realized that his commander would not speak to him.

Cortes knew that the soldiers of the Palace had not eaten for many days and were weak with fatigue and hunger. So he clenched his jaws and shouted, "Where is this dog of a king who suffers us to starve before his eyes?" And together with Pedro de Alvarado and Velásquez de León he burst into our chamber and confronted Montezuma.

The Great Speaker was somehow able to lift himself from the floor and stand with a desperate show of dignity, supported by Itzcuauhtzin and me. He looked at Cortes with contempt and then he said, "My Lord, your soldiers have turned on us and killed our warriors and our unarmed boys as they danced. My Lord, your soldiers—"

But Cortes shouted a curse and Montezuma drew back in dizzy astonishment. He was so weak that he hung upon our arms like a dying man.

"You are a traitor!" Cortes yelled at my Lord. "Your spies sent information to my enemy Narváez in the hope that he would defeat me! And now you suffer the markets to be closed and leave us to die of famine!"

Then, turning fiercely to Itzcuauhtzin, he exclaimed, "Tell your master and all his barbaric people to open the markets at once, or we will do it for them and they will suffer the consequences!"

The soldiers of Cortes drew their swords and stood threateningly before us. I clutched the arm of Montezuma, hoping I could somehow protect him. And as I gazed at the faces of those savages, I kept repeating their names to myself. I wanted to remember them forever. I wanted those loathsome names to remain in my memory as long as I could breathe, so I could shout them out to all the people of the world, so I could warn them, so I could tell them the names of those who murdered Mexico!

Fernando Cortes! Juan Velásquez de León! Pedro de Alvarado!

If you hear of such men, I beg you kill them! Strangle

them! Burn them alive! But first whisper to each of them the sacred name of my poor Lord Montezuma!

At just this moment a cannon roared and Montezuma collapsed. The soldiers turned from us at once and rushed away, for the people of the city were insane with rage and the cannons had opened fire on them as they rushed the gates of the Palace. There were many war cries and great showers of arrows and stones fell upon the Españoles. The entire population of Tenochtitlan and all of the allies descended upon the strangers. Cuitlahuac, Lord of Ixtapala, had been elected Great Speaker in his elder brother's place and now he came with thousands of warriors to break the bodies of the Españoles and drive them into the water.

On the third day of fighting, when the strangers knew that the rage of the people was so strong that it would not vanish, Cortes came to the doorway of the room where we were imprisoned. His ferocious expression melted away now as he addressed us ceremoniously, requesting that Montezuma speak from the roof terrace of the Palace and urge the people to retreat and to restore order in the city.

Montezuma waved us away when we attempted to lift him to his feet. He squatted on the floor in his soiled mantle, and in a hoarse voice he muttered, "What have I to do with Cortes? I do not wish to hear from him again. I only wish to die. I do not wish to hear his name. My belief in him has brought me to this terrible state! What more does he want of me?"

Padre Olmedo came forward and urged Montezuma in the name of the white man's god to speak to the people. My Lord gave a hollow laugh when he heard this, and on his hands and knees he crawled to the priest and said, "It is of no use to talk to me about your god. I have heard about your god already! I have heard you call us barbarians for making sacrifices and then I have seen you steal away our bodies and our hearts to feed the hunger of your terrible god! Every deed you have told us is sinful you yourselves have committed in our city. And whatever you have told us is evil in our lives you have committed in your own lives! There is no truth in you! You are false and you are evil and you will never leave these walls alive!"

Cortes suddenly bellowed a curse and rushed at Montezuma where he lay helpless on the floor, kicking and cursing him until Padre Olmedo attempted to restrain him. But Cortes had gone mad with rage at my Lord's refusal to obey him. His soldiers wanted to murder Montezuma. They despised him as a weakling and they called him a traitor to his own people. Velásquez de León scoffed at my Lord, while Alvarado berated him and would not withdraw despite the pleading of Padre Olmedo. They fell upon Montezuma and would have killed him had Itzcuauhtzin not interceded with a promise that our Lord would ascend to the roof terrace and address his people.

"But we beg you," Itzcuauhtzin murmured, "to leave us now so we may prepare our Lord. And we plead with you to remove his fetters, for the sight of him chained will only enrage his people."

Reluctantly Cortes agreed. The commander and his captains hovered over us threateningly, their faces filled with brutality so great they could hardly control themselves. Only the urging of Padre Olmedo finally managed to coax them from our chamber. And at last we were alone.

Montezuma was unconscious. Itzcuauhtzin and I crept to a corner and, panting from exhaustion and fright, we whispered to each other.

"My Lord," I told Itzcuauhtzin, "I fear that Montezuma does not possess the strength to climb to the roof. . . . I do not think he can speak, my Lord. . . . I do not know if he can summon the words, and if he should speak, my Lord, what can he say to his people?"

"It does not matter, Nanautzin. His people do not wish to hear him anymore. But if he speaks, at least he can live."

"No, my Lord," I murmured, "this day is a dark day and I do not think that many of us will live beyond it."

"Montezuma and I are safe while they still need us and as long as the soldiers do not turn their hunger and anger upon us. If Montezuma will speak, we will live another day. But you, Nanautzin, you will not remain here with us. We will hide you away, and when the soldiers are flocking around the windows to hear what Montezuma will say, you will slip away. And with you will go this message to Cuitlahuac, the brother of Montezuma who is now our Great Speaker. You will tell him that Montezuma Xocoyotzin has fought well and has spoken truly. You will tell him that we shall never know what was within his heart when he saw the white men and we will never understand all the things that have come into his mind in the terrible days since the strangers came. We shall say he was evil and we shall say he was good, and we shall say that he was strong and that he was weak, but we will never really know what was in his heart. We will never really know this lord named Montezuma."

Then we dressed Lord Montezuma in his imperial

robes. His chains were removed, and with our aid he stood falteringly on his feet. While I supported him, Itzcuauhtzin pulled the white and blue mantle over his hunched, lifeless shoulders. Upon his feet were slipped the golden sandals in which he had first met Fernando Cortes. Then upon his head Itzcuauhtzin placed the diadem of the Great Speaker of Mexico.

When he was finally dressed the soldiers stepped forward and pushed us aside. For a moment Montezuma II staggered, but then he summoned whatever life remained in his body and, standing erect, he turned proudly toward his enemies.

I gazed one last time at my Lord as he stepped forward to the cadence that beats within the hearts of our whole race of people. Then Montezuma ascended the central turret of the Palace.

I watched after him for a long moment, but then Itzcuauhtzin gave me the signal to slip out of sight while the enemy was taking Montezuma away from us. I could not take my eyes from him and I could not move. I trembled with foreboding. But when Velásquez de León impudently took my Lord by the shoulder I turned away in revulsion and ran headlong down the stairs toward the gates.

When Montezuma stepped into the afternoon sunlight his magnificent costume glistened high above the throngs of people who surrounded the embattled Palace. For just a moment a great hush fell over them when they looked up and saw him standing glowing in the sunshine. But then a single voice shouted, "Traitor!" And suddenly the whole mass of people bellowed at him in a roar of contempt.

For a moment there was silence once again as Montezuma raised his arms and began to speak. Then a single stone smashed into the turret just next to him—then another and another. One stone struck the diadem from his head, and he made a feeble motion to save it, but it slipped away and fell into the crowd below. Then a stone struck his cheek and another his forehead. He fell without a sound.

The crowd gasped. Thousands upon thousands of people gasped. They stood limply, gazing up silently and stunned at the roof terrace where Montezuma lay. Then slowly, as the white soldiers carried Montezuma to his apartments below, the people silently turned away and slowly retreated from the Plaza.

It is said that Lord Montezuma would not lie down, but sat upright against a wall and would not accept medicine or bandages. It is told that when his wounds were bandaged he tore the bandages away, slowly and deliberately, and would not allow the white men to touch him. Itzcuauhtzin begged my Lord to live, but Montezuma said nothing. He just leaned against the wall and laboriously gasped for breath.

It is said that for three days Montezuma sat upright against the stone wall of his chamber. For three days the Españoles threatened Montezuma and commanded him to call his war chiefs to council and convince them to return peacefully to their homes. But Montezuma gave no response. He stared out into the distance and did not hear their voices. Even when Juan Velásquez de León put his hands around the throat of Itzcuauhtzin and threatened to strangle him, Lord Montezuma would not consent to their demands. He stared fixedly upon something in the air. And he smiled strangely and then he began to laugh.

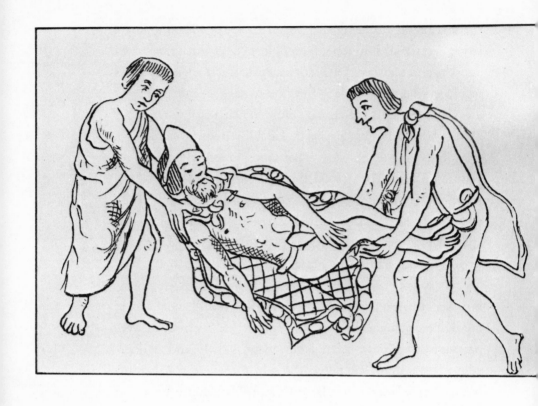

The body of Montezuma II is carried away
by his people. *Codex Florentino*.

Juan Velásquez de León could not tolerate the smirk on those royal lips. He shouted and madly sprang to his feet and rushed at my Lord, thrusting a knife into his heart.

The smile lingered on the lips of Montezuma until blood filled his mouth. It slowly spilled over his clouded face, which glowed in death like a winter's Moon.

At night the warriors of Tenochtitlan discovered two bodies thrown down at the water's edge at the place called Teoayoc. They moaned when they saw the faces of the corpses, for they recognized Montezuma and Itzcuauhtzin. The war chiefs came and they shook their heads. Then they took Montezuma into their arms and they carried him to the place called Copulcou, where they built a great pyre and placed his body upon it and ignited it. The fire crackled and flared, sending long flames into the sky. The slender body of Montezuma turned, and an arm fell and dangled with a delicate, open palm as the flames nibbled at the fingertips. The corpse sizzled noisily and it smelled foul as it burned. Black smoke poured from the mouth of Montezuma and fluid dripped from his ears. As the fire consumed him, the people gathered around and they muttered, "This man was evil! This man was cruel and deceitful. Now he has been murdered by those who are more cruel and deceitful than he!"

They watched with grim faces as the fire attacked the corpse. It burst open and slowly spread its entrails over the ravenous coals. And when the fire was gone, every trace of Montezuma Xocoyotzin had vanished.

Twenty-two

And when night had fallen, and when midnight came
into the darkest region of the sky, then the ravening
hounds with pale faces and dirty hands opened the gates of
the Palace and crept out into the city. In the darkness they
hoped to slip away from us. The Españoles and the
Tlaxcalan warriors came sneaking in closed ranks on silent
feet.

The clouds filled the sky and rain fell all night. In the
darkness the gentle shower twisted in the breeze and threw a
fine mist into the soiled faces of the enemies as they tried to
crawl out from under the rage of Tenochtitlan. They moved
like serpents in the shadows, along the walls, carrying
planks on which they hoped to cross the canals where the
bridges had been torn away. They whispered like thieves as
they laid down the planks, crossed over them, and then
raised them again. They prayed humbly to their god, but in
their mantles and on their backs they carried away the gold
they had stolen from Mexico. They groaned under the
weight of their plunder while they searched the night for
Mexicans and prayed fervently to their god.

252

They were able to cross three canals, the Tecpantzinco, the Tzapotlan, and the Atenchicalco. This they did under the cover of the night and the rain. And their cowardly faces were gradually overcome by looks of self-satisfied glee as they safely neared the fourth canal, the Mixoatechialtitlan, and dreamed of their undetected escape. But the rage of the people of Tenochtitlan was so great that they could not sleep. The anger burned in the hearts of the people and transformed them into jaguars. They could see in the dark! Their ears heard every sound in the night! In our brutalized city the loathing of the people was so immense that they lay awake and dreamed of capturing the dreadful enemies. They sniffed the grass for the foul scent of them. They crouched down flat on their bellies and gazed out into the darkness for the slightest sign of them, for the slightest movement.

Just as the Españoles reached the fourth canal their retreat was discovered!

A woman drawing water at the edge of the canal saw them. She shouted, "O Mexicans, come, all of you! They are here! They are trying to cross the canal! Our enemies are escaping!"

Next, a priest on top of the pyramid of Huitzilopochtli cried out. His chanting voice echoed across the entire city: "O warriors and Mexicans! Our enemies are escaping! Chase them! Run after them and pursue them in your canoes!"

Suddenly the dark city was glittering with torches and a massive outcry rose into the sky. Warriors leaped into their boats and sent up howls as they set out in pursuit. The young boatmen paddled with all their might, releasing their rage in their arms and lashing the water with their oars, beating the lake until it boiled with their fury. Their

253

muscles ached and their limbs were swollen with hatred for the dogs who had urinated on their temples and soiled their gods. The veins in their necks throbbed as they threw back their heads and howled.

The canoes came from every direction, madly racing toward the sounds of the fleeing enemies. Then suddenly they could see the Españoles, who were running for their lives, and everywhere they ran they were followed by the clanking and clattering of golden treasure that fell from their bags. It scattered like fireflies in the darkness, bouncing, rolling, plunging into the canals.

The canoes and warriors converged on the Españoles from all sides of the causeway and cut them off. At once the cannons burst and torrents of arrows buzzed like hornets in the air. The Mexican warriors fell like the rain, but behind them came more brave men and behind them still more. The women and children of Tenochtitlan ran into the bombardment with sticks and spears and anything with which they could fight the enemies. They wept and screamed as they fell upon the Españoles. They hammered upon their heads with knives until their ugly faces disappeared in blood. They spat on them and cursed them as they destroyed their eyes and drove spears into their throats. Tears of fear and rage and sorrow ran down their cheeks as they battered the white men, as they trampled upon their limbs and shouted again and again the names of those whom the Españoles had murdered.

When the Españoles reached the Canal of the Toltecs, they hurled themselves headlong into the water, as if they were leaping from a cliff. The Tlaxcalan warriors, the white foot soldiers, the mounted men in their armor, and the brown women who accompanied them, all of them ran to the brink of the canal and plunged over it. The gold dragged them down as they beat the water with their arms. Their armor tangled around their bodies and pulled them down. The horses screamed and thrashed as they plummeted into the canal, their frantic hoofs bursting the heads of drowning soldiers.

My own shout joined the massive outcry of my people as we ran at the fleeing enemies. I had no sword or spear, but I did not care.

I did not know who I was as I bellowed, but I was no longer Nanautzin. I did not know how I became so strong. The rage of the people was like a wind and I was sucked up by the blast of it. It blew me in front of it and it engulfed me. It swept into all of us and it came back out of us stronger than before. Our shouts flew out of us like a storm and our shouts made mad the wind that drove us into the bodies of our enemies.

Our women tore the hair of the brown mistresses of the Españoles and beat them and filled their loins with smoldering torches. They screamed as I struggled through the tangle of limbs and beat at the white sweating bodies that reeled around me. Everywhere was a wild clamor in which horrid groans and shouts of vengeance rose in deafening bombardments. I snatched up a club and swung it recklessly in the darkness, splattering blood and crushing heads and bursting pale bodies as I staggered forward. Horses slipped and collapsed and screamed as they pounded down upon the ground and helplessly thrashed their legs in the air. The unmounted soldiers were buried alive in the avalanche of Mexicans that fell upon them as they lay stunned. Then

The Españoles are driven out of Tenochtitlan. *Codex Florentino*.

suddenly I caught sight of a familiar face. It was the dog called Juan Velásquez de León, and he was crying out commands as his horse lunged and staggered and slipped beneath him. He tore the heads off the Mexican warriors who tried to kill him. With wide sweeps of his sword he brought them down like saplings in a storm. And as I glared at him, he gave a victorious shout and wiped the blood from his face.

I could not bear to see the look upon his hateful face. And I could not breathe while he was still alive. For he was the dog who had murdered Montezuma.

I charged him and swung my club with all my might. His horse swerved and staggered. The animal uttered a terrible sound and its eyes glowed mysteriously as it stood transfixed before me. Then it slowly rose up as if to greet me, its delicate legs dancing in the air and its head tossing wildly in the wind. It stood up very tall and it shook its whole body and whinnied proudly! And it victoriously threw Velásquez de León from its back and galloped away to freedom. Velásquez crashed to the ground.

"Montezuma!" I cried. "Montezuma!" I shouted as I fell upon him. "Montezuma!" I wept as I brought my club down again and again upon his skull and crushed it. *"Montezuma!"*

His body twitched. For a moment it writhed wildly. Then it stopped. And it seemed so fragile and harmless as it lay there that I could not help but pity the man who had been Juan Velásquez de León.

The Canal of the Toltecs was choked with the bodies of men and horses. The drowned bodies filled the gap in the causeway like a bridge of the dead, and the white foot soldiers scampered over the corpses of their friends and fled to the other side. The last to escape were Pedro de Alvarado and a handful of his soldiers who were chased by the endless, shouting tide of my people. I watched hypnotically as Alvarado was thrown from his horse.

"Kill him!" the people shouted as they raced toward him. But he managed to get back on his feet, and he swung his long lance around with fantastic power, which knocked down the warriors and sent them flying.

"Kill him! Kill him!" I screamed as I ran in the midst of the throng pursuing him. "He murdered our young warriors! He killed them in cold blood!"

Alvarado began to run. He dashed toward Cortes and his horsemen, who urgently beckoned to him from the brink of the canal. He raced toward them with all his power and attempted to leap to the saddle behind a comrade, but one of my people grabbed his arm and threw him to the side. Cortes and his men called again and again to Alvarado, but he could not reach them. We cut him off and we bellowed as we closed in on him. Cortes could wait no longer, and with his soldiers he plunged into the water and retreated, leaving Alvarado alone in our midst.

Panic came into the white man's eyes as we descended upon him. But then he lurched suddenly, managing to evade us, and ran to the very edge of the canal, where he froze and stared down into the wide canal filled with our canoes and warriors. Suddenly Alvarado cried out and swung full circle with his long lance. He crouched down like some fantastic beast, and then abruptly he thrust his lance firmly into the bottom of the canal and sprang forward with all his might, miraculously clearing the wide gap in a single leap!

In a moment he was back on his feet on the other side of the water, where his comrades swept him up and galloped away.

We stared after him dumbly, our bloody hands dangling at our sides. Fernando Cortes had escaped. Pedro de Alvarado was also safe. And the brown woman named Ce Malinalli was alive. We sighed in dismay and gazed at one another, hardly recognizing the ferocious people we had become. Now we were truly barbarians. Our hatred had turned us into savages. Now we were the people the Españoles had always said we were. Now we had gone mad with grief and bitterness. We had been destroyed by our own wrath. Our minds were filled with nothing but the horrible atrocities and crimes of the white men. We loathed them in our precious memories where only the dead are buried, but now that our rage was spent we were forlorn.

I was ashamed to be Nanautzin. I gazed at my bloody arms and I was ashamed to be a man of Mexico, for now we were as evil as the strangers.

The Españoles fled into the darkness. The river called Tepzolatl separated us, and then two more rivers. They forded the Tepzolatl River, and then they crossed the Tepzolac and the Acueco rivers. When the dawn came the strangers were far away and Tenochtitlan was covered with blood.

The people moaned as they covered their wounds. The men fished the limp bodies of the Españoles from the canals. They pulled off their clothes and stared in amazement at their soft white skin and the hairs that grew on their chests and their limbs. They loaded the corpses of the Tlaxcalan enemies into canoes and took them far away where the rushes grow and there they threw them away without respect or honor. They also threw away the bodies of the brown women who had been the companions of the Españoles. When their mantles were stripped away these women were the color of ripe corn, for they had painted themselves yellow like the Dirt-eating Women. And their filthy mouths were painted black. We despoiled each of them and left them lying bare among the rushes.

And then we removed each of the deer called "horses." And when this was done the warriors laid out the corpses of the Españoles, arranging them neatly in many rows. In the daylight their bodies were as white as the buds of the maguey, as the white maize stalks in the early spring. No one human had ever been as white as these strangers.

Then we gathered up everything the Españoles had abandoned in their flight. We gathered up whatever we could find and searched the waters of the canals for the gold disks and ingots and the treasure of Montezuma.

We also collected many weapons that had been abandoned or had fallen into the canals and littered the causeway: the cannons, swords, spears, bows and arrows, the iron helmets and coats of armor and breastplates and shields. Everywhere Tenochtitlan was strewn with broken arrows.

And when we had washed away the blood and when we had vomited up the evil we had swallowed in battle, the conch trumpets sounded in the temples atop the pyramids and the fires rose into the evening. One by one the white prisoners were dragged up the steps to the altars, where they were given to the gods in thanksgiving for our victory over the strangers.

I had already seen too much blood and I did not wish to stand among the cheering people in the Great Plaza when they watched expectantly as the Españoles whimpered and were pulled to their deaths.

I walked away silently and, after crossing the Plaza, I stood alone in the entrance of the dusty Palace of Montezuma. The magical painted book in which my Lord had once read the secrets of the future lay abandoned on the floor. I cautiously crouched in the dimness over the mysterious paintings and gazed at them. But of the future of Tenochititlan I could see nothing.

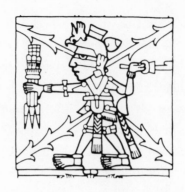

Twenty-three

A cry of joy went up and there was laughter and celebration. When the eighth month, called *uei tecuilhuitl,* arrived, the city of Tenochtitlan held the feast day with renewed hope. The Españoles had been driven out forever! They had been humiliated and beaten, and now they would slouch away in shame and leave the land of Mexico, never to appear again!

Despite the great loss of life and the destruction in the city, the people were jubilant as they adorned the ceremonial dancers in their godly disguises: the feathers and turquoise masks, wondrous mantles and sacred ornaments of gold that they had safely hidden away from the hunger of the Españoles. Everywhere there was joy and solemn prayers of thanksgiving. The people embraced one another as friends and shared the special foods of the festival. They recounted tales of heroic actions in the defeat of the strangers, and they also lamented in songs the warriors, the women, the fragile young boys who had died with weapons or sticks in their hands. The people of Tenochtitlan truly loved each of them. But they did not love Nanautzin, for I had been the voice of the Lord whom they now despised and I was a man of hateful Tlaxcala where even now the Españoles had taken refuge from our pursuing warriors. The great Lord who had transformed me was gone, and with his death I was committed to the endless silent contempt of his people. I was thrown back down into poverty. I was abandoned, but I could no longer be what I had once been. I did not have that humble woodcutter within me anymore. I was someone else now, but I did not know for certain who I had become. The people of the city did not embrace me, for to them I was a Tlaxcalan, and to the Tlaxcalans I was Montezuma's voice and I was therefore a traitor.

I wandered among the celebrants, but no one embraced me. No one offered me festive food. They turned away and their warm smiles suddenly faded when they looked upon me. And since Cuitlahuac, the brother of Montezuma, had been chosen to succeed as Great Speaker by the Council of the Four Lords of the Four Quarters, I went to him to recite what poor Itzcuauhtzin had commanded me to say of the last hours of Lord Montezuma. But I was turned away at his gate, and Cuitlahuac would no longer allow me to be the voice of Montezuma. Like him, I was dead.

In the shadows behind the abandoned houses of the dead I sat alone and gazed out into the Great Plaza where the rituals of the feast were performed and where the people sent up shout after shout in honor of the Lord Cuitlahuac who had led them to victory and crushed the horrendous white barbarians.

Then I felt a curious motion in the air, and a deep, foul fragrance swept around me. In the distance and in the darkness I could see someone slowly approaching. As the figure came nearer I could make out a handsome young woman dressed in strange clothes and ornaments. Upon her face was a thick white chalk that made her the color of the Moon. And under her nails were silvery crystals that glistened in the night. Though her body was very slender and her face was very beautiful, I dreaded this woman as she approached me slowly, limping slightly as if she were crippled. The moonlight followed dutifully behind her at a distance, leaving her in a perpetual shade.

"What is your name?" the strange woman asked in a toneless voice.

"I am called Nanautzin," I said.

"And what are you doing sitting here alone in the dark while all your people celebrate their victory?"

"I have lost the great Lord who protected me," I murmured. "I have become nothing to his people." Then I peered into the woman's pale face and tried to discern her features in the deep shadows that surrounded her. Gradually I could see countless little sores that covered her handsome face. Tiny worms crept lugubriously out of her nostrils before they wiggled helplessly in the light and slipped back out of sight. Her long black hair was matted with excrement, dried pus, and urine. Her eyes possessed no iris or color but were blank and milky white.

"Who are you and what is your name?" I asked fearfully.

"My name is Smallpox," she said tonelessly. "I am the mat woman of the strangers. I came here with them and they have left me behind."

"Ah," I murmured. "And what is it that you do for the Españoles?"

"I bring death," the woman said. "Come sit near me, Nanautzin." She sighed as she squatted upon the ground and lifted her mantle and spread her legs. "Come lie down beside me."

I cringed as her chalky hand reached toward me. I knew that if she touched me I would die, but I did not dare run away. I tried to give an appearance of friendliness while I searched my mind for some means of evading her.

"I am deeply honored," I said with a lavish smile, "to be the one man of these thousands of men of Tenochtitlan with whom you wish to lie down. But I am Nanautzin, the Ugly One, who fell into the fire. My body is covered with scars. My face is repulsive to all women. I have no wife and I have no home. I have no children and I have no desire left within my body, for it has grown cold with neglect."

"Then you will not lie down with me?" the woman asked.

"I am honored, but surely you would rather have one of the strong men whose virility is praised by his many wives. Surely you would prefer a young fellow and not a cold old man like me," I stammered as politely as possible.

"You are right!" the woman snapped with annoyance as she covered her face and withdrew. "I was only pitying you, for you are ugly and alone. But if you will not come to me, there are many men in the Great Plaza, and I shall find far better welcome among them!"

Then she limped slowly toward the crowded Plaza. The sweet odor of decay flew into the wind and followed after her. The obedient silver moonlight trailed doggedly in her footsteps. I breathed a deep sigh when she had gone, but the long twisted shadow that her body had made lingered on the ground long after her departure, making a terrible blemish upon the Earth.

So it was that in the thirteenth month many people began to fall down and rave with fever. Sores appeared on their faces and chests. They no longer could walk. They groaned and lay helpless. The smell of decay came from their mouths when they collapsed. They stank as if they were already dead, and their sores ran and spread over their entire bodies. They screamed with agony and they lay motionless. And they closed their eyes, one by one, and they died. One by one they closed their eyes until thousands had died. And many also died of starvation on their mats, for no one dared attend the sick and no one dared approach them. For seventy days the strange sickness of the Españoles decimated the people of Tenochtitlan, and those who did not die in agony were blind.

Then the fever went away, satisfied with the lives it had taken. And Smallpox went back to her people, the Españoles. She joined them in Tlaxcala, where the Four Lords had given the defeated strangers an exuberant welcome and had offered them shelter.

Then the many days of the year followed one another, *oxcotl uetzi* followed *tlaxochimaco*. And *ochpaniztli* brought its twenty days, and then *teotl eco* and *tepeilhuitl* and the other times called *izcalli* and *nemontemi* and *atl caualo*. Now a year had passed since many of the Españoles had died at the Canal of the Toltecs.

I, Nanautzin, the Ugly One, had survived. I lived in the crumbling houses of families that had been killed by the Españoles or by the fever. I ate the refuse that women left in

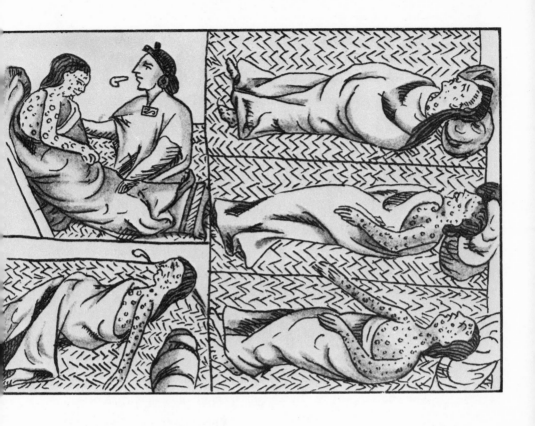

The sickness called smallpox destroyed many of the people of Tenochtitlan. *Codex Florentino.*

the streets. I begged for their buckets of slop before they dumped them into the canals. They hated me and they took pleasure in feeding me their garbage. They watched as I gobbled up sewage and laughed: "Do you see how the Tlaxcalan eats our dirt? Do you see how this savage lives on our garbage?"

But the lords who surrounded Cuitlahuac, the Great Speaker, were not so haughty and smug, for they knew that the strangers had not left Mexico but remained not far away under the protection of the vast armies of Tlaxcala. So one day six lords of Tenochtitlan were sent to hold council with their ancient enemies, the Tlaxcalans. The emissaries of Cuitlahuac announced to the council of Tlaxcala that they must bury their grievances and enter into a treaty. All the tribes of Mexico, they declared, must make a common cause in defense of their land against the white men. All this was conveyed to the four lords and the war chiefs of Tlaxcala. The messengers of the Great Speaker of Tenochtitlan told them that they would surely bring down on their own heads the terrible anger of the gods if they harbored the Españoles who had violated and destroyed the temples. And if perchance the Tlaxcalan lords hoped for the friendship and loyalty of the white man, they should take warning from the fate of Montezuma, who had received the strangers kindly and, in return, had been murdered and whose city had been ravaged and left in blood and ashes. The proclamation of Cuitlahuac begged the Tlaxcalans, in respect for their common faith and heritage, not to allow the disabled white enemies to escape from their hands, but to capture them now while they were weak and sacrifice them at once to the gods whose temples they had profaned.

After these words were spoken in council there was

much argument. The Tlaxcalan lord called Xicotencatl urged his people to embrace the proposals of Tenochtitlan. He declared that it was better to unite with their kindred, with those who shared their own language, their faith, and their ancient history, than to throw themselves into a continued alliance with the fierce strangers, who, however they might speak of their pale god, worshiped nothing but gold. The young warriors of Tlaxcala shouted their accord with Xicotencatl, for they had come to disdain the falseness and greed of the Españoles. But the blind old father of Xicotencatl, who was one of the four rulers of the tribe, defied the alliance with the people of Tenochtitlan, for he hated them more than he hated the white men.

"Yes, now the Great Speaker wants peace and alliances," he exclaimed. "But when we have driven the white men away the men of Tenochtitlan will forget their promises as they have always done, and they will devour us and trample us, they will exact tribute, and they will take away our people for sacrifice as they have done for hundreds of years! I say, Better the white men than the lords of Tenochtitlan!"

The alliance was rejected, and the envoys of Tenochtitlan made their escape before the shouts of their ancient enemies could inform the Españoles that they had secretly come to beg peace with Tlaxcala.

In the late afternoon, I was crouching over my miserable dinner when the ambassadors returned with word that the Tlaxcalans refused to unite with Tenochtitlan. The news spread quickly over the city, and the hatred for Tlaxcala was greater than ever, and I hid myself in fear of being torn apart by the enraged people.

The Sun was still lingering above the western hills and

poured wide beams over the whole Valley of Mexico, lighting up the towers and temples of Tenochtitlan with a golden radiance. Then suddenly the great drum in the temple of the War God sounded. A long procession began to wind slowly up the massive stairway of the pyramid, climbing high into the transparent evening air. As the long file of priests and warriors reached the flat summit, I could see several men stripped to their waists. I could tell by the whiteness of their skin that some of them were Españoles. They were the prisoners for sacrifice, whose heads were decorated with coronals of brilliant plumes. They were urged along by blows and compelled to take part in the dances that honored the gods. Then the white captives were stripped of their finery and stretched over the altar one after another and cut open, and their hearts were torn from them. The bodies were hurled down the steep stairways in such numbers that they piled up at the base of the pyramid. The great drum resounded and the priests sent up prayers that begged the gods to forgive the desecrations of the white men who had profaned the temples. Hour after hour, as the night came over the city, prisoners were led up the stairway to the great altar while Tenochtitlan blazed all around me with the illumination of a thousand bonfires, on the terraced roofs of the houses and in the plazas and temples. The grand pageant of purification was clearly visible through the fiery glare and brought hope to the fearful people who longed for the renewed protection of the gods. But I am Nanautzin, and I do not hope any longer. For me the gods are dead.

I sat in the rubble and I looked across the river and beyond the vast valleys, searching for the faces of people who were gone forever. I could not help thinking about the day that was coming down upon us when everything would die and all that had been could be no more. I sat in the crumbling city under a storm of Stars, watching them burn their separate fires in the enormous black lake of the sky, and always as I watched, some forlorn Star died. It made a great flash and then it fell. There will surely come a night when all the Stars must fall. One day even our father the Sun will fall. For all the Stars are fathers and all of them must die. I do not understand it. I do not try. I only know that there is a thing called Death and we cannot understand how good it is to be alive until we have seen the Stars, the birds, our fathers fall.

Twenty-four

Thirteen sailing ships appeared in the distance upon the misty lake. The drums of the Great Pyramid called out to Tenochtitlan, and the people trembled, for the white men had come back from the dead to fight them again.

The Palace was in mourning for Lord Cuitlahuac, who had died with a terrible fever, walking away to the Region of the Dead while he was still a young man and leaving his throne empty. The drum resounded and the lords hurried to the Council Chamber, where they quickly chose a boy of barely twenty, Cuauhtemoc, to be the Lord of Tenochtitlan.

Then the drums beat louder as the Españoles sailed across the lake in ships that thousands of porters had brought in hundreds of pieces on the long overland march from Tlaxcala to Texcoco, where the vessels were reassembled on the lake and outfitted with the fearful cannons. It was this alliance between Tlaxcala and Texcoco—the former ally of Tenochtitlan—that made possible the ruinous attack by the ships of the white men. Fernando Cortes had made his floating islands called battleships appear upon the lake that surrounded Tenochtitlan. Now nothing could save us!

The mighty ships came out upon the lake from Texcoco. They rushed over the water proudly and then they anchored near Acachinanco. I watched them bitterly from across the water as they mounted their cannons and raised their sails and moved out onto the lake. The soldiers on the ships beat their drums and blew their trumpets. Then the ships rapidly approached the Zoquiapan quarter, where the people gathered their children into canoes and fled across the water as fast as they could paddle, leaving all their possessions behind and abandoning their gardens.

Soon the enemies overran the village, seizing everything they found. They gathered up their plunder and loaded it into the ships in large bundles. They stole our blankets, our battle dress, and our drums, and they carried everything away. When the Españoles reached Xoloco, near the entrance of Tenochtitlan itself, they found a barricade that had been built across the causeway in the hope of blocking the white men, but they destroyed it with four shots of their cannons. Then two ships attacked our canoes, firing their cannons directly into the thick of the flotilla and sending up spouts of water and many broken bodies. Those who were not killed drowned because they were too crippled to swim. The water was thick with human limbs. Brown bodies with their arms outstretched in stunned horror and their long hair fanned out in the crimson water sank slowly to the bottom of the lake.

Everywhere was the gagging sound of men dying. They vomited blood in the streets and screamed in pain until their hearts collapsed and terror froze in their eyes. The babies no longer cried but sat silently in the broken houses where the cannons had blown away the lives of their parents. A little boy giggled and shook his hands joyously as he watched the canoes capsize in the lake, until a cannon burst sent up a cloud of fire and dust and he vanished within it.

The ships with their roaring cannons pursued our war canoes out into the open lake, but when they had almost run them down, suddenly they turned away and sailed at full speed toward the main causeway of Tenochtitlan, which led from the gates of the city to the Great Plaza. The ships began to bombard the houses, whose thick adobe walls exploded into the air and crumbled to the ground and into the canals. The Earth shook with each blast of the cannons and our warriors fled as walls tumbled down all around them. The warriors of Tenochtitlan ran blindly, howling with desperation as our city collapsed.

Then the clatter of iron armor resounded in the streets as the Españoles came out of their ships and chased the warriors. The Tlaxcalans began to throw stones and adobe bricks and roof beams from the broken houses into the canal to fill it. They ran around in the dust and shouted and worked quickly until they had filled the canal to the level of the causeway. Immediately a band of horsemen galloped forward, crossing over the bridge the Tlaxcalans had made and searching all around for signs of the Mexican warriors. But all the soldiers of Tenochtitlan were fighting on the lake. However, the brave men of Tlatelolco were lying in wait for the Españoles, and when they saw the horsemen they rushed forward with shouts and war cries. The lead horseman lunged forward and stabbed one of the Tlatelolcos, but the terribly wounded man grabbed hold of the lance and would not let it go. The horseman tugged fiercely at his lance, but the warrior clutched it until his comrades came running to his aid and twisted the lance from the white man's hands. They swung their battle clubs, filling the air with whistles, and they knocked the horseman from his saddle. He crashed to the ground with a great clatter and tried to get to his feet while the Tlatelolcos beat and kicked him, and then there was a violent chop and his head rolled away from his body.

The Tlatelolco warriors cheered as they brushed the gore from the blood-spattered cotton armor. Then they quickly retreated as many vengeful horsemen pursued them.

The warriors fought hard for Tenochtitlan, but already they were surrounded. The Españoles joined all their forces into one massive unit and began the march toward the Eagle Gate, where they set up the cannons and pointed them directly into the heart of the city. We were already locked in a death trap, but we fought with all our strength. Black clouds of smoke filled the air as the cannons fired repeatedly. Even as the great city slipped away from us, house by house, street by street, the warriors continued to fight with all their hearts. They resisted wave upon wave of enemy soldiers, a massive force of opponents and cannons and swords that destroyed and trampled everything. Our warriors wept as the city was gradually wrenched from us, but they did not retreat. They fought on valiantly with tears in their eyes.

Our whole race of people was dying in the streets of Tenochtitlan. Our whole history was being buried alive under the rubble. The stones that our ancient forefathers had shaped from rude rock fell into the dirt as our entire world came down around us. Our very faith came tumbling

The Españoles and their Tlaxcalan allies
besiege Tenochtitlan. *Codex Florentino*.

down as the gods were heaved from their temples. The Españoles had brought forward their largest cannon and set it up on the sacrificial stone. The priests of Huitzilopochtli went out fearlessly into the storm of iron arrows, for they could not endure the desecration of this holiest place. They began to beat their huge ritual drums from the top of the pyramid as the white soldiers raced panting toward them up the long stairway. The throbbing of the drums went out over the city, calling the warriors to defend the shrine of the great god Huitzilopochtli, incarnation of the Sun. But before they could come to the aid of the priests, the Españoles reached the top of the pyramid and tore into the holy men and cut them down with their swords and pitched them headlong over the brink. Their black-clad bodies tumbled down the steps as the gods cried out in pain and covered their faces.

"Mexicans! They have killed your priests!" the warriors shouted as they came running to save the temple. The great captains and warriors who had been battling from their canoes now returned to the land and rushed into the Great Plaza. "Mexican warriors, find the enemies and kill them!" they shouted.

The Españoles, seeing the massive counterattack, tightened their ranks, loaded their cannons, and raised their hundreds of glistening swords. Their Tlaxcalan allies shouted their war cries and hunched in the posture of battle, their clubs clenched in their hands. The next moment, there was nothing but noise and confusion, shuffling, jabbing, screaming, and dying. The warriors of Tenochtitlan and all their brave allies charged into the Great Plaza from every direction. The air turned dark with gun smoke and arrows.

Almost all the noble families perished. There remained alive only a few lords and princes. For eighty days the battle raged, and more than two hundred and fifty thousand Mexicans of Tenochtitlan fell. The battle for the Great Plaza was so furious that both sides retreated in exhaustion and pain. The Mexican warriors withdrew to Xoloco, and the Españoles and their allies retreated to an encampment in Acachinanco, abandoning the huge cannon they had set up on the sacrificial stone.

Now the refugees wept as they left their homes and gardens. The great city was no more. The bodies rotted among rubble. White men and brown men intermingled in death, their limbs pulverized into a pathetic, stinking refuse. I staggered out into the dismal evening as the Mexicans deserted the Tenochtitlan quarters and sought refuge in the district called Tlatelolco, whose warriors swore to hold out against the Españoles. All around me were weeping people. Husbands went searching for their wives, and fathers carried the limp bodies of children over their shoulders, the blood running down their chests and bellies. Tears of grief streamed from their faces as they went silently through the ruins of the great city.

The world was changed. Where women had ground maize in the afternoon sunlight there was now a gray, smoldering wreckage. The great canals that once ran abundantly with good water were soggy with sludge and blood. The air was filled with ash, the flowers were gone, and the children who had played among the terraces lay rotting under the debris of their homes. The artists of precious stones had vanished, the farmers were gone, the maize did not grow, and the birds of the sky had left our city. No glistening temples rose against the vast blue sky of Mexico; the sky was forever gray and the temples were gone. There were no people in Tenochtitlan, and all the fires had gone out.

"The end of the world has come," I muttered as I trailed after the retreating Mexicans who loathed me. "The world in which I live is dying, and soon my people will also be gone."

But when the refugees arrived in the Tlatelolco quarter there were no tears or lamentations from the warriors there. They beat their fists on their chests and roared defiantly at the Españoles, for they refused to be defeated. They raced past us and charged back into the Plaza of Tenochtitlan to fight whatever enemies remained there.

At that very moment the golden demon named Pedro de Alvarado launched an attack against the Point of the Alders, in the direction of Nonohualco. But the Tlatelolcan warriors were too much for him, and his troops were shattered as if he had sent them against a wall of stone. Alvarado was forced to retreat to Tlacopan, and the Tlatelolcos celebrated their victory. But soon the Españoles attacked again.

They beat their drums and played their drums. Their banner-bearers waved their flags in the air defiantly. The massive armies of the Tlaxcalans and the other allies followed close behind the Españoles. The Tlaxcalans were livid with arrogance as they held their heads high and pounded their breasts and sang songs as they marched. But the Mexican allies of Tenochtitlan were also singing. And it was as if each side were challenging the other with the magic of their sacred songs!

The Mexicans hid themselves carefully until the enemies reached solid ground. They crouched down and waited for the signal of their war chief: the shout would tell them it was the moment to attack. And I trembled as I hid among them.

"What are you doing here?" Hecatzin, the captain of the Tlatelolco warriors, barked at me as I cowered behind him. "Why aren't you out there with your Tlaxcalan brothers? Get away from me or you will poison my spirit and bring me bad fortune!" he hissed under his breath as the enemy came closer.

"I was once the voice of Lord Montezuma," I said. "And I will die on the side of Montezuma."

"Get down or you will die an early death! Stay out of my way! I have no time to fight for a Tlaxcalan."

Then suddenly the signal was heard: "Mexican warriors, defend our land!"

Captain Hecatzin leaped up at once and raced toward the Españoles, yelling frantically, "Warriors of Tlatelolco, come with me and save our people! Destroy these barbarians!" And he crashed violently into a white soldier and knocked him off his feet with a single blow. But then the white man leaped back to his feet and with a powerful thrust knocked Hecatzin to the ground. Blood poured from a wound on Hecatzin's shoulder, but he did not remain on the ground for more than a moment. Almost at once he rebounded magically and clubbed the Español again.

Suddenly the whole mass of Mexican warriors sprang up and charged into the enemy. The Españoles were so astonished by the force of the attack that they staggered to and fro as if they were drunk, and then they raced through the rubble-choked streets with the warriors in pursuit. But the Tlaxcalans would not retreat. They made a vast circle in the marketplace and rushed forward, stabbing and killing our warriors and trampling everything underfoot. People ran in every direction, but they could not escape the murderous circle the Tlaxcalans had made around us. Captain Hecatzin shouted commands and his warriors bravely followed him as he crashed again and again into the unbroken wall of enemies. Arrows flew over our heads as we crouched behind anything that might protect us. I dodged the crashing blows of clubs and twisted around to get out of the way of the onrush of soldiers, who clashed and clattered as they fell upon one another.

Then suddenly I heard a furious war cry, and when I spun around I saw a Tlaxcalan warrior with his club braced over my head.

He stopped and stared at me in recognition for just a moment.

"Wait!" I shouted at him. And he turned and looked at me again. "Why don't you kill me?" I exclaimed in a rage. "Go ahead!" I screamed at him. "Why don't you kill me!"

"No," he muttered. "You are one of us . . . you are Tlaxcalan."

"Kill me, you fool!" I screamed as he fled from me. "I am not one of you, you savage! I am not one of you!" I sobbed. "I am not a barbarian! I am not one of the savages who have murdered Mexico!"

A moan arose from the very ground. And as the enemy hurried away the people of Tenochtitlan slowly arose with their hands upon their faces and stared at the Great

Pyramid. And they moaned in one grief-stricken voice so that the sound flowed everywhere across the city. The Españoles had set fire to the temple. In the evening the flames quickly enveloped the entire structure, and smoke swirled into the air. The glorious gilded and painted shrines of precious cedar crackled in the flames and turned into ashes. The angry fire summoned the thunder and the sky filled with storm clouds and the gods roared above us. We wept and cried out as we fell to our knees, and the awesome shape of Huitzilopochtli arose in the rushing flames and hastened shrieking into the storm.

At nightfall it began to rain. Then the final omen appeared. It blazed like a giant bonfire in the heavens. It wheeled in immense spirals like a whirlwind of fire and sent showers of sparks into the sky. The omen growled down at the world, rumbling and hissing. It circled the wall nearest the lakeshore and then hovered above Coyonacazco. Slowly it moved out over the middle of the lake, where it abruptly vanished.

No one whimpered or shouted when the omen came into the sky. All the people of Tenochtitlan knew what it meant and they watched it in utter silence.

Now we were tormented by hunger. Our bones stood out from our flesh and people who had once been robust stumbled along like old men. There was no fresh water to drink, but only the stinking water of the canals, which were littered with decaying bodies. Many people died of the sickness that made them throw up and soil themselves because they could hold nothing within them, and everything poured out of them.

282

Our only food was lizards, dried corncobs, tiny dead birds, and the salt grass of the lake. Now all the people of Mexico ate refuse. Those who were made with hunger also ate the corpses. Women chewed pieces of leather and deer hides. Old men ate water lilies and insects. We ate anything to stay alive. We ate the bitterest weeds. We ate worms and roaches. We ate dirt.

Our warriors were so weak with hunger that, little by little, stone by stone, the enemies forced them to retreat. Little by little we lost our world and we found ourselves against the walls of Tenochtitlan.

Then once again the Españoles came.

They started killing and destroying us. And many people died. And when they could endure no more, the frenzied flight from the dying city began. The people cried out, "We cannot suffer anymore! Let us run away! Let us live on shame and bitter weeds forever!"

Some fled across the lake while others ran along the broken causeways. But even as they ran away, defenseless and without weapons, the enemy attacked and killed them. The people fled in every direction. Some whimpered insanely and went out into the water, wading up to their chests and chins, and then disappeared under the water.

When the fighting was at an end, Fernando Cortes demanded the gold his men had abandoned in the Canal of the Toltecs during their escape from the city. He would not talk of peace until the gold was surrendered. He called the wounded chiefs of Tenochtitlan together and he demanded all the gold they were hiding in the city.

But we had no gold. We had no food. We had nothing.

The Españoles were stationed everywhere along the roads as the refugees trailed away from the flaming city. We could not look at one another, and we did not speak as we fled in rags. At last we came to the road where the waters divide. At this place there was still fighting. All was in confusion and only on the high ground could we take refuge, for the water was full of men fighting and the roads were also crammed with warriors.

And so it was that the Mexicans ended . . . and we abandoned our city. There where the waters divide we were reunited. Those who had survived stood huddled together. We had nothing, no shields or swords. We had nothing to eat. We ate no more. The whole night it rained down upon us. And when our war chiefs and lords were taken from among us as prisoners, we knew that our lives were over. And so we wandered away helplessly. We did not know where we could go. We did not know where we might find shelter from the rain. And even as we went away in our rags, the soldiers stopped us and searched in our most secret places. The conquerors searched everywhere upon our bodies, and they unwound the skirts of our women, and they felt everywhere with their hands, searching for gold in our mouths, our ears, our hair. And the people were scattered everywhere and they could not look at one another, so great was our shame and humiliation in the hands of the conquerors.

The warriors who were still alive needed our help, and we carried them and dragged them away with us. But the Españoles came and took these once-strong warriors away from us and they branded them with hot irons upon the cheeks and upon the lips. The warriors made no sound when their flesh sizzled and sputtered under the iron, but when it was over they covered the terrible brands that were a humiliation to their spirits.

Then the Españoles left us alone and went in search of our Great Speaker, Cuauhtemoc, in order to take him prisoner. The conquerors tied white handkerchiefs over their noses as they went because they were sickened by the stench of the rotting bodies. And after a while they came back on foot, dragging Lord Cuauhtemoc through the mud behind them.

The white man called García de Olquin brought Lord Cuauhtemoc before Fernando Cortes. The chief of the Españoles was angered by such rude treatment of the Great Speaker of Tenochtitlan and ordered that he be unhanded at once and treated with dignity.

Lord Cuauhtemoc raised his boyish face toward Cortes and then he spoke in grief-stricken words: "I have tried desperately to save my land from your hands. My people have given their lives in defense of their city. But we cannot survive. I now beg you to take my life, for this would bring an end to all the lords of Mexico, and it would be as it must be, for you have already destroyed my city and killed my people, and I have become the Lord of a world where nothing lives. So it is better that I die."

Cortes would not kill our Lord, but he ordered Cuauhtemoc to send out the command for all his warriors to surrender. And without waiting, Lord Cuauhtemoc climbed to a tower and shouted across the city that the battle had ended and that we had lost. Of the three hundred thousand warriors who had defended our city, only sixty thousand were still alive. When they heard their Lord call out to them, they dropped their weapons to the ground and fell to their knees and wept.

On the same day the Españoles began looting the city. And they went about without expression upon their faces and committed terrible atrocities. Only Prince Ixtlilxochitl of Texcoco, the ally of Cortes, wept for the conquered people and had compassion for us. We were of his own race and homeland, and so he protected us from his warriors and commanded that the women and children should not be mistreated.

We gathered upon the rooftops of the crumbling houses and stared at the ruins of our city in dazed silence. There was nothing left but rubble. Even the Great Pyramid was darkened by death, and upon its summit the gods lay dead.

All this befell us. We saw it all around us and we shook our heads and wondered how it was possible that a whole world could die. Worms inhabit the corpses and multiply in our streets and plazas. We are dead. Our world and its proud heritage is nothing. We are dead and can fight no more.

> We have pounded our hands in despair
> against the broken adobe walls.
> We have filled our mouths with ashes
> and the sound of the lamentation is everywhere.

This song of sorrow came in the wind. Occasionally there were screams. For when the Españoles could not find enough gold, they put many people in chains. They tied Lord Cuauhtemoc to a stake and they burned his feet until they were gone, but he could not tell them where the gold was hidden. Later they seized chiefs and commanded them to reveal the whereabouts of the gold they were guarding, but they possessed nothing and could confess nothing. They had no gold. So the Españoles hanged them in the middle of the Mazatlan road and left their bodies there. They murdered the priests and they set the huge dogs on the warriors. The lords were beaten and the women were carried away by their hair.

All of this I saw. I saw Mexico die, and then I came away in misery and anger.

The temples were in flames and the city of Tenochtitlan
was destroyed forever. *Codex Florentino.*

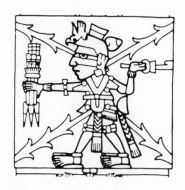

Twenty-five

Call me Nanautzin, and weep for me, for I am the last of my race which has fallen forever into a reckless night. Call me *tlamatini,* for I am one of the wise men, a broken, smoky mirror in which the world makes its imperfect shadows.

Once I was an ignorant woodcutter. Once I was stupid and unschooled and I did not know that I understood nothing. But now I know. Night falls upon my words, for I am old and filled with nothing but black thoughts and terrible memories. I have covered my face with soot. Nothing but broken flowers and songs of sorrow are left to me. In the road are broken arrows. The houses are torn apart, and their walls are red with the blood of the Mexicans. We have chewed twigs and sour grass. We have filled our mouths with dust. And though we have perished, we are still alive. The last day dies slowly.

All around me are the strangers. They growl. They spread their thick saliva everywhere and they multiply like beetles. They roar; they hunt us down and destroy us. Where can I go and how can I survive?

The strangers are coming for me. The padres would take my soul just as the priests would have my heart. I can hear them scratching among the boulders, searching for gold, barking as they sniff the ground for the scent of Mexicans and gold. Soon they will find my cave and throw themselves upon me.

Great Huitzilopochtli stumbles as he strides across the darkening sky, and his dream of bright yellow plumes is shattered. The Sun strangles on the darkness, weeping great silvery tears as he falls to his knees and cries for Mexico.

I cannot breathe, for I am dying of hunger and I cannot raise myself. Once I was surrounded by the splendor of my people but now I am surrounded by my own waste. I am filled with shame and my spirit tumbles down the steps of the pyramid. When I look up I see only the face of my Lord Montezuma gazing peacefully into my eyes.

"And what did you learn, Woodcutter?" he asks softly.

"They say that it is just a bit of sand that makes the pearl," I whisper. But my Lord does not hear me when I speak to him.

"We thought that these strangers were gods," I murmur as I curl up on the floor and groan. "And we worshiped them and we relinquished our lives to them. We were sent into a dream by their power and their cunning. But then our priests told us that they were not deities. My Lord, the priests were wrong. For these Españoles, they are truly gods. They are the same gods of war who have lived upon our blood for generations. They are the great ones whose coming we have always awaited. They are the same gods we have worshiped since the day long ago when Huitzilopochtli led us out of Aztlan on our long pilgrimage in search of Tenochtitlan. Now Tenochtitlan is dead and buried under the bodies of its own people. Now the white gods are triumphant. They are the last of the gods, my Lord. They are the mirror before us in which we finally see ourselves truly. These terrible strangers, these Españoles, are the same hungry gods of our forefathers. And now they have come down to live upon our land and upon our bodies."

The barking of the dogs is very loud now. The chatter of the Españoles is closer. And I will lie quietly and I will sing my last song, for I was once the voice of Montezuma and upon my song my world shall survive. I, the singer, raise myself upon my songs. And I will sing until this longest night is over and all that I have known can be no more. I will sing of the New Fire and the new years. Of the days when our proud city ruled the world. When great Montezuma was Lord and his prayers kept the heavens turning. All this I shall sing in my final song. Of the Four Suns and the ones called Toltecs who carried with them the books and the music of the flutes. Of the Lord named Quetzalcoatl, and the long journey to this good land. All this I will praise in my songs. And I shall tell of these many beautiful things before the last day is ended and all of our fires have gone out. All this I shall keep alive in my songs!

Resource Materials

Afterword and Notes on Sources
Maps
The End of the Aztec World
Aztec Names and Terms from the Text
Selected Bibliography

Afterword and Notes on Sources

¿Qué es la historia de América toda sino una crónica de lo real-maravilloso? (What is the whole history of America but a chronicle of the marvelous-real?)   —Alejo Carpentier

When the story is ended there is nothing more for the storyteller to tell. But since my story comes out of folk history as well as the academic history of Western civilization, I think I should try to tell those who might be interested a bit about how I wrote this book. Because these source materials are not part of the *real* story, they are placed here at the conclusion.

To a certain extent *The Sun, He Dies* is a companion to another book I have written, called *Anpao,* and much of what I said in the afterword of that book bears repeating here.

Among the Indians of the Americas the teller of stories is a weaver, the creator of *cultural autobiographies*. His designs are the threads of his personal saga and the history of his whole people. Though the designs are always traditional, the hands that weave them are always new. These stories, like ancient Indian designs, have been passed from one generation to the next, and sometimes they were written down by sixteenth-century priests who had a curiously profound interest in the culture they were anxious to eradicate.

Very little in this book has been invented in the sense that fictional scenes and events are usually invented. The words are mine and even the characters are largely elaborations of my own making, but the pre-Columbian folk history and the post-Columbian academic history of the Aztec world existed long before I undertook the writing of this book. In fact, the most extraordinary tales are always substantiated historical events, as, for instance, the transformation of Nanautzin into an orator of Montezuma. Don Alvaro Tezozomoc, a descendant of Montezuma, told this story to Spanish padres. I have retained the gist of his account faithfully, though in the original it was a humble farmer (not a woodcutter) named Xochitlacotzin whom Montezuma caught stealing wood from a royal forest, and in recognition of this peasant's candor he magnanimously elevated him to the post of the Town Chief of Atzcapotzalco (and not the post of Chief Orator).

All the other events of this book are equally substantiated in historical documents. The ten years of omens, the astrological warnings reported by the priests, the prophecies of the bearded white god, Quetzalcoatl, and every other episode and concept of this book are tangible and real aspects of Aztec history. I have invented virtually nothing, but I have focused the factual events into a continuous and intellectually focused narration. I have tried to use these actions and happenings to present the viewpoint of those who were destroyed by the invasion, and I have made use of everything the survivors of the siege of Cortes left to us as well as all the interpretative resources now available to us in the twentieth century. In this way, perhaps it becomes a bit clearer that what I have done in *The Sun, He Dies* is to use the wholly invented character called Nanautzin as the needle with which I could dramatically interweave many different events from the massive fabric of factual and folk history that has survived in the literature of Mexico. I put Nanautzin at the center of events or I placed him in the crowd as a dramatic observer of major events in the last years of the Aztec world. This book, therefore, is my effort to use the vast facilities of the tradition of written literature to convey the energy, uniqueness, and imagery of Indian oral tradition. I have approached my effort, however, not as a stenographer or as an ethnologist or as a historian, but as a writer.

It is possible that readers will wonder what I have contributed to the stories and events of *The Sun, He Dies* other than collecting them from countless tellers. I suspect I have done the same thing that many prior generations of tellers of history have done, only the creative process in my effort is much more like the methods used by contemporary American Indian painters than the techniques of ancient storytellers. Like modern Indian painters I have made use of new potentials of technique and imagination that I have learned through the education available in the twentieth century. I believe, as do contemporary Indian painters, in the existence of some sort of transcendent Indian sensibility, and I believe that its power and its truth can be expressed in modes typical of our day as well as in the venerated, unique styles of the older traditionalists. Just as young Indian painters with a command of modern methods have reinterpreted Indian iconography and history in a new style, so I have recounted the folk history in a prose that tries to merge the old and the new.

I believe that there are images and ideas which are uniquely Indian and remain uniquely Indian no matter what mannerisms are used to present them. These Indian ideas are central to the events in *The Sun, He Dies*. My aim has been to illuminate them as self-contained realities, without drawing parallels to non-Indian rationales or attempting to "apologize" for them or to "explain" them. I have presented these ancient memories neither as curiosities nor as naïve fiction, but as an alternative vision of the world and as an alternative process of history.

History is always the account of events as seen and preserved by the dominant culture. Laurette Séjourné has made this fact very clear in regard to Mexico: "Thus it came about that Tenochtitlan, the center of the Aztec world, was destined to be known to the West only through the reports of those who destroyed it." *The Sun, He Dies* is an alternative vision of the same history.

You may notice that I am disinclined to refer to "myths" and "legends" when I talk about this book and its events. It is because these words tend to express the dominant culture's disregard for the beliefs of other peoples, just as I would be expressing a nonchalant superiority were I to speak to Christians of their "Jesus myths." *The Sun, He Dies* is not concerned with myth but with a reality that seems to have escaped the experience of non-Indians. The omens that appear in this book, the "deer" that the strangers ride, the apparitions and powerful events of nature—these are facts from another scheme of reality. They are not products of a lavish imagination but products of the vision of a people whose experience is fundamentally different from that of the white man's civilization.

298

Most of the stories and historical events in *The Sun, He Dies* exist in many versions. There are twelve surviving documents, written or painted, in which Native Americans described the coming of the Spaniards, the events just prior to their invasion, and the terrible conflict that ensued after their arrival. Some of these documents were assembled as few as seven years from the 1521 defeat of the Aztecs; other manuscripts date from later times. The most important among these primary sources are the *Songs of the Conquest* (1524), *Unos anales históricos de la nación mexicana* (1528), and the *Codex Florentino* (1555). The last of these sources was the most important in the creation of this book. It was written under the supervision of Fray Bernardino de Sahagún in Nahuatl, the language of the Aztecs, by his Indian students from Tlatelolco and elsewhere, who made elaborate use of the reminiscences of old native people who had actually seen the defeat of their land. This extraordinarily important manuscript had been translated into both Spanish and English in editions published by Miguel León-Portilla as well as Arthur J. O. Anderson and Charles E. Dibble. These sources, as well as other valuable works that have greatly contributed to my writing, are found in the selected bibliography.

The major pictographic records of the conflict between the Aztecs and the Spaniards are also found in the texts of Sahagún's informants, and some of these unique drawings serve as the illustrations of this book.

I think it might be of interest to trace various versions of the stories I have recounted in *The Sun, He Dies* and to discover their sources. In one case, the description of the first time any of the Aztecs experienced the burst of guns or cannons, I have reprinted five versions of the event, since the various texts are short and perfectly demonstrate the kind of language that results when several different writers approach the same sixteenth-century event. And these examples give a good basis for seeing what I have done with the story in my own version.

In the various tellings of the story of the "first burst of the cannons," all the writers (and translators) intend to report the same event and all of the accounts intend to be history. But what we find when we read these versions is five strikingly different "visions" and not the objective reporting that we are led to believe is the basis of "objective" history. Between these vastly different versions there exists, not misjudgment, not exaggeration or fraud, but a real and fundamental variance in the way different people *see* reality. Each version is an expression of a cultural bias that shapes the way we anticipate and experience and remember events.

The version transcribed from reports of Aztec survivors, ca. 1547, by Fray Bernadino de Sahagún in the language of the Aztec, Nahuatl:

> Niman tlanaoati in capitan injc ilpiloque, tepoztli imjcxic qujntlalilique, yoan inquechtlan: in ie iuhquj njman ic qujtlazque in tomaoac tleqjqujztli: auh in titlanti in jquac in vel iolmjcque, yoan cocotlaoaque, vehuetzque, nenecuj-liuhtivetzque, aocmo qujmatque: auh in espanoles quj-meeuhq qujmeeoatitlalique, qujmonjitique vino: njma ie ic qujntlamaca, qujntlaqualtique, ic imjhio qujcujque, ic oalihiocujque.

The translation from the Aztec into English by Arthur
J. O. Anderson and Charles E. Dibble:

> Then the Captain commanded that they be bound. They
> put irons on their ankles and their necks. This done, they
> then shot the great lombard gun. And the messengers,
> when this [happened], indeed fainted away and swooned;
> they each fell: each one, swaying, fell; they knew no more.
> And the Spaniards raised each one, raised each one so that
> he sat; they made them drink wine. Thereupon they gave
> them food; they made them eat. Thus they restored them;
> thus they regained their strength.

The version translated from Nahuatl into Spanish by
Angel María Garibay K, re-created in Spanish by Miguel
León-Portilla, and rendered into English by Lysander
Kemp:

> Then the Captain gave orders, and the messengers were
> chained by the feet and by the neck. When this had been
> done, the great cannon was fired off. The messengers lost
> their senses and fainted away. They fell down side by side
> and lay where they had fallen. But the Spaniards quickly
> revived them: they lifted them up, gave them wine to drink
> and then offered them food.

The version of the same event as recounted by the
famous soldier of Fernando Cortes's invasion forces, Bernal
Díaz, in his memoir entitled *The Conquest of New Spain* (this
translation by J. M. Cohen):

> The display was carried out in the presence of the two
> ambassadors [of Montezuma], and in order that they
> should see the shot leave the gun Cortes pretended that he

wished to speak to them and some other Caciques again, just before the cannon was fired. As it was very still at the moment, the balls resounded with a great din as they went over the forest. The two governors and the rest of the Indians were frightened by this strange happening, and ordered their painters to paint it, so that Montezuma might see.

The same event as reported by William H. Prescott in his famous *The Conquest of Mexico:*

. . . [Cortes] ordered out the cavalry on the beach, the wet sands of which afforded a firm footing for the horses. The bold and rapid movements of the troops, as they went through their military exercises; the apparent ease with which they managed the fiery animals on which they were mounted; the glancing of their weapons; and the shrill cry of the trumpet, all filled the spectators with astonishment; but when they heard the thunders of the cannon, which Cortes ordered to be fired at the same time, and witnessed the volumes of smoke and flame issuing from these terrible engines, and the rushing sound of the balls, as they dashed through the trees of the neighboring forest, shivering their branches into fragments, they were filled with consternation, from which the Aztec chief himself was not wholly free.

Unquestionably in matters of fact and, alas, in terms of humanity, the victors and the victims saw the same events very differently—to such an extent that, more than three hundred years after the Spanish reports of the invasion, Prescott (who was essentially very fair-minded) nonetheless sustained the bias of the victors even though he possessed all the conflicting accounts of the Aztecs themselves in the works of Sahagún, Durán, et al. To the Indian "writers" the ambassadors of Montezuma were chained and brutalized; while to the non-Indian writers the messengers of Montezuma were simply given a harmless demonstration of military might. Of course both versions are correct, but we do not really comprehend what happened unless we are in possession of the various responses to the same event. There is no "truth" to be found here. What is discovered in history is a cultural viewpoint.

Besides the variance in our experience of history there is also a variance in the way we experience ourselves. The conception of "characterization" in Western literature and the literature of primal cultures is sometimes at odds. Primal people and the people of the dominant cultures tend to understand themselves as persons in quite different ways. Pre-Columbian literature is tribal rather than individuated. But this tribalism is not limited to American Indians or the peoples of Oceania and Africa; it is also found in various European traditions, such as that of Homer. The "characterizations" in both the European sagas and those of Native Americans are similar in many ways, and they are fundamentally different from later notions of personality in literary works. The *dramatis personae* of tribal literature are essentially external. The reader tends to know a character by his actions and not by an outpouring of feelings and various internal states of mind. To the cursory view such characters might seem to be stereotypes, but in the long view they are actually archetypes. To the primal mind, truth is not inclusive but essential. In folk literature the "truth" is made up of what lies at the bottom of various events, while to the

Western mind the "truth" is *everything* that makes up an event.

Gradually, however, a change comes over traditional folk literature. In post-Columbian times the attitude toward character changes markedly without ever relinquishing its primal focus. Literary characters tend to be individuated in much the same way that Native American painters, who once depicted tribal "beings" rather than "individuals," begin to represent specific persons in their paintings. This "Shakespearean" perspective of human psychology is not necessarily the result of white influences, but probably evolves from the pressures and cultural shock of confrontation between radically different peoples. Whatever the cause, the result is substantially Indian. The archetypes have become diversified and evasive, but they are never caricatures of ideas and persons. They never turn into allegorical figures, but remain characters in the Homeric sense. Unlike Studs Lonigan or Stephen Dedalus, who are individuals in terms of the Western view of personality, the characters of Indian and other primal literatures are Platonic models rather than psychological case histories. For primal peoples tend to strive for the depiction of essences rather than appearances.

My challenge in *The Sun, He Dies* was to start with the ancient form of the epic and to end with its post-Columbian form. In the shattering transition from one notion of the "self" to the other is found whatever meaning this book might possess.

The story of the end of the Aztec world is fascinating, for it is truly *fabulous* history, with numerous "coincidental" events that are quite beyond the reach of naïve reality. That story is also a metaphor for a wider idea. It speaks to us in terms of how really different we are from one another and yet how very curiously similar.

> Now I know that it is not out of our single souls we dream. We dream anonymously and communally, if each after his fashion. The great soul of which we are a part may dream through us, in our manner of dreaming, its own secret dreams, of its youth, its hope, its joy and peace—and its blood-sacrifice. [Thomas Mann, *The Magic Mountain.*]

It is part of that dream that we find in the history of the Aztec world.

Jamake Highwater
Piitai Sahkomaapii

Santa Fe, New Mexico
1979

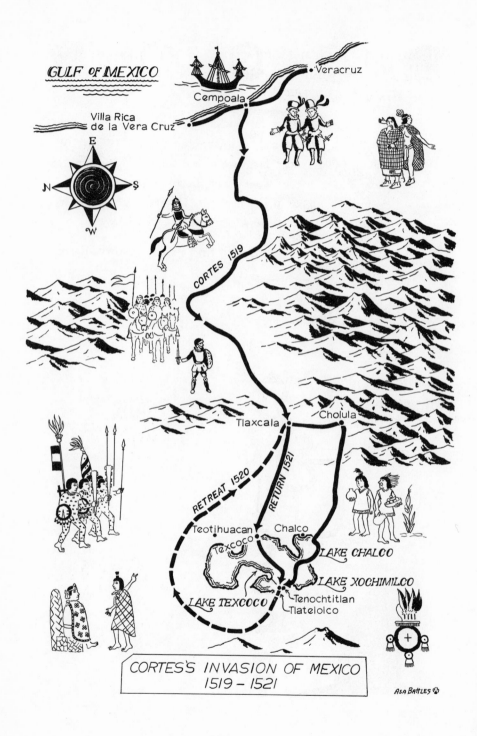

GULF of MEXICO

Veracruz

Cempoala

Villa Rica
de la Vera Cruz

CORTES 1519

Cholula

Tlaxcala

RETREAT 1520

RETURN 1521

Teotihuacan

Chalco

Texcoco

LAKE CHALCO

LAKE XOCHIMILCO

LAKE TEXCOCO

Tenochtitlan
Tlatelolco

CORTES'S INVASION OF MEXICO
1519 – 1521

Asa Battles

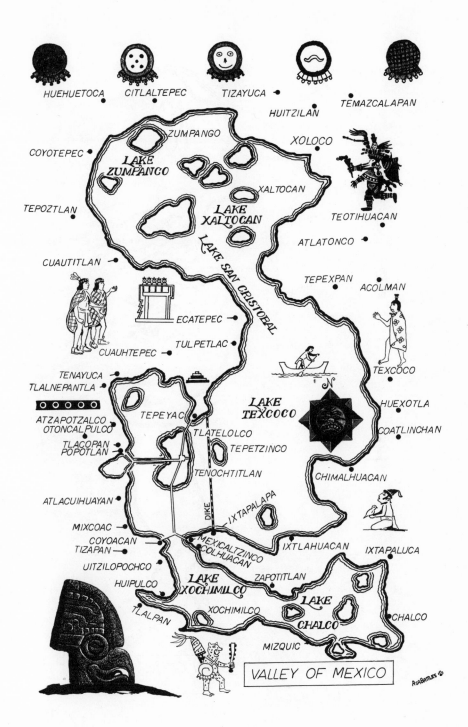

HUEHUETOCA   CITLALTEPEC   TIZAYUCA   TEMAZCALAPAN

HUITZILAN

ZUMPANGO   XOLOCO

COYOTEPEC

LAKE ZUMPANGO

XALTOCAN

TEPOZTLAN

LAKE XALTOCAN

TEOTIHUACAN

ATLATONCO

CUAUTITLAN

LAKE SAN CRISTOBAL

TEPEXPAN   ACOLMAN

ECATEPEC

TULPETLAC

TEXCOCO

CUAUHTEPEC

TENAYUCA
TLALNEPANTLA

LAKE TEXCOCO

HUEXOTLA

ATZAPOTZALCO
OTONCALPULCO

TEPEYAC

COATLINCHAN

TLACOPAN
POPOTLAN

TLATELOLCO

TEPETZINCO

ATLACUIHUAYAN

TENOCHTITLAN

CHIMALHUACAN

DIKE

IXTAPALAPA

MIXCOAC

COYOACAN
TIZAPAN

MEXICALTZINCO
COLHUACAN

IXTLAHUACAN

IXTAPALUCA

UITZILOPOCHCO

ZAPOTITLAN

HUIPULCO

LAKE XOCHIMILCO

LAKE CHALCO

TLALPAN

XOCHIMILCO

CHALCO

MIZQUIC

VALLEY OF MEXICO

AsaBattles

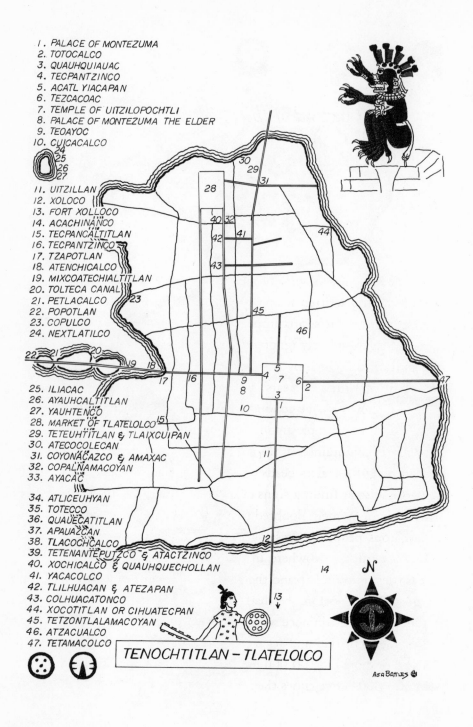

1. PALACE OF MONTEZUMA
2. TOTOCALCO
3. QUAUHQUIAUAC
4. TECPANTZINCO
5. ACATL YIACAPAN
6. TEZCACOAC
7. TEMPLE OF UITZILOPOCHTLI
8. PALACE OF MONTEZUMA THE ELDER
9. TEOAYOC
10. CUICACALCO
11. UITZILLAN
12. XOLOCO
13. FORT XOLLOCO
14. ACACHINANCO
15. TECPANCALTITLAN
16. TECPANTZINCO
17. TZAPOTLAN
18. ATENCHICALCO
19. MIXCOATECHIALTITLAN
20. TOLTECA CANAL
21. PETLACALCO
22. POPOTLAN
23. COPULCO
24. NEXTLATILCO
25. ILIACAC
26. AYAUHCALTITLAN
27. YAUHTENCO
28. MARKET OF TLATELOLCO
29. TETEUHTITLAN & TLAIXCUIPAN
30. ATECOCOLECAN
31. COYONACAZCO & AMAXAC
32. COPALNAMACOYAN
33. AYACAC
34. ATLICEUHYAN
35. TOTECCO
36. QUAUECATITLAN
37. APAUAZCAN
38. TLACOCHCALCO
39. TETENANTEPUTZCO & ATACTZINCO
40. XOCHICALCO & QUAUHQUECHOLLAN
41. YACACOLCO
42. TLILHUACAN & ATEZAPAN
43. COLHUACATONCO
44. XOCOTITLAN OR CIHUATECPAN
45. TETZONTLALAMACOYAN
46. ATZACUALCO
47. TETAMACOLCO

TENOCHTITLAN – TLATELOLCO

ASA BATTLES

The End of the Aztec World

"From the point of view of what we know today," Laurette
Séjourné has written in her highly perceptive study of the
Aztec world, "it seems impossible that Europe could have
remained completely ignorant until the sixteenth century of
a civilization which by that time had existed in Mexico for
over fifteen hundred years. Equally surprising is the indif-
ference shown by the conquerors toward the universe it was
their fate to stumble upon. Nothing shows Cortes's inner
attitude, maintained up to the end of the conquest, better
than his gift of glass beads to the Aztec leaders: in spite of
his surprise at finding signs of great cultural refinement, he
never for a moment doubted that he was in the presence of a
barbarous people interesting only because they were fabu-
lously wealthy. Nowhere in his writing does he show the
least desire to understand them; in fact he condemned them
out of hand before he had made more than the most
superficial acquaintance with them."

Tenochtitlan and its neighboring city Tlatelolco consisted of more than 60,000 houses and a population in excess
of 300,000—five times the size of Henry VIII's London. In

little more than five years the exquisite city and its massive population had been destroyed. And this stunning destruction was somehow achieved by a force of not more than six hundred Spaniards and their numerous Indian allies.

Fernando Cortes was born in 1485 in Medellín, a provincial Spanish town. His first biographer, Francisco Lopes de Gomara, depicts him as "restless, haughty, mischievous and given to quarrelling." Broad-shouldered, medium in height, and pale-complected, Cortes developed a social air of affability but was still haughty and aggressive when his authority was challenged. His lofty ambitions were perfectly suited to the imperialistic mood of Spain in the fifteenth and sixteenth centuries. After Ferdinand and Isabella united Aragon and Castile in 1479, Spain became the most formidable military power of Europe. The non-Christian Moors who had long been the loathed enemies of Spain were driven from their last Spanish foothold in Granada in 1492. The resolutely Catholic and expansionist Spanish nation looked with unbridled greed at the "new" lands stumbled upon by Columbus. In 1511 the Spaniards invaded and subjugated Cuba. Cortes was among the conquerors. Here he married and resettled. When Isabella and Ferdinand died, the Spanish throne passed to Charles V, who eventually also reigned as emperor of Austria, Germany, Luxembourg, the Low Countries, and part of Burgundy. An extravagant Hapsburg, Charles was always looking for new sources of funds to lavish on his munificent tastes, and the Western Hemisphere and its legends of immense riches fascinated him.

Cortes saw his moment and promptly volunteered to lead an expedition in search of riches. He was appointed commander of such an expedition by the governor of Cuba,

Diego Velázquez, who was as ambitious as Cortes and did not trust the independent young commander. He therefore cautiously authorized Cortes only to explore, not to conquer. One clause in the governor's instructions, however, indicated that Cortes, in the event of emergencies, could take whatever measures would conform with "the services of God and their Highnesses." The cunning Cortes interpreted these words to suit his purposes, gaining from them a very doubtful legality to what became his brilliant act of insubordination to the authority of Governor Diego Velázquez.

When Cortes landed on the coast of Mexico in February 1519, his flotilla consisted of eleven ships, about five hundred soldiers, one hundred sailors, numerous servants, and sixteen horses. Eight months later he had already reached the heart of the Aztec world, the great city of Tenochtitlan, and had been received there as an honored guest. Absolutely nothing of a militaristic sort was done to prevent Cortes from entering Mexico despite the fact that the Aztecs and their allies constituted an awesomely large and fierce military force. The march of Cortes through the Mexican countryside can be explained mainly, as Laurette Séjourné has pointed out, by the undoubted talents of Cortes for intrigue and betrayal, which enabled him to orient himself very quickly in the maze of Mexican politics. "Soon after his arrival, he discovered resentment and rebellion simmering among Montezuma's subject tribes, and at once formed the military alliances that made his dazzling victories possible. An indomitable will, not shrinking from assassination or wholesale massacre, accomplished the rest." *(Burning Water.)*

In his first landfall, at Cozumel, Cortes had encoun-

tered a shipwrecked countryman named Jeronimo de Aguilar, who had lived among the Indians for about eight years
and had therefore learned their language. While among the
people of Tabasco, Cortes also acquired a second interpreter
as well as a cohort with as much cunning as Cortes himself.
Her name was Ce Malinalli or Malinche (or Doña Marina
after her baptism), a young native woman who spoke
Nahuatl as well as the languages of the Yucatan that Aguilar
understood. Ce Malinalli quickly learned Spanish from
Aguilar and became the consort of Fernando Cortes.

Using Ce Malinalli's exceptional abilities to turn her
own people's religious faith and political dissatisfaction to
the advantage of Cortes, the Spanish commander was able to
impose the despotism of Spain on the vast Mexican territory
by posing as a liberator of tribes oppressed by the Aztec
overlords. Cortes also possessed the advantage of his fanatical Catholic missionary zeal as a justification of his exploi-
tation of the Mexicans. He made a good case against the
Aztecs by pointing out their use of human sacrifice and
cannibalism. Those accusations shock the twentieth-century
sensibility, but they have a somewhat different impact when
viewed against the gross inhumanities practiced in Europe
at the time Cortes invaded Mexico. The Inquisition, which
flourished in southern Europe from 1237 to 1834, is famous
for its wholesale use of torture and the horrendous violations
of human decency in the name of the "true faith." Spain was
a stronghold of the most unconscionable acts in the name of
God. The expulsion of the Jews from Spain and the defeat of
the Moors were two long-term struggles involving staggering cruelties and inhumanities. Though Cortes and his
soldiers made the most of their shock and consternation over

human sacrifice, it must be remembered that in Cholula the Spanish commander ordered the slaughter of hundreds of unarmed religious celebrants. A man capable of ordering six thousand throats to be cut in less than two hours must certainly earn a reputation for blood-letting no less shocking than that of the Aztec sacrificial priests.

At this point Cortes ordered his most curiously daring stroke: the destruction of his own ships, which would prevent any conspiracies within the ranks led by those loyal to Governor Velázquez of Cuba. Then the army of Cortes marched inland. On August 31, 1519, it entered the lands of the Tlaxcalans, an Indian people who loathed the Aztecs and had long fought with them. The stalemate between Tenochtitlan and Tlaxcala was useful to the Mexican religious scheme, for its "flowery wars" provided sacrificial prisoners for both cities. Cortes easily won the alliance of Tlaxcala against Montezuma, and thus secured the massive forces required to subjugate all Mexico. The horses, cannons, muskets, and European battle techniques were doubtless of great assistance to the Spaniards in defeating Mexico, but without the fierce dedication of Montezuma's Indian enemies it is extremely doubtful that Cortes could have survived his unbelievable ambition to subdue the vast and powerful realm of Montezuma II.

No one will ever really know what prompted Montezuma to allow the Spaniards to march across Mexico, to enter the capital and then wander freely in the great city without the least resistance. All we know is that for some shadowy reasons the great Lord of Tenochtitlan, who was absolutely unyielding in his political aggressions against native cities, somehow offered the white strangers scarcely any opposition. Eventually the massacre by the Spanish soldiers of the unarmed warriors at their sacred feast infuriated the Aztecs and they drove the Spaniards out of Tenochtitlan, where they had been encamped peacefully for about five months.

During this time, Cortes had to leave Tenochtitlan to fight a battle against his own countrymen. He ordered his troops to attack the forces sent by Governor Velázquez of Cuba to arrest Cortes for insubordination—in short, for acting like the monarch of Mexico. Cortes defeated these Spanish soldiers and then, with promises of gold, managed to win over most of Velázquez's troops to his own cause.

After the Aztecs had driven the Spaniards out of their city, Cortes had several boats built and transported overland, in sections, to the lake where the "floating" capital of Mexico was located. Nearly a year passed while the Spaniards were preparing their siege of Tenochtitlan. The rigid war ethics of the Aztecs assured the war chiefs that, once formally defeated, the humiliated white strangers would depart for their own land and never return to Mexico again. But Cortes did not know the Aztec rules of war and he certainly did not accept the defeat of the "Night of Sorrow" as final.

With the boats he needed to attack Tenochtitlan from the water, Cortes marched back to the capital. The terrible siege lasted seventy-five days (the native accounts claim it was eighty days). And by the time the city surrendered, it no longer existed. Its temples and houses were rubble. Its magnificent works of religious art were destroyed. Its treasures were stolen and melted into ingots, and the population had been decimated. In 1525 the Aztec world ended.

Aztec Names and Terms from the Text

Ahuitzotl	ah-WEET-sohtl
Anahuac	ah-NAH-wahk
Axayacatl	ash-ay-AH-catl
Cacama	KA-ka-mah
Chalco	CHAAL-co
Chapultepec	cha-POOL-te-pec
Cholula	choh-LOO-lah
Cuauhtemoc	kwow-TAY-moc
Cuauhtemoctzin	kwow-TAY-moc-tzeen
Cuitlahuac	quit-la-WHO-ach
Huechuetlan	way-WAYT-lan
Huemac	weh-MAHC
Huitzilopochtli	wee-tsee-loh-POHTCH-tlee
Itzcuauhtzin	eetz-kwa-UHT-zeen
Itzcoatl	eetz-CO-atl
Ixtlilxochitl	eesht-leel-SHO-cheetl
Mexica (Mexicans)	meh-SHEE-ka
Mictlan	MEEK-tlan
Mictlantecuhtli	meek-tlan-tay-COOT-li
Mixteca	mees-TEH-cah
Montezuma (Moctezuma)	mohc-teh-SOO-mah
Montezuma Ilhuicamina I	il-wee-cah-MEEN-a

Montezuma Xocoyotzin II	sho-coy-ot-SEEN
nahual	NAH-wahl
Nahuatl	nah-WAHTL
Nanautzin	na-na-U-tzeen
Nezahualpilli	ne-zoo-al-PEEL-li
Oaxaca	wah-HAH-cah
Pinotl	pin-OOTL
Quetzalcoatl	ket-sahl-COH-ahtl
Tenochtitlan	ten-och-TEE-tlahn
Texcoco	tes-COH-coh
Tezcatlipoca	tehs-cah-tlee-POH-cah
Tizoc	tiz-OCK
Tlacopan	tla-CO-pan
Tlatelolco	tlah-te-LOHL-coh
Tlaxcala	tlash-CAH-lah
Toltec	TOHL-tec

Selected Bibliography

Primary Sources

Codex Mendoza (Aztec Manuscript), commentaries by Kurt Ross; Miller Graphics, Productions Liber S.A., CH-Fribourg, 1978 (Spain); based on the manuscript at the Bodleian Library, Oxford.

Cortes, Fernando. *Conquest: Dispatches of Cortes from the New World* (abridged). Irwin R. Blacker, ed. Grosset & Dunlap, 1962. Republished as *Fernando Cortes: His Five Letters of Relation to the Emperor Charles V, 1519–1526.* Francis Augustus Mac-Nutt, trans. New introduction by John Greenway. 2 vols. Rio Grande Press, 1977.

Díaz del Castillo, Bernal. *The Conquest of New Spain.* J. M. Cohen, trans. (Slightly abridged.) Penguin Classics, 1963.

Durán, Diego. *Book of the Gods and Rites and the Ancient Calendar.* Fernando Horcasitas and Doris Heyden, trans. and eds. University of Oklahoma Press, 1971.

————. *Historia de las Indias de Nueva España, et Islas de Terra Firma.* Ramirez, ed. Mexico, 1867–80.

Ixtlilxochitl, Fernando de Alva. *Obras Históricas.* Mexico, 1891–92.

Sahagún, Bernardino de. *Historia general de las cosas de Nueva España*. English-Nahuatl edition. Dibble and Anderson, eds. School of American Research at Santa Fe, and University of Utah Press; in progress. Part XIII, "The Conquest of Mexico," 1975.

Tezozomoc, Hernando Alvarado. *Cronica Mexicayotl*. Leon, ed. Mexico, 1948.

Secondary Sources

Bernal, Ignacio. *Mexico Before Cortes: Art, History and Legend,* Willis Barnstone, trans. Rev. ed. Doubleday/Anchor, 1975.

Bierhorst, John. *Four Masterworks of American Indian Literature.* (Includes "Quetzalcoatl.") Farrar, Straus & Giroux, 1974.

Burland, C. A. *Montezuma: Lord of the Aztecs*. G. P. Putnam's Sons, 1973.

Caso, Alfonso. *The Aztecs: People of the Sun*. Lowell Dunham, trans. Oklahoma University Press, 1958.

Davis, E. Adams, ed. *Of the Night Wind's Telling: Legends from the Valley of Mexico*. University of Oklahoma Press, 1946.

Keen, Benjamin. *The Aztec Image in Western Thought*. Rutgers University Press, 1971.

León-Portilla, Miguel. *Aztec Thought and Culture*. Jack Emory Davis, trans. University of Oklahoma Press, 1963.

———. *The Broken Spears, Aztec Account of the Conquest of Mexico,* Lysander Kemp, trans. Beacon Press, 1962.

———. *Pre-Columbian Literatures of Mexico*. Grace Lobanov and Jamake Highwater, trans.; University of Oklahoma Press, 1969.

Paz, Octavio. *The Labyrinth of Solitude*. Allen Lane, 1957.

Prescott, William H. *The Conquest of Mexico* [1843]. Repub. Modern Library, 1943.

Séjourné, Laurette. *Burning Water: Thought and Religion in Ancient Mexico.* Repub. Shambala Press, 1976.

Soustelle, Jacques. *Daily Life of the Aztecs.* Weidenfeld and Nicolson, 1961.

Vaillant, George C. *The Aztecs of Mexico.* Revised by Suzannah B. Vaillant. Penguin Books, 1972.

Von Hagen, Victor W. *The Aztec: Man and Tribe.* New American Library, 1961.